HOPE ADRIFT

HOPE ADRIFT

A GREY'S HARBOR STORY

LARK GRIFFING

WIND LARK
PUBLISHING

GREY'S HARBOR SERIES

GREY'S LANDING
A Grey's Harbor Story
by Lark Griffing

GREY'S HARBOR
A Grey's Harbor Anthology
By Carol Cassada
Lark Griffing
Piper Malone
Jennifer Sivec
J.C. Wing

HOPE ADRIFT
A Grey's Harbor Story
By Lark Griffing

Coming Soon ~

HARBOR TIDES
A Grey's Harbor Story
By Lark Griffing

HARBOR SONG
A Grey's Harbor Story
By J.C. Wing

PERFECT SEAS
A Grey's Harbor Story
By Jennifer Sivec

ISBN-13: 978-0-9988719-6-7

Edited by Wing Family Editing

Cover Design by Wicked Whale Publishing

1

Hope stepped onto the dock suddenly beginning to question the impulsive decision that landed her here. The last two months were one snap decision after another, some without any thought whatsoever. It wasn't like her. She was always the methodical one, the planner, the one who looked at every aspect before moving forward on anything.

Until two months ago.

When she walked in on Gary.

With his admin.

On his desk.

And it wasn't shorthand she was doing. More like some kind of oral dictation.

Hope shook her head to rid herself of the image that was burned on her brain. The first snap decision was the call to her brother, the attorney. The second was the quick divorce. The third was accepting a job halfway across the country. The fourth, renting a houseboat to live on.

She had lost her mind. Rapidly.

She glanced at the paper in her hand then looked down the wooden dock. It was in the last slip, a small boat, suitable for the river and estuary, but not the sea. Three pontoons and a flat deck with a small cabin situated in the center. A sundeck graced the top of the cabin with deck chairs and a cheerful flag sporting what looked like a hurricane cocktail. Hope grinned at that. A hurricane sounded good about now.

She looked harder at the boat. A curious, dubious expression flitted across her face. Something about the vessel…like it was home-made or something. Was that possible? Do people make boats? How safe would that be?

"What, you don't like her?"

Startled, Hope jumped at the voice. As she turned, her heel caught in the crack between the dock boards and she lost her balance. A strong hand grasped her wrist and averted a disaster.

She tried to gain her composure as she looked into the bluest eyes she had ever seen.

"If you changed your mind and don't want to rent her, you can just tell me. You don't have to jump in the water for a quick getaway." The blue eyes were crinkled at the corners, and the lips on that face were quirked up in a crooked smile.

"No, I, um, sorry. I've just never seen a houseboat that looked quite like that," Hope said with what she hoped sounded like a non-critical voice.

"And what kind of houseboats are you more familiar with?" the blue eyes asked.

"Well, actually," Hope blushed, "I'm not really familiar with any…" Her voice trailed off.

"Okay, let's get you familiar, and I am Bridger, by the way." He held out his hand waiting for her to take it.

She was still mesmerized by the color of those eyes.

He cleared his throat and started to lower his proffered hand.

Hope managed to blush again, then reached for his hand while murmuring an apology.

"Hope, Hope Elliot, um Chandler. Hope Chandler," she said firmly.

"Are you sure, Hope Chandler?" the eyes asked, trying to suppress a smile.

"Positive," Hope answered, attempting to sound a little frosty but only managing squeaky instead.

"First rule of house boating," Bridger started, "heels are not a good plan." He kept hold of her hand and led her safely along the dock and helped her board the boat. Once on the gleaming wooden deck, he gently let go of her and started the grand tour.

The cabin had a porch roof that extended over the front of the boat. Under that roof was a gas grill, a patio table and a rocking chair. A sliding glass patio door led into the cabin. The deck had a narrow walkway on each side of the cabin leading to the stern. Here there were two more chairs, a steel-banded cooler and several fishing rod holders attached to the railing. A metal spiral staircase led to the top sun deck.

There was another sliding patio door off to the side of the spiral staircase that led into the master bedroom. That door was locked.

Bridger led Hope around to the fore deck again and slid open the patio door. Hope gasped in surprise. They stepped into a beautiful open floor plan. A dinette was in the corner with a L-shaped bench seat, complete with storage in the benches. The living area had a deep, comfortable reclining love seat with a sea chest as a coffee table, and more cleverly hidden storage. A tiny wood burning stove sat in the corner.

A cheerful well-appointed galley was adjacent to the dinette. It was small, but cleverly designed to have maximum counter space and cubbies for kitchen appliances and cookware.

A small hall led out of the living area to a compact but comfortable head with a shower and the bedroom lay beyond. The beautiful space was bathed in light from the patio doors and ingeniously placed high port hole windows that lined the wall just below the ceiling. Golden knotty pine bead board graced the walls, polished to a soft glow.

Hope turned to Bridger, her eyes shining, her hands clasped in front of her with pure joy. She had found a home. She knew it. She could feel it in her bones. This little boat was the start of her new journey. She would start a new teaching job on Monday, and the sale of the home she and Gary had shared would close on Tuesday. One door opening, another closing with a hard slam.

"You'll be okay here," Bridger said softly. He watched her subconsciously rubbing the white line around her finger where a ring had resided for years.

*H*ope signed the paperwork at the galley counter and Bridger handed her the keys. She hugged herself smiling, thinking she had just made an amazing decision, one that she never would have made in her former existence.

"Do you have things to move in? Can I help you with any bags?" Bridger raised his eyebrows in a question, watching this woman take in the world that was once his most precious place; the first boat he built with his dad.

"Actually, I only have three suitcases and a backpack. Which is a good thing, I suppose," she said, as she looked around at the small space she was going to have to get used to. "Everything should fit in the closets and those built in drawers," she gestured to the storage drawers she could see down the hall in the bedroom, "but I don't know what I am going to do with the empty suitcases." A perplexed look settled on her face as she tried to puzzle out a solution.

Bridger was surprised to find himself attracted to the scrunched-up nose and furrowed brow that came with Hope's solution searching. He wanted to reach out a finger and stroke her forehead, smoothing the thought wrinkles.

It was getting warm in the cabin.

He was starting to think of reaching out a finger to stroke some other parts of her body that he was certain weren't wrinkled, that looked, in fact firm and taut, like that flat abdomen of hers right where it transitioned into a hip bone, right where that sundress draped just so...*Shit.*

"The suitcases are no problem. I have some storage lockers over in the boat building. You can store them there. Let me help you get your stuff on the boat."

"You really don't have to do that," she told him. "But thanks for letting me store my suitcases. That will really help."

The moved out of the cabin and onto the deck in the afternoon sunshine. Hope stretched her head backward and let the sun warm her face. She purred like a cat, with a very self-satisfied smile on her face.

For a brief moment, Bridger thought of laying her down on the top deck and making her purr even louder, her body naked in the sunlight.

Hope looked at him suddenly, electricity snapping between them. She gave him a little smile and moved to the gangway. She knew what she just did to him, and she liked it.

He knew she knew, and he wasn't sure how he felt about that.

*B*ridger followed Hope to her car and helped her remove her suitcases from the trunk. Realizing it was too much for her to handle on her own, she gratefully accepted his offer to help. She held up one finger to Bridger, asking him to wait a minute as she slipped her feet out of her high heels. Scrounging in the back of her car, she came up with a pair of flip flops. Grinning at Bridger, she slid her feet into the sandals and wiggled her toes, enjoying the freedom.

He stared at Hope's toes, the bright pink nail polish contrasting nicely with the smooth tan on her feet. His eyes traveled up her legs—wait, upgrade that—her truly fantastic legs and let his imagination run wild when his eyes were stopped at the hemline of her short sundress.

When his eyes met hers, she was still smiling, like she had won something.

"What are you smiling at, and why do you look so smug?" Bridger asked Hope, not sure he wanted to hear her answer.

She blushed despite her cocky demeanor.

"I was just thinking," she cleared her throat, all the bravado she had a minute ago slipping away. "Never mind what I was thinking. Let's just say that I am starting a new life in a new town. I have a new job, and I am feeling pretty good about things right now."

"Hmmm," Bridger said, knowing full well that was not what she was thinking but deciding to let it go. "Since you now have a new friend, would you like to go grab a bite to eat at a diner that is new to you?" He picked up her suitcases, leaving the backpack for her to carry, and started down the dock toward Hope's new home.

"Maybe. Is the food good?"

"If you like homestyle."

"Is the company nice?"

"If you like casual and relaxed."

"Then I will take that friend up on the offer. When do I meet him?"

Bridger turned to set her straight, but when he saw the teasing smile turning up the edges of that very kissable mouth, he turned around quickly, just in case his trousers gave him away.

He carried the luggage into the bedroom and placed the suitcases on the mattress. Hope stared at the mattress, a realization dawning on her.

"What's wrong?" Bridger asked, looking around in case he missed something when he cleaned the place before her appointment.

"I just realized. When I left, I left everything. I packed my bags with my favorite clothes, but I left everything else. I have to find a store if I want sheets, and towels, and kitchen supplies..." Her voice trailed off.

Bridger figured there was a story there, but it was the wrong time and place.

"The kitchen probably has everything you need, so that shouldn't be a problem. There's a mall out by the freeway, so you should be able to pick some stuff up there. I can take you there before we go eat, or after. Or I can meet you, whatever you want."

"I don't want to impose, and I would like to find my way around. What time did you want to eat? Are you starving now?"

"I'm easy," Bridger said, "Is an hour enough time?"

"Female here. No way I can shop in an hour. Can you give me two? Will you starve before then?"

"No, I'll live. He drew a quick map to the mall for Hope and then left her to settle in and get what she needed. Two hours would give him enough time to take a quick shower and check in on his mom.

When he left the boat, Hope was looking through the kitchen cupboards and making a list. She was humming happily and looked content and at home on his boat. He liked the fact that she was on his boat.

*O*nce her list was made, Hope left the boat, carefully locking the front sliding door. She checked it to be sure she did it right. She laughed at herself. What was she worried about? She had absolutely nothing to steal. She hopped into her car and studied the map. She recognized that she was going to be heading back the way she had come, so she was confident that she would find her way to the mall without any mishap. She thought for a minute, trying to remember if she saw any evidence of a shopping plaza, but she didn't remember anything like that. No worries, she was confident she would find it. As she pulled out of the parking area and drove down the gravel lane, she passed a large blue steel building surrounded by boats on cradles and trailers. In the doorway, Bridger was talking of the phone. He raised his hand in a lazy wave as she drove by. She smiled and waved back. Maybe things really were going to be okay. She was determined to not look back, only forward, and the man waving to her right now was not a bad thing to be looking forward to. *Dinner that is*, she reminded herself. *You're just having dinner.* She shook her head. She was never one to be forward, but damn, maybe she needed to look at herself and perhaps try to be a little less reticent.

*B*ridger watched Hope leave as he listened to his newest customer drone on and on about what he might want on his boat. They had already been through this, but the man needed a weekly update and constant assurance that the boat would be to his exact specifications. Bridger had to continue to remind him that it was too late to change anything but the cosmetic details, as the hull was already formed, and Bridger was beginning to apply the planking. Sometimes he wondered why he got into this business in the first place, but as he walked back into the building and he caught sight of the boat lit by the sunlight, he remembered why. *Wooden boats are beautiful*, he thought. *They have graceful curves like a woman.* His mind flashed to Hope and her curves. *Yep, women and boats have a lot in common.*

Once he managed to get the man off the phone he hopped into his truck and headed out the drive on the way to the home where he grew up. His mom lived alone in a rambling house south of town and he checked on her daily. He glanced at his watch. Now he only had an hour and a half to visit with his mom, get back to his boat, and get a shower before he met Hope for dinner. As long as Mom didn't create a chore for him, he would have plenty of time.

3

*H*ope unloaded her shopping bags on the small galley counter. She smiled at the blue and white nautical towels she bought for her bathroom. *Cheesy*, she thought, but she couldn't help herself. *Why not?* In her past life, Gary was all about sleek and modern. Appearances were everything. Well, maybe she was rebelling, but she loved the stupid towels.

The sheets made her happy, too. They were also navy and white, but they were a field of forget-me-nots on a white background. Clean, crisp, and feminine. She tore open the package and realized she didn't know where she was going to do her laundry.

The boat didn't have a washer and a dryer.

Well that was dumb of her. She was so enamored with the idea of living on the boat, she had overlooked that little convenience. She wondered what else she overlooked. She looked around her and was instantly charmed again by the boat. *What if she slept on unwashed sheets? Would it kill her?* She rubbed them against her face. They were soft, but still…

Hope heard footsteps on the dock and Bridger's voice.

"Permission to board?"

Hope giggled and opened the sliding screen door.

"By all means. Welcome to your boat, but my new home."

He stepped inside and looked at her. She was still holding the top sheet against her.

"Planning on going to a toga party?" he asked, his eyes sparkling.

"Sure, why not?" she teased back.

He liked that about her. She could laugh at herself.

She was refreshing.

"Seriously, it just dawned on me that my floating apartment doesn't have laundry facilities." She pouted a little.

Bridger cleared his throat. *Damn she was cute.*

"There are laundry facilities in the white marina building. You haven't seen it, yet?"

"No, but it looks like I need to find it." She gestured to the pile of new towels on the counter."

"Well, gather your stuff and you can throw it in the washer before we leave. No one will bother it."

"Are you sure?" Hope looked at him, not trusting that she could just walk away from her things.

"Positive. There are only three of us living at the marina, you, me, and Old Clarence. I'm not doing laundry tonight, and I've never seen Old Clarence do laundry. I suspect he coerces his lady friends to help him in that department."

"Lady friends?" Hope raised her eyebrows.

"Wait until you meet him. He'll probably try to ask you out or invite you over for drinks and a toss in the sheets."

Hope burst out laughing.

"A toss in the sheets? A guy named Old Clarence? You're kidding, right?"

"Not at all," Bridger said solemnly. "Swear."

"Hmmm, does he have money?" Hope asked, a glint in her eye.

"So, you have a price, huh?" Bridger's eye's darkened and Hope felt a flush rise to her cheeks. It wasn't the only part of her body getting warm.

"More than you could afford, I suspect," she teased.

"Did you remember to buy laundry detergent," he whispered in a menacing voice.

Damn it.

He was quick to register her reaction.

"Well, sweetheart," he started in a terrible Bogart impression, "what's it worth to you?"

He leered at her, wagging his eyebrows, trying hard to look sinister.

"For a cup of laundry detergent, I'll buy you a drink. After all, these are clean sheets, not dirty underwear. Not worth much more than a beer."

She stared him down, her hands on her hips in mock anger, the sheet still draped across her body in an odd garden toga motif.

"Okay, I'll take the beer. Are you ready?"

Hope stuffed the towels and the sheets in a shopping bag and followed Bridger out of the cabin, carefully locking the door behind her. She tested it.

Bridger watched how careful she was about making sure the boat was locked.

"Things are pretty quiet and safe here. It's a small town, and people respect other people's property."

"It's a habit. In the city, someone would steal everything out of your car before you could get it locked behind you." She smiled apologetically.

"Not a bad idea to keep things locked, but I didn't want you to worry. You're safe here."

"Thanks, now where is that cup of soap?"

"That's my boat in the first slip. We'll stop there first then I'll take you to the marina building. Can I carry that for you?" He reached to take the bag from her.

"No, I've got it okay, but thanks." She smiled at him making sure he knew she wasn't militant about denying his offer. "If it was heavy, you can bet I would have you carry it."

They stopped at the first slip and Hope stared up at the huge sailboat.

Her mouth dropped open. It was a beautiful wooden boat with graceful curves and brass portholes. Bridger took her hand to help her onto the deck. It required her to climb several steps. Once on deck, it took Bridger a second to drop her hand. She noticed but chose not to say anything.

Bridger's boat was stunning. Easily twice the size of hers, maybe more, it gleamed in the sun, the brass and teak deck highly polished. The mast rose high above her, and she got dizzy looking up as the boat moved gently underneath her. Bridger reached out to steady her.

"I get more movement at this dock than you do, plus a sailboat rides in the water differently. You'll get your sea legs soon."

"Your boat is beautiful," Hope said in a hushed whisper. "You live here?"

"Yep, here or in the houseboat in the next slip."

"Oooh la la..." Hope said, raising her eyebrows. "Two homes next to each other, huh? Pretty impressive!"

"That's also where my office is," Bridger pointed out. "Here, come on below." He shoved the slide-open hatch to the companionway and led Hope down the stairs into the interior of the boat.

They entered a generous salon. There was a small galley to the right of the stairs and a bathroom to the left. A dinette was further in on the right, and a seating area was opposite of the dinette. The fore cabin was where the captain's berth was, and Bridger showed Hope that there were guest accommodations in the aft cabin.

She loved it but felt confined, thinking that her little houseboat was better suited for living. Bridger read her mind.

"The houseboat is more comfortable for staying in the river and hanging out in one place, but this boat can sail the world. I can live in her and travel all I want."

"Have you done that?" Hope asked, curious, but thinking she already knew the answer.

"No." Bridger sighed, "The business hasn't allowed me the luxury." But his face brightened in a smile, "I have taken her to the Virgin Islands and spent some time there, then brought her home." His eyes held a faraway look.

"I bet it was amazing. I've never sailed before," Hope said as she looked at all the electronic equipment wondering what it all did.

"Well, that is going to have to change. I would love to take you on a cruise down the coast." He reached into a cabinet above his head and tossed a laundry pod at Hope. "Here, don't eat it."

She laughed and tossed it in her bag and added the dryer sheet Bridger handed her. Turning, she headed back up the stairs to the deck. Bridger followed and helped her down the steps and back on the dock.

"Aren't you going to close the hatch thingy?" she asked.

"Hatch thingy? No, I'm going to air out the cabin a bit. No one will bother my boat. Let's get this laundry in and get going. I'm getting hungry."

Bridger showed her the marina building complete with laundry and shower rooms in case she didn't want to use the one on the boat. She threw the towels and sheets in the washing machine and added the laundry pod, but only after offering it to the hungry Bridger. He passed.

Satisfied, they made their way to Bridger's truck. As he helped her in, he noticed she didn't have anything in her hands.

"No purse or anything?" he asked, sure they were going to have to go back to her boat.

"Nope, everything I need is in my pocket. I'm good." She smiled at him and he shut the truck door.

Damn, he was beginning to like this woman. She didn't carry a purse. That alone was a big star in his book.

4

*B*ridger pulled out of the marina and headed toward town. On the way he pointed out landmarks to help Hope get acquainted with the area.

"I'm a little turned around," she mused out loud. "Where's the high school from here?"

"We can swing by on the way to the diner, if you want."

Hope nodded enthusiastically, keeping her eyes on the road, her bottom lip caught between her teeth. Bridge smiled at the fierce concentration on her face. He knew she was memorizing the route.

"You start school on Monday, right?"

Again, she nodded and turned to him, flashing a smile.

"I do, and I'm very excited, but a bit overwhelmed. I haven't had time to prepare, I haven't seen my classroom, and I have nothing ready to start the year. I just got an email this morning letting me know what classes I'm going to be teaching." She pouted a little, considering the monumental task in front of her. "Eh, I'll just wing it!" she said, laughing

Bridger was delighted with her spirit and the sparkle in her eye. Plus, he wanted to pull that bottom lip in-between his and bite it himself.

Hope didn't seem like other women he had known; self-absorbed and traumatized by the slightest thing. Of course, he had sworn off women for some time, but this was refreshing.

He stopped in front of the high school, an old brick building with updated windows and cheerful flowers in the flowerbed surrounding the giant flagpole. This was truly a small-town USA high school.

"Do you think you know your way? Can you get here Monday morning?"

"Yep. Left out of the marina. Follow the river. Turn right on the first road and cross the river on the bridge. Go straight passing a couple of roads that look like they lead back to the river. Turn left and follow Elm until you turn right on Maple and voila...school."

She bounced on her seat grinning madly at Bridger.

"I should've figured you're smart. After all, you're a teacher. Now, I'm hungry. Are you ready to eat?"

"Starved. Where to now?" Hope's eyes sparkled in anticipation. She was enjoying herself. She felt free and unencumbered. Gary was always worried about appearances. He would frown at her if she acted silly. She always felt like she was reined in, like she was pretending to be someone she wasn't. She wasn't the perfect businessman's wife, with the perfect hair and the perfect makeup. Sometimes she didn't know the right things to say. Sometimes she just wanted to grin like a maniac and bounce up and down on the front seat of a truck.

"What?" asked Bridger, grinning himself and not really knowing why.

"Nothing. I'm just happy."

"I like your kind of happy. Let me ask you a question. How do you feel about really thick, hand-spun dark chocolate malts?"

"I feel deeply about them!" she said solemnly. "The difference between a malt and a shake is a religious experience. You know what I mean?"

Bridger nodded his head reverently.

"Why do you ask?" She looked at him in earnest, hope in her eyes. "Are you telling me the diner we are going to can make such a delicacy?"

"The best on the east coast. But you have to pair it with a bacon cheeseburger with grilled onions and hand cut fries. Does that sound good, or do you need a salad or something?"

"Um, no, I don't need a salad or something. I need that burger, those fries, and the malt. How long before you can make that happen?"

Bridger swung into a parking space on Main Street.

"How about now. Welcome to the Cathead Diner."

Bridger got out of the truck and walked around to let Hope out, but she had already jumped down from the seat and was waiting for him to lock up.

Damn, this girl doesn't carry a purse, doesn't need rabbit food, and can get out of the truck all by herself. Bridger opened the door of the diner and allowed Hope to walk in before him. She spun around to face him as he let the door close.

"Oh my God, it smells amazing in here. I didn't realize how hungry I was until this very moment."

"Hello stranger." A beautiful blonde woman walked up to Bridger and kissed his check. She gave him the once over, then glanced at Hope. Realization dawned on her as she registered the dopey grin plastered on Bridger's face.

"Hey, Maeve," said Bridger affectionately as he returned the kiss.

Hope felt an interesting ping in her heart. Why did she care that this Maeve chick was hanging on Bridger? Hope just met him today. But still. For some reason, she didn't like it. Not at all.

"Maeve, this is Hope Chandler. She just moved into town, and she's renting my old houseboat. Hope this is Maeve Wynn. She owns this greasy spoon."

They sized each other up for a second, then Maeve gave Hope a warm smile.

"Welcome to Grey's Harbor, Hope. Let me know if there is anything I can do to help you feel at home."

"Thank you, Maeve. It's nice to meet you. Actually, you can make me feel at home." She looked steadily at Maeve, the corners of her mouth tipping up slightly.

Maeve was surprised. Most people just glossed over the polite offer. She liked this girl and her moxie.

"Okay, I'll bite. What can I do for you?"

"Make me the chocolatiest. thickest, maltiest malt known to man, and I will feel surrounded by love and think I may have found my new home. Can you do that?"

Maeve laughed and gave Hope a hug.

"That I can do. Bridger take Hope over to the corner table while I get started on the malts. I know you want one."

"You know me so well Maeve. Too bad you and Tank are still an item."

"I heard that, Bridger." A well-muscled man made his way across the diner and shook hands with Bridger. "How are you doing, man, and who is this?"

Hope looked at Tank with interest. *This town certainly had amazing looking men. Were they all this well built and good looking? What the hell was in the water here?*

Bridger narrowed his eyes at Tank and Tank grinned a lazy grin back. Tank was well aware of his effect on women. It was also very obvious that Bridger wasn't taking too kindly to it.

Bridger made the necessary introductions while guiding Hope to the corner table.

Maeve joined the group, setting two tall malts on the table accompanied by two metal vessels which held the rest of the malt that didn't fit into the glasses. Hope groaned out loud.

"If this tastes half as good as it looks, I may never leave here. And I'll need to buy all new clothes in a larger size before school starts on Monday."

Hope bent to the straw and worked hard to get a taste of the thick malt, crossing her eyes in the process.

"Hope just got hired to teach at the high school," offered Bridger before he tackled his malt.

Tank nudged Bridger over in the booth and slid in next to him.

"I heard that the board hired a bunch of new people."

Hope slid sideways and patted the seat for Maeve to join her.

Maeve glanced around the diner, satisfying herself that all was well before she took a load off and joined them.

"They did," offered Maeve. "Mrs. Pincher finally retired, so they had to replace her, to the delight of all the students yet to take senior English, and Susie Baker got married and moved to Boston, so the counselor position opened up. Plus, I think they needed a new first grade teacher and gym teacher at the elementary."

Hope looked at Maeve in awe.

"You're certainly in the know around here."

"Yep, I am and so is Izzy Edwards, the bartender at the Mizzen Mast. In a small town you can get all your local news from the bartender and diner."

"Don't forget the barber," Bridger said as he ran his hands through his hair.

"Who you obviously need to see," said Tank as he looked disapprovingly at Bridger's longer hair. Tank's was close cut and tidy while Bridger looked like a kid who had come in from a day playing at the ocean.

"I'll tell you a lot of people are angry with the new board president."

"Why?" asked Hope in between sips of malt.

Bridger gave Maeve a warning look. Maeve waved her hand at him.

"She might as well know. She is going to be taking the brunt of the displeasure. Please don't take offense, but I think you should know what you're up against. The board president, Gaylord Fornby is an out of towner. He feels like the schools need a wider range of experience than what the local teachers can deliver. Most of our teachers were born and raised here. They went to college and came home to teach in the local schools. Grey's Harbor is like that. People come home to it."

"I can see why," Hope said, encouraging Maeve to continue talking and to let her know that she wasn't offended by the conversation.

"Fornby insisted that all new hires come from the outside, to 'weave a new thread into the fabric of our community'. The locals call it bullshit. The board members bought it hook, line, and sinker. There are a lot of people who are unhappy, because they felt those jobs should have gone to their sons and daughters."

"I can understand that sentiment," said Hope as she considered Maeve's words. "I also know how hard it is to get a teaching job, so their kids will have to leave Grey's Harbor just to make a living. That's sad."

"What teaching job did you land?" asked Tank

"My guess is Mrs. Pincher's. I am teaching senior English."

"Oh crap," said Tank, just as a waitress came to the table, so he didn't finish his sentence.

"Maeve, would you like me to take everyone's order?"

"Thanks, Jenny. Please do."

They all ordered the bacon cheeseburger with fries special and before Jenny left, Maeve introduced her to Hope.

"Jennifer is building a home on the bank of the river." Bridger explained. "She's on the other side from where your houseboat is, but down around a bend. You can't see the place from the marina. She's dating my friend, Ryker. He's the one who's building the house, and he's Maeve's brother."

Jennifer blushed a little but extended her hand to Hope.

"Welcome to Grey's Harbor, Hope. I think you'll like it here. You've already met some of the best people I know."

With that she hurried to the kitchen to deliver their orders.

"Okay, Tank, you don't get off that easy. Spill it." Hope leveled a stare at the attractive man sitting opposite her.

He squirmed

"Damn. You have the teacher look down pat, don't you!"

"It comes with the territory. Now start talking."

"Okay, but it might end up being nothing. Ralph Cotter's daughter had her eye on that job. He was talking up and down the town that when Pincher retired, his baby girl would be the newest institution at the school. She had been dreaming about that job since she was in high school. Daddy was sure she would get it. After all, Ralph Cotter is old money and owns half the new Whale Watch Cove development just north of town. He thinks money talks and doesn't take no for an answer. When he discovered that his daughter was passed over for the position, he made noises that there would be hell to pay. My guess is you have made two enemies already without even trying."

"Two? Ralph Cotter and who else?"

"Why, his spoiled rotten daughter Clara."

"What a pretty old-fashioned name," Hope murmured.

"That's all you have to say?" Tank stared at her, open-mouthed.

"Don't worry, Tank," Hope reached over and patted his hand. "I'm used to it. Everyone hates the English teacher."

Bridger snorted a half-laugh and Maeve shook her head.

"I can't disagree," said Bridger, after drawing another taste of malt. "I wasn't too fond of mine either."

"Yours never looked like Hope," said Jennifer, as she delivered the cheeseburgers to the table. "Old lady Pincher was old when Bridger was in school. He hated her and so did Tank."

"Did you?" asked Hope, her mouth watering as she eyed the giant burger in front of her, onions glistening beneath the melted cheese, large slabs of bacon peeking out from under the bun.

"No," said Jennifer. "I loved her. She was sweet and kind and always had time to read my writing. She was a great woman. On the other hand, she was a tough old bird, with a narrow face and hooked, beak nose, and she wouldn't take any crap from any student. She also knew when kids were trying to pull a fast one. Like the time Bridger and Ryker tried to convince her that they were reading *The Great Gatsby* on the beach when a shark was sighted near a girl in the water. As the story goes, both boys plunged in the water to save the damsel in distress, and when they got back to their towels, their books had disappeared. She called foul and gave them both detentions after school for a week. They had to sit in her room as she read to them for an hour and a half each night until they had listened to the entire novel."

"Longest damn week of my life," complained Bridger.

"Poor boy," Hope replied. "I hope you learned something."

"Yeah, the movie was better."

Hope shook her head and bit into the burger that was waiting on her plate. For the second time that day, her eyes crossed. *Damn, it was good.*

"Can I get you guys anything else?" Jennifer asked the table.

"Mmmm, no thanks," Hope said as she savored the food. Swallowing, she told Maeve it was the best burger she had ever eaten.

"You must really be hungry," Maeve protested, but glowed with the praise. Hope didn't need to worry about the rest of the townspeople or her students. She would easily win them over with kindness and her sweet sense of humor. She had a feeling the school was lucky to snag a teacher like Hope. Maybe Gaylord Fornby got something right with his hiring practices.

5

*B*ridger pulled the truck up to the dock and put it in park. He turned to Hope, about to speak, but she beat him to it.

"Thank you so much for an amazing evening, and thank you for introducing me to some new friends and for paying for dinner. It wasn't necessary." She smiled at him. "I don't know if you have anything else to do this evening, but I have some questions about the boat and a bottle of rum that needs opened, so would you like to join me on the deck of my new rented boat and help me with both?"

"I think I can fit that into my schedule. What exactly do you plan on doing with the rum?"

"We have options. I don't see you as a strawberry daiquiri kind of guy, and I don't have any mint for mojitos. So, you can have it neat, with cola and lime, a regular daiquiri, or a Hemingway Special."

"What's a Hemingway Special, other than the perfect sounding drink for an English teacher to serve?"

"It's a modified daiquiri, but not as sweet, and it's made with grapefruit juice. And maraschino liqueur. You have to like grapefruit juice. I can make it with orange juice, but it's not the same. Good, but Hemingway wouldn't approve."

"Okay, I wouldn't want to piss off Hemingway. I can give the original a try. I'm not picky. I'm happy with cheap beer."

Hope looked at him dismissively. "Strike one," she said, then laughed and started down the dock toward the little houseboat.

Bridger lit the kerosene lamps that hung from brackets on the outside of the cabin, casting a soft light over the deck. He swept the inevitable spider webs off the chairs and popped his head in the sliding door to ask Hope if she needed help.

She met him at the door with two icy drinks and a dish of salty mixed nuts. Bridger took them from her and led her to the chairs.

"Oooh, I love the lights," Hope said softly, "They're so much nicer than electric ones."

"You have electric ones too, but these help keep bugs away." Bridger remained standing, waiting for Hope to sit in one of the chairs. As she was lowering herself, he casually remarked, "Oh, and I wiped all the spider webs off that chair for you." He grinned as she stopped herself mid-sit and checked the chair, a look of distrust plastered all over her face.

"I'm not sure whether to tell you that you are mean or to thank you," she said as she cautiously sat on the chair, not looking comfortable at all.

"I wondered if you had an aversion to spiders. I never mentioned it, but you're living on a boat on the water. Spiders are inevitable. They eat other bugs, so you have that going for you."

"Which is nice," she said, trying for light-hearted, but it fell flat.

"Just wipe down the webs when you see them, and you'll be fine. You'll get used to them."

She looked dubious and nervously sipped her drink. The self-assured sparkle and bounce had left her, and now she sat huddled on the chair looking dismal.

"Oh crap. I'm sorry Hope. I didn't realize you hated spiders that much. I'll spray tomorrow if you want. I usually avoid insecticides, but if they bother you that much, I'll take care of it."

"No," she said, trying hard to be brave. "If this is part of the deal with living on a boat, I'm going to have to try to get used to it." She took a huge slug of her daiquiri, relying on liquid courage to get her through the night.

"Okay, but I will get some mothballs over here and we can set them out."

"Mothballs?"

"Yep. They help control spiders. Does the smell bother you too much?"

"Not at all. Actually, I kind of like it in small doses. It reminds me of my grandmother's house. Does it really work?"

"Some people swear by it. I think it helps, that's for sure. Trust me, Hope. You'll be fine, and if you're really bothered, I'll take care of it." He smiled reassuringly at her and leaned back in his chair taking a tentative sip of his Hemingway Special. "This is pretty good."

"You really like it?"

"I do. It's also pretty strong. Is yours as strong as mine?"

"Of course. Hemingway wouldn't have it any other way."

They sat in a companionable silence, each enjoying their drinks as the boat moved gently on the water. Hope asked her questions about the boat and what amenities were in the area.

"I'm going to love this," Hope said as she relaxed back in her chair. "Are those frogs I hear?"

"Yep, and that croaking warbling sound is a heron."

"I wondered what the heck that was. Oh, look, a fish just jumped," Hope said excitedly. "I've never caught a fish in my life. I always wanted to."

"We'll try to remedy that sometime if you'd like."

"I would very much like," said Hope, as she stifled a yawn.

Bridger drained his drink and stood to leave.

"You don't have to leave. I'm not really tired."

"You've had a long day, and I have an early morning tomorrow. I'm meeting with a client first thing."

"Tomorrow is Saturday."

"I am fully aware, but my client said he will be in the area bright and early and he wants to check on the progress of his boat. He's a pain in the ass, and I guarantee he'll want to make changes that are too late to make."

"That sucks. Thanks again for tonight and for sharing a drink with me."

"It was my pleasure, Hope. Remember, if you need anything, I'm just down the dock. I'm sleeping on the sailboat tonight. Just come on down the dock and holler. I'll hear you and come running."

"I'm sure I'll be fine," she said, suddenly coming to the realization that she was sleeping on a boat, floating on the water, out in the country, not near the city or the city lights, and there were freaking spiders on the boat. *No problem at all.* She sighed.

"Of course, you will. Just remember, the boat moves with the water. It dances, and it creaks. You'll hear animals and fish. Something might even bump against the boat at night. Nothing out here will hurt you. Spook you maybe, but not hurt you. You have my phone number. Call or text anytime. The first night can be unnerving. Deal?"

She stiffened her upper lip in a comical way.

"Deal," she announced.

Damn, he had a sudden urge to kiss that stiff upper lip and melt it into submission.

"What?" she asked.

"Nothing," he murmured in a husky voice. She had no idea what she did to him. None at all.

6

*H*ope woke to the sound of someone whistling and footsteps on the dock. It took a minute to orient herself. Then she remembered she was sleeping on a boat, floating on a river.

She stretched and sat up, moving the curtain aside to peek outside. The sun was shining on the water while two kayaks glided silently toward the ocean. The footsteps on the dock faded with the whistling.

She dropped back in bed lazily and smiled at the ceiling. She hadn't been attacked by a giant spider in her sleep. In fact, she had slept like a baby, gently rocked by the movement of the river.

As much as she wanted to lay in bed and relish this quiet time, she knew she had a lot to do to be ready for Monday morning, so she got up and padded to the bathroom. The head, she reminded herself. This is a boat, not an apartment. When she was done, she looked at the compact shower. Well, might as well try to figure out the routine, especially how to shave her legs in such cramped quarters.

She turned on the shower, relieved to discover the water pressure was perfect. Once she turned around a couple of times in the tiny compartment, she found a ledge to prop her toes on as she carefully shaved each leg. Yep, this was going to work just fine.

A half hour later, Hope was on deck sipping a cup of coffee and concentrating furiously, squinting at her laptop. She had angled the little table so the sun didn't shine on her screen, but it was still a little difficult to see. Still, this was such an amazing place to work on her school preparation that she was perfectly willing to squint a little.

She heard the whistling approach again with the fall of footsteps. She detected a slight limp in the sound. Saving her document, she looked up from her computer to see a slightly stooped elderly gentlemen making his way down the dock.

He saw her looking at him, so he waved and continued on to her slip.

"Morning, pretty lady."

Old Clarence, she thought. It had to be.

"Good morning. I bet you're Clarence."

"Pretty and smart. And you are Hope."

"Smooth and informed," she replied.

He threw his head back and cackled, delighted she was willing to spar with him. He gestured toward her boat, so she motioned him aboard. He was surprisingly nimble for his age, despite his limp. He bowed slightly toward her and formally introduced himself. She took his hand and solemnly shook it. His eyes twinkling, he raised her hand to his lips, his eyes never leaving hers.

"Perhaps I could have a chance with you," he suggested. "Especially if I do away with Bridger." He tapped his temple with a crooked index finger, contemplating the dastardly deed.

"I'm not interested in a jail widow romance," she quipped, shaking her head with disapproval.

"Then I will just have to out charm him," Clarence snorted. "Won't be hard to do. Young men have no idea how to woo a woman. Too wrapped up in themselves. I was going to invite you over for a spot of tea and a scone, but I see you drink coffee. Too bitter for me. I am sweet through and through." He smiled again, encouraging her to engage. He was having fun.

"I would, but I think you have company. Maybe?" Hope pointed down the dock at a heavy-set woman in a pair of wedge sandals and a tight skirt making her way toward them. Her stretchy shirt pulled tightly across her ample bosom that was held up with obviously straining bra straps. The clingy fabric of the top emphasized the divots in her shoulders. Despite her ample size and her tight, curve-accentuating clothing, she was attractive and looked pulled together with a large tote that complimented her shoes. She was waving one hand while trying to smooth her hair with the other. Her bright red lipstick sparkled in the sun. Hope wasn't sure if it was wet or actually had some kind of glitter in it.

"Yoo-hoo. Clarence, yoo-hoo."

Clarence did not turn around.

"That would be Mabel. She is my eight o'clock. She likes mornings. She says that's when she is the most energetic. I hate to break up our little party, but I have to attend to her and get her out before Vicky shows up at eleven. Vicky is more of a nooner type. I do like Vicky." Clarence's eyes twinkled as he thought about Vicky. "Perhaps I could interest you in four o'clock?" he said winking.

Hope had a brief, unwelcome visual image of bony Clarence in a pair of boxers, his knobby knees pointing in two different directions, moving toward her in a lurid, leering way while smiling and offering her a bouquet of daisies. *Where the hell did that come from,* she thought shaking her head slightly.

She kept the plastic smile pasted to her face and politely declined.

"I'm sorry, but I have an engagement at four o'clock." She abruptly decided she would need a malt at the Cathead Diner around four. "I wouldn't keep Mabel waiting though. She looks a little jealous."

With that comment, Old Clarence's head snapped around. He jumped up and waved enthusiastically as Mabel came closer. He winked at Hope and quickly limped his way off her boat. In seconds he was next to Mable, his palm cupping her elbow. She tittered about and allowed him to lead her onto the houseboat two slips down from Hope's. As Clarence let Mabel into his cabin, he popped his head out for a last look at Hope. He gave her the thumbs up and disappeared inside.

Hope's mouth dropped open in disbelief. Bridger wasn't kidding last night when he mentioned Old Clarence just might suggest a toss in the sheets.

Hope settled back at the table and woke her laptop, ready to finish her twelfth grade regular English syllabus when her phone whistled at her. Who would be texting her? Her ex-husband was out of the picture, her brother was her only family left, and he never texted. All of her friends, rather ex-friends, were now allied with Gary. She was alone and essentially friendless. For a moment she felt a pang of panic in her gut.

She was alone.

She leaned across the table and snagged her phone.

Bridger.

A slow smile spread across her face.

She did have a friend, maybe more, if last night's diner crew was true to their word.

She moved the phone to reduce the glare so she could read Bridger's text.

`What time did Old Clarence pencil you in for? Do you need rescued?`

Hope grinned and looked around. She didn't see him anywhere on the deck of the sailboat at the other end of the dock.

She heard a whistle and turned toward it.

Bridger waved at her as he leaned against the huge metal building on the other side of the marina.

She texted back.

`I made a snap decision that I needed a malt at four o'clock. Coincidentally the same time he had an opening all set for me.`

`He might follow you. I'd be careful. If you need a chaperone, let me know. I can rescue you.`

`My hero.`

Bridger waved again and disappeared into the building. As she watched, a white BMW pulled up next to the building. A man stepped out of the car. He was on the phone, gesturing angrily.

Hope watched with interest. The man was impeccably dressed for a day on the golf course impressing businessmen and women.

She didn't like him.

She texted Bridger.

I think your client is here. I think he's pissed off at someone already. Brace yourself.

Shit. Thanks.

Bridger came out of the building glancing over at her and nodding, a lazy smile on his face.

He approached the man, ignoring the fact that he was obviously angry at someone on the other end of the phone. Bridger wasn't going to waste his Saturday waiting on this douche bag.

The man turned away from Bridger while he finished the call. Bridger looked over at Hope, grinning in a satisfied way.

Hope was enjoying the power play. She liked the fact that Bridger wasn't intimidated by the man's demeanor.

The man put the phone in his pocket and shook Bridger's hand, but it was obvious to Hope that the man was being dismissive. In his eyes, Bridger was subordinate to him.

Hope liked the man even less.

Bridger and the man disappeared into the building.

Hope drained the last of her coffee and went back to work.

Twenty minutes later she sensed a movement at the big building. The man came out walking quickly, clearly irritated. He got into his car and left, spitting gravel behind him as he sped away. She smiled at Bridger, who was now leaning lazily against the building, looking as insolent as one of her teenage students who refused to do his homework.

She laughed out loud.

Bridger was a manipulator and an instigator, and he enjoyed playing the game. It was written all over him.

She liked that.

7

*H*ope moved quickly to keep up with the tall, efficient principal who was taking her down the hall to her new classroom. Her head was spinning with all the introductions. She knew she wasn't going to be able to keep all of the teachers, office staff, and administration straight in her mind. There were too many names, but at least the names went with smiling faces, people who wanted to be where they were.

Mr. Fender unlocked the classroom door and handed Hope the keys.

"Well, Ms. Chandler, here's your classroom. I'm sure you'll find what you need in there, but if there's something you require, please let Charlotte know and she will take care of it."

Charlotte. Which one was Charlotte? Hope cast around in her memory banks, running through the myriad of people she met that morning.

"Charlotte is the lady in charge in the main office," Mr. Fender said kindly. "Actually, Charlotte is in charge of the whole district, but we don't let that get out. We especially don't let the new superintendent get wind of that. We love Charlotte. She's efficient."

Charlotte. Unnatural redhead, soft comfortable body, warm smile, certainly a force to be reckoned with if you piss her off...

"Yes, thank you. I remember Charlotte." Hope smiled back, gratefully. "I'm sure everything is in order. My room looks wonderful. Did you need a copy of my lesson plans for the week?"

Mr. Fender looked startled.

"Ms. Chandler. You are now teaching in a small-town school district. It's not that we're backward, but we're a little more relaxed about things. If you have your lesson plans on your desk or in a planner where they can be accessed in an emergency, and if you have sub plans in a folder in the office, then I don't require you to turn in your lesson plans to me. Although, do expect me to pop in unannounced occasionally. I enjoy catching a lesson or two from my teachers. I learn a lot." He turned to leave. "Have a good day, and let me know if you need anything."

"Thank you. Please have a good day, too."

Mr. Fender left and Hope turned to survey her room. She didn't have a chance to get it ready, having been hired at the last minute. It made her sad because it wasn't warm and welcoming to her new students. It wasn't like her. But it couldn't be helped. She would have to order some posters tonight.

"Welcome, Hope." A tall, willowy blonde stood in the doorway, her arms full of posters and bulletin board border. "I'm Pepper Wilde, and I have the room across the hall. I teach freshman English and a public speaking class. Welcome to the English department. Do you need some stuff? We have about a half an hour before the hoards show up. If you want, I can help you get some things up on your walls so they don't look so naked."

"Wow, thanks. You're a lifesaver. I don't have anything yet, and I hate it. Are you sure you don't mind sharing your stash? I know how we teachers can be."

"I'm happy to. Besides, I am sure I'm going to steal stuff from you. I'm a shameless thief."

Pepper dumped the pile on the table near the windows, and

together they quickly decorated the room with punctuation posters and inspirational phrases.

"There, that's better." Pepper stood back surveying their work.

"I can't thank you enough."

"Well, it's generic, but it'll work until you can put stuff up that reflects your own style."

A loud clanging sound filled the halls.

"There's the first bell. Good luck. If you need anything, just holler. Did they tell you how to take attendance? Make sure you get that in within the first five minutes or Charlotte will be calling you out. Whatever you do, don't get on Charlotte's bad side."

"Yes, I'm familiar with your system, so I've got this. Check back after first period to see if I'm still standing."

Pepper waved backward as she hurried to her own classroom yelling to a student as she crossed the hall.

"Get off the top of the lockers. What are you thinking? Sheesh." She turned and winked at Hope, then disappeared into her room.

Hope moved to stand in the hall next to her door. Her students began to file into her room. Hope said good morning to each one of them, trying to get a feel for each individual. It was a typical group. Some were quiet, some were chatty and exuberant, others were so caught up in their conversation that they completely ignored her. One young man looked particularly sullen and withdrawn, almost angry. She figured he was going to be a tough case, so she made a mental note to get to know him and try to engage him.

A new year had begun, and she was excited. She loved teaching, and the new school felt like a good place. She closed the door to her classroom and turned to her class smiling.

"Good morning, guys. I'm Ms. Chandler. Welcome to my class."

*T*hird period class dismissed with a loud ring and Hope collapsed into her desk chair, her head spinning as she swiveled around and stared at the whiteboard behind her. It was covered with writing in bright colors. She read the statements from her three classes.

"I hate English. It's pointless."

"I love to read."

"I write poetry."

"Do we have to learn how to use commas?"

They were all pretty typical. Some students were happy to express their fears while others jockeyed for position of favorite student. It was obvious some just put something on the board to satisfy the requirement. As she skimmed over three classes worth of statements her eyes rested on one written in black.

"Leave me alone."

Hmmm. Good to know, but the statements were anonymous, so she was going to have to figure out which student felt this way. Because it was written on the left-hand side of the board, she assumed it was from her first period class. The image of the sullen looking boy flashed in front of her eyes. Yep, she thought. Probably him.

"Hey, are you coming to lunch, or do you need some alone time?" Pepper dangled her brightly colored lunch bag by the tip of her index finger and beckoned Hope to join her.

"Oh, I am definitely ready for lunch." Hope swung back toward her desk and opened the bottom drawer. She pulled out the sad looking plastic grocery bag. She showed it to Pepper.

"I'm pathetic," she laughed. "Let's go. Please tell me there's a pop machine."

"If you mean a soda machine, yes, we have one in the faculty lounge. Teacher's only. Whatever you do don't let Fender catch you getting a soda for a student. He hates that."

"My guess is you found out the hard way."

"Yep, more than once," Pepper admitted with a laugh.

Pepper led Hope to the faculty lounge, and they sat together at a table near the window. It was a sunny room, full of light. The walls were painted a cheerful light blue, and there were several round tables placed around making the space feel like a pleasant bistro. There were two microwaves, a refrigerator, and the much-anticipated soda machine in the tiny galley area.

"Wow, this is the nicest teacher's lounge I have ever seen," said Hope appreciatively.

"You should've seen it last year. This place was a dump. We complained to Fender and he took it to heart. Over the summer he worked in here for a week behind closed doors. No one was allowed to come in except for Bridger and Ryker. They helped him. We were blown away when he opened the door and let us take a look. He hosted a summer luncheon to show off his handiwork. We were very appreciative. He really is a good guy."

"I'd say so. The last place I worked had a room that looked like a dungeon. That was our teacher's lunchroom." Hope took a bite of her sandwich, thinking. "Bridger, as in Bridger Cadigan?"

"How many guys do you know named Bridger?" Pepper asked, teasing.

"Good point," said Hope, coloring slightly.

"Yes, same Bridger. How do you know him?"

"I'm renting a houseboat from him."

"Wait, you're living in his old houseboat, the one he built with his dad?" Pepper's eyes widened with surprise.

"I...I don't know. Maybe, I guess. It looks kinda like a homemade boat, and it is parked at the last parking spot."

"Honey, it's not parked, it's docked, and you have the last slip, not parking spot. Girl, you are not from the east coast, are you?"

Hope laughed good-naturedly.

"That obvious, huh?"

Pepper grinned and nodded.

"So why are you so surprised that Bridger rented me the house-boat? Is there something wrong with it?"

"No, not at all. It's just Bridger loves that boat with all his heart. When we were young and dumb in high school, we used to try to convince Bridger to have parties at that boat. Small ones, you know, just a few of us. He never let that happen. That boat was like a sanctuary to him. He was afraid we would get drunk and something would happen, one of us would fall off the boat and drown and he would lose it or something. Bridger is smart like that. He's probably right. It would have happened. As it was, Johnny Macomber was drinking one night with his friend Stan Larding. They decided to joy ride out on Stan's dad's fishing boat. They got very drunk. Johnny fell overboard. It was bad. It was two weeks before they found Johnny's body. You can't imagine what that was like after having been in the ocean for two weeks."

Pepper shuddered at the thought and Hope put her sandwich down, no longer hungry.

"That's horrible. I can't imagine how hard that was on the family and the community," said Hope, shaking her head with the thought.

"It was beyond horrible. Then Johnny's family sued Stan's family. Stan's family lost everything, their business and their friends. They moved out of town and have never been back. That caused a shockwave through the Harbor. It put the fear of God into Bridger. His dad had already passed away, and he was trying to run the family business with his mom and finish school. He wasn't taking any chances, so the houseboat and the marina were off limits for parties."

"That sounds very smart of Bridger, but I know how teenagers are. Did he still have friends?"

"Oh yeah. None of us held it against him. We all loved Bridger. We still hung out at the marina, but it wasn't a party spot."

"Gotcha. Well, I will tell you that the paperwork I signed made my eyes cross. My guess is I can't sue him for anything."

"I'm sure you won't need to. He's a really nice guy."

Hope looked at Pepper carefully. Was that wistfulness in those eyes?

"So, did you ever go out with him? I kinda sense…"

"Yeah, I did. For a very short time." Pepper ducked her head to take a bite of her sandwich, chewing it slowly. "But then Bridger had to deal with another tragedy, and we were over before we started."

Hope waited. Suddenly sorry she had asked.

"So, how much longer do we have for lunch?" Hope asked as she popped the last bite of her sandwich in her mouth.

"About three minutes. The bell will ring in five, but I like to beat the horde in the hall, so I leave a few minutes before the bell."

"That's a sound plan," said Hope as she drained her can of soda.

"Oh, and Hope, it's okay that you asked about Bridger and me. Don't feel bad. We dated. It was nice. He's a wonderful man. It just wasn't meant to be. He and I are still friends. I just wish it would have worked out for us. He really is a great guy."

"Thanks, Pepper. I didn't mean to make you feel badly."

"No worries. I'm over it, mostly. I just need to find another great guy to sweep me off my feet. He's out there. I'm sure of it."

8

"Hey Mom, how's it going?" Bridger crossed the kitchen and landed a kiss on his mother's cheek. She reached up and embraced him, clinging just a little.

"Hello, honey. Are you hungry? I was just going to have a cup of tea. I can make you a turkey sandwich if you'd like." She looked so hopeful that Bridger couldn't break her heart. He'd have to start working out harder if he was going to keep eating two lunches.

"Sure, but if you could make the sandwich on the light side? I'm trying to watch my figure." He smiled and struck a pose, pushing his gut out as far as he could. His mother's mouth twitched upward and slapped his gut lightly, but the smile didn't reach her eyes. For a minute, they looked a little vacant. It was fleeting, and maybe he was imagining things.

His mother busied herself in the kitchen, setting out a teacup and two plates.

"I'm going to check some things in the office for a second. Do you need help, or can I go over Livingston's accounts for a minute? He said he paid me for the upholstery upgrades, but I don't trust the man."

"Of course, dear. I'm fine here. Do you want a soda or iced tea?"

"Iced tea please, and please don't dump any sugar in it."

His mother scowled at the thought of unsweetened tea. Bridger laughed and went into the small home office just off of the kitchen pantry. He opened the old wooden file cabinet and flipped through looking for the folder marked Livingston.

It wasn't there.

That was odd. His mother was meticulous with her filing. She had been a librarian before she quit her job and stayed home to run the office side of the marina business with his dad. The woman was positively anal.

He carefully started again, working his way through the folders one by one. No, it wasn't there. Wait, it was under the W's. W for Wendell? Wendell Livingston. That was odd.

He turned to take the folder to the desk when the phone rang.

"Would you mind getting that, dear?"

Bridger picked up the receiver.

"Cadigan Marina, this is Bridger Cadigan."

"Hey, Bridger, it's John Horvath, how are you? You don't usually answer the office phone. Is your mom okay?"

"Hey, John. Mom's fine. She's just making me a sandwich. What can I help you with?"

"Well, Bridger. This is just a little awkward."

"Spit it out John. You know me. Cut to the chase. What's the problem?"

"Well, I just want to say, if you've found yourself in some financial difficulty, I understand. We can work something out, if you would just talk to me about it, but ignoring an invoice this long. I mean, if you need to make payments, or..."

"John, what are you talking about? What invoice?" Bridger furrowed his brow and slid open a drawer looking for the Horvath Iron Works account.

"You haven't paid the invoice for the custom railing work you ordered."

"John, that boat was finished three months ago. I don't understand why you weren't paid. Can you give me some time to check with

Mom and find out what's going on? You know she handles the accounts side of the business, and I apologize. I will make certain you get paid immediately. Can you email me personally the invoice?"

"Of course, Bridger. I figured there was just some kind of mix-up. I'll email that to you today. Let me check, yep, I have your email address. Thanks for checking on this. I appreciate it."

"No, thank you, John. I'm truly sorry and will remedy it immediately."

Bridger walked back into the kitchen, holding the Horvath Works folder in his hand.

"Mom?"

"Who was that on the phone, dear?"

"That was Howard from Horvath Iron Works. He says his invoice for the custom railing for the Spencer boat was never paid."

"Nonsense. Of course, it was paid."

"Well, Howard claims he doesn't have it. Let's check the accounting after lunch and see if we can figure out what went wrong. I'm sure there's just some misunderstanding or something," Bridger said carefully as he noticed the slight tremor in his mom's hands. The teacup rattled against the saucer she was carrying to the kitchen table.

Bridger gently took the tea from her and set it down at his mom's customary seat. He took her shoulders in his hands and turned her to look at him.

"Mom, don't worry. Howard's a friend. We'll figure it out and set it right. Now let's have lunch. I'm hungry," he lied kindly.

They sat down to lunch, his mother picking at her sandwich. The teacup rattled softly in the saucer when she set it down. He could see her mind working.

"Mom, it'll be okay. We will figure this out."

"Of course, it will be okay," she snapped. "I've been doing this job since before you were born. I know how to run this office."

Bridger looked shocked but recovered quickly. His mom rarely raised her voice, and when she did, she was always contrite. This time she was looking at him defiantly.

"And you do a damn fine job of it! Finish eating and we'll figure it out." He raised his iced tea glass and took a long draw. "Now that's how you make tea for a man!" He grinned at her knowing she thought he was a heathen. She was from the South and sweet tea was sacred.

"Your lack of taste must have come from you father," she teased back. Suddenly, everything seemed alright.

Bridger helped his mom clean up the dishes and then the two of them went into the office. His mom was now on a mission to figure out what went wrong. She expertly flipped to the duplicate check she had written which covered the amount of the invoice Bridger had in his email.

"Okay, so let's check if it hit the bank yet," said Bridger, relieved that he didn't have to have a difficult conversation with his mom.

Emmeline quickly accessed the business checking account and began searching for the check. Her brow creased in a deep furrow.

"What's wrong?"

"It looks like the check has not been cashed. That's odd."

"Something must have happened to it. Maybe it was lost in the mail. I'll call Howard and let him know that he can expect another check out first thing."

"You will do no such thing," Emmeline said sternly. "I handle the office end of things. You go build a boat and keep the marina running. I will do my part here, now scoot. I have things to do."

Emmeline picked up the phone, dialing as she dismissed him. He kissed her cheek goodbye as she started speaking, waving him away like a gnat.

"Howard? Emmeline Cadigan here."

Bridger crossed through the kitchen and quietly closed the back door behind him. *Well, that was taken care of, but still...the Livingston upholstery upgrade issue was not resolved.* Bridger had left the folder on the desk when Howard called, and he had forgotten to pick it back up and refile it. His mom was going to chew him out for leaving a file out. *Well maybe she would file it under H this time where it belongs.* Not a mistake his mom usually made.

9

"So, how was your first week at Grey's Harbor High?" asked Bridger as he took a swig of beer from the bottle.

"Please tell me that's a craft beer at least," Hope teased as she lifted her Hemingway Special to her lips.

"It is, actually. It's a Crab Pot Porter from the local microbrewery."

"Crab Pot? That doesn't sound appetizing. What's the name of the brewery, although I'm afraid of the answer? Maybe Whale Spit Brewery?"

"No, but they do have a Sperm Whale Ale. No lie."

Hope groaned as she lifted the bottle from Bridger's hand. Sure enough, the name was Crab Pot Porter, but the brewery name was borderline respectable, Naked Beach Brewing.

"Isn't it a little warm for a porter?"

"They were all out of the Island Goatfish IPA."

"Of course," Hope smiled and lifted her glass in a toast, settling back in the deck chair and relaxing.

It was Friday evening and Bridger had stopped over to see if the mothballs he had provided were working enough for her. Hope admitted that she was still bothered by the spiders but was getting adept at using her little broom to make them disappear.

Bridger had walked down carrying two beers, but Hope had turned him down gracefully, preferring her rum drink. They sat companionably sipping and watching the pleasure boaters heading down the river and out into the open ocean.

"So, seriously, how's the job? Making friends? Enemies?" Bridger took another sip, looking over the neck of the bottle at Hope, making eye contact.

She shivered a little. *Damn he was seriously good looking.*

"No enemies, yet. I did make friends with Pepper Wilde. She was a lifesaver the first day. She came into my room with an armload of bulletin board stuff to help me decorate."

"Pepper's a very special lady. I'm glad you guys are friends. She'll take care of you and watch your back. She's smart and funny, and all around a great person."

"Just not the person for you?" asked Hope, softly. She knew she was treading on personal territory, but it wouldn't be fair for him to not know she knew they had a history.

"I'm afraid I hurt her. I never wanted to do that." Bridger looked off over the river watching a heron fish for dinner.

Hope waited for him to continue.

He didn't.

"That heron has the right idea."

"What's that?" Hope asked as she drained her drink.

"Dinner. Are you hungry?"

"What do you have in mind?"

"It's Friday. That means Izzy is frying fish."

"What's an Izzy?"

"Izzy is a character. You'll love her. She owns the Mizzen Mast."

"Mizzen Mast? Oh wait, that's right, you guys talked about Izzy when we were at the diner. She knows what's going on in town just like Maeve. Got it. I'm definitely up for fish fry. Are her fries as good as Maeve's?"

"You're going to have to be the judge of that. I know when to keep my mouth shut."

The parking lot was full when they arrived at the Mizzen Mast, so

Bridger had to pull around the crowded patio and park in the back. Hope could hear the band doing a sound check. She smiled at Bridger. She liked this town, and this man wasn't too bad either.

Bridger led her to a table on the deck on the other side of the building.

"Why are you pouting?" asked Bridger, stopping himself before he touched her lower lip with his finger.

"I liked the little patio where the band is setting up. You didn't want to sit there?"

Bridger smiled knowingly.

"I sit there a lot, but tonight's band is Trevor Hammond's band. He's a local high school kid, and he only knows one volume. Trust me, you'll have enough sound back here by the river. They're young and not so good. Not terrible, but Izzy gives them a venue for Friday night. Friday fish fry is crowded so the loud music just kinda fits."

"Gotcha."

A woman approached the table, laying her hand on Bridger's shoulder. Hope stared at the brightly colored tattoos that graced the woman's arms. Hope's eyes slid up to meet the cool gaze of the person who had to be Izzy. Their eyes locked. Izzy waited to be judged. Hope took in the piercings and the ink.

Bridger watched, amused.

Hope gave Izzy her most dazzling smile, hoping to disarm the tension that was starting to swirl around the table.

"Hi, I'm Hope...."

"Hope Chandler, the new English teacher. You rent Bridger's houseboat, you aren't from around here. Shit, you call a boat slip a parking spot. Most of your students like you, but a couple don't. Not your fault, they're just related to Clara Cotter, and they think you don't deserve the job. You like chocolate malts, and you don't like spiders. Yes, I know everything about everybody, but I mind my own business. Unless you screw with my friends, then it becomes my business. I don't have the stuff to make a Hemingway Special, so would you like a beer or some other drink that borders on normal? I'm Izzy, by the way. It's a pleasure to meet you."

With that Izzy and Bridger broke out laughing and Hope's composure fell to hell, her mouth hanging open, her mind swirling.

"Well, there's one thing you don't know, Izzy," said Hope, pulling herself together.

"What's that?"

"You're losing one of your piercings. Left ear. Yep, that's the one."

Izzy grinned at Hope and offered her hand.

"Seriously, what would you like to drink?"

"Do you have Sperm Whale Ale?" asked Hope cautiously.

"Sure do, Bridger?"

"Make that two, Iz." He swatted her ass as she turned. She stopped dead in her tracks and turned looking at Bridger, her face darkening.

"That's for giving Hope a hard time," he drawled as he leaned back in his chair.

"You just wish you had a piece of this ass. Bridger, you're sweet to look at, but you're just not the man for me. Now keep your hands off my ass and pay attention to the lady at your table. I've got a bar to run."

A young man delivered their drinks and took their orders, both deciding on the Friday fry. Hope took a cautious sip of her beer.

"Well?" asked Bridger as he took a long draw from the bottle.

"It's very good. I'm not a beer drinker, normally, but it goes with fish fry and Izzy scared me."

"Don't let Izzy scare you. Granted, she's tough and can out swear any sailor, but she has a heart of gold. I don't want to get into her personal business. It's a small town and you'll figure things out on your own, but that tough exterior has a soft spot or two inside. If she decides to make you her friend, she'll be a friend for life."

"You guys are obviously close. It's generally frowned upon to slap a woman's ass, even if you're dating her."

"Yeah. Izzy and I go way back. She knows she can count on me, and I can count on her. "

"It must be nice to have friends like that," Hope gazed wistfully out over the river.

"You lost a lot when you came here, didn't you?" It was a statement, not a question.

Hope thought for a minute, wanting to make sure the answer she gave was what she really felt.

"No, not really. What I left behind wasn't worth hanging onto. Material stuff doesn't matter, and people aren't important if they don't have your best interests at heart." She took another sip of her beer and thought about the man sitting across from her. "Besides, I am making new friends here, and they seem to be of a more solid stock. Like Izzy. My guess is she has strong morals and is loyal to a fault. I'm going to be her friend. Just watch and see."

"I have no doubt." Bridger briefly reached across the table and gave Hope's hand a reassuring squeeze but released it quickly.

A slow smile moved across Hope's face. Yeah, he was feeling it, too.

Their dinners arrived and Hope dove in with gusto. The fish was perfect, fresh from the sea and lightly battered, the inside creamy and flaky at the same time. Bridger watched with wonder as Hope devoured the meal. Once again, he was astounded at her. She was real. He liked that.

"Hello, Hope."

They both looked up from their dinners.

"Oh, hi, Chris. How are you?"

"Doing well, thank you. I heard that this is the place for fish on a Friday night, but being new in town, I wasn't sure..."

Bridger frowned, then tried to hide it. Hope was too quick for him. She caught it and grinned wickedly.

"Why don't you join us, Chris. The more the merrier, right Bridger?"

"Of course. Hi, I'm Bridger."

"Oh, I'm sorry. Bridger, this is Chris Komat. He's the new counselor at the high school. So, he's new, just like me," she emphasized just to see if Bridger squirmed. "Chris, Bridger Cadigan." Hope grinned at the two men. This could be interesting, she thought.

"Yes, please have a seat," said Bridger, surprised that it was difficult to be gracious.

"If you're certain I'm not intruding," Chris said, as he was already sliding into the seat.

"What can I get you to drink?" asked Bridger as he stood up. "I'm heading inside for a minute anyway."

"Whatever you're drinking is fine, and thank you," said Chris as he turned his attention to Hope, effectively dismissing Bridger.

Bridger scowled as he made his way through the open garage doors into the bar. Izzy watched him out of the corner of her eye as he made his way to the men's room.

When he came out, she had three Sperm Whales ready for him.

"How'd you know?" Bridger asked as he leaned on the bar with his elbows.

Izzy raised her pierced eyebrow.

"Remember, I can read lips. It's a gift."

Izzy gestured with her chin and watched Bridger's face darken.

"Pretty boy has an eye on your lady, doesn't he?"

"She's not my lady."

"Bullshit," snorted Izzy. "She's very obviously your lady, or should be. But let me tell you, if you aren't careful, that man is going to swoop in and carry her off."

"What makes you say that? Why do you think she would fall for him?"

"You mean why would she fall for him over me. Well, she's here alone. It gets old, being alone. She's new, he's new. Now, it looks like she has two suitors. Which one will provide her security, protection, and entertainment? He looks pretty entertaining."

They watched as Chris gestured wildly and both he and Hope broke into gales of laughter.

"Here, take your beers and see if you can salvage the evening. I take it she likes my fish fry?"

"Yes, ma'am. She loves it."

"Good. She just moved up a peg."

Bridger gathered the three bottles in his hands and turned to make his way back through the crowded bar to the deck. He felt his ass get a sound pinch.

Without looking back, he replied.

"I deserved that."

revor Hammond's band was in full swing when Chris finished his dinner. He looked up from his plate to see Bridger studying him. He also noticed that Hope's foot was tapping lightly under the table.

"Hope, care to dance?" he asked her, not bothering to look at Bridger. He wasn't interested in letting Bridger think he was asking for permission.

"I'd love to." She patted her lips with her napkin and left it on her plate, indicating she was done.

Bridger stared at the napkin. She was done. With him? He watched the two disappear around the side of the bar heading to the patio.

"Smooth move." Izzy appeared next to Bridger and put another beer in his hand. "After this, you're cut off. I'll let Chris keep drinking for a bit. You'll be the one who can drive her home. Deal?"

"Thanks, Iz."

"I always take care of the ones I love. Especially when they are screwing their life up on their own." She laid a hand on his shoulder and squeezed. "Bridger, this one isn't going to come easy. You're going to have to work for her. But if you get her, it would be really shitty for you to hurt her. Understand?" Izzy looked hard into Bridger's eyes, making sure her point was clear.

"Aye aye, Cap'n."

"You're a dork, Bridger." She lightly kissed his cheek and disappeared into the bar, leaving him to think about Hope, his future, and his messed-up past.

10

*H*ope made her way back to the table, her cheeks flushed, eyes sparkling. Chris was close behind, his palm on the small of her back.

He moves fast, Bridger thought. He was really beginning to not like this guy.

Not at all.

"You're right, Bridger," Hope exclaimed, the excitement still showing in her face, "Trevor and his friends only know one volume, but they have a lot of heart. The drummer is in my second period class, Jimmy something."

"Jimmy Stevens, Ron Steven's boy. Ron owns the auto repair garage just north of town. Good guy, Ron. You can trust him with your car."

"That's right. I am so bad with names. Please excuse me for a minute. I'll be right back." Hope smiled at the two men and left them alone, working her way through the crowd into the bar. She was on the hunt for the ladies' room.

"So," Chris leaned back in his chair and took a swig of the beer that had just appeared in front of him. He didn't look surprised or think to thank whoever had been generous. "I'd be happy to run Hope home this evening. I'm sure you have something to do tonight."

"I do have something to do tonight," said Bridger with a gleam in his eye, "and that's staying here until Hope has had enough and then driving her back to my boat where she is staying."

"You mean renting," said Chris, rising to the challenge.

"I didn't say which boat," Bridger took a sip of the water Izzy had left for him in a highball glass, leveling a gaze at Chris over the rim.

"Interesting," said Chris. "Hope said you guys are just friends, unless you are suggesting friends with benefits." Chris's face held a smile that made Bridger's blood run cold.

"I think you'll find that Hope is not that kind of lady," said Bridger, fervently hoping that he was right.

Hope pushed out the ladies' room door, careful not to touch the handle with her clean hands. There were enough germs in the high school, she didn't need another place to pick up something and get sick at the beginning of school. Izzy gestured to her from the bar.

"I understand you liked my fish."

"Izzy, your fish was delicious and so were the fries. I'm so glad Bridger brought me here."

"Me, too. About Bridger. He is a very, very good friend of mine. Please be careful. I won't take too kindly to someone hurting him or using him. Now before you get your back up, I don't know you. I don't think you're the type, but I can see trouble brewing already, and I think you might be enjoying it." She gestured out toward the deck. The stormy look on Bridger's face told one story, the self-satisfied look on Chris's told another.

"Oh, Izzy. I'm not that kind of girl. I'll be honest with you, when Chris asked to join us, I thought it might be interesting, you know, to see if there was anything…" she stammered uncomfortably.

"I understand. Nothing different than any normal woman might want to find out. Just don't play him. You just met him and you're new in town. There are a lot of eligible bachelors here. Bridger might not be the one for you. That's okay, but please don't play him along and hurt him. Got it?"

"Yes ma'am. I won't. I think he's sweet and a good person. I'm not ready for a serious relationship right now, but I'm not opposed to dating. Maybe dating around. Is that bad of me?"

"No, it's adult and the only way to get to know people. Just make sure Bridger knows where he stands. That's all I ask. Now get out here before that guidance counselor pushes all the wrong buttons on Bridger."

Izzy wiped the bar with her rag, fuming because she knew a counselor would know exactly what he was doing, so he was doing it on purpose. Hope seemed a little naive to Izzy. Almost like she didn't realize she was setting those two men up to come to blows.

Hope hurried back out to the table.

"What'd I miss?" she asked brightly, allowing Bridger to push her chair in for her. Both men had sprung up, but Bridger won the round.

"Nothing important," said Bridger raising his glass to Chris. "Chris offered to drive you home if you wanted."

"Why thank you, Chris, but I always leave with the one I came with." She smiled up at Bridger and the tension in his gut started to loosen.

Hope didn't catch the dark look on Chris's face, but Bridger didn't miss it. Something didn't feel right about this guy.

"Well, maybe some other time," said Chris. "We can do dinner." He congratulated himself on making a date in front of Bridger. He was certain it wouldn't backfire on him.

"That would be lovely, thank you."

"Great. I'll see you at school on Monday." He emphasized the last part, making certain Bridger didn't miss the fact that he would be spending every day with Hope.

"Goodnight," said Bridger, and he watched as Chris left the deck. He wondered briefly if Chris left the bar altogether, but he didn't worry about it. He knew Izzy would give him any information he would need to know later. Now he turned his attention on Hope. The band was attempting a slow song. He figured they would butcher it, but what the hell, it was Fish Fry Friday.

"Hope, would you care to dance?"

"I would love to."

Bridger took her hand and led her to an empty spot on the deck near the river. Despite the tempo of the song, the band still played it hard rock loud. A few other couples joined them as they swayed to the music, the river moving lazily beside them.

They made small talk, but mostly were quiet, wincing at the wrong notes and the tripped-up rhythms. When it was done, Hope leaned over the rail and looked into the dark swirling water.

"This is the river that runs past the marina, where I live, right?"

"Yep."

"It doesn't make sense to me."

"That's because it twists and turns. It's not a straight shot. Here..." Bridger walked over and snagged a carnation from the vase on the nearest table. "Izzy won't mind."

He dropped it in the river, and they watched as the current took it.

"Now, whenever you're ready, we can drive back to the boats and we can sit and wait for that flower to float past."

"Don't we need to hurry?"

"No, it'll take a while. We may have to sit together out there waiting if you want to see it."

"I don't have to be anywhere, and I've got nothing better to do. I would love to sit out there with you and wait for that flower to float by."

Together they went inside to settle the bill. Izzy gave Bridger a swift kiss on the cheek and a hug. Hope wondered if Izzy would hug her, too. All she got was a warning glance and a good night with a tight smile. She was going to have to work harder if she wanted Izzy for a friend.

11

*M*onday came too quickly. When the alarm went off, Hope had a hard time waking up. She stretched and listened to the rain falling on the roof of the little boat. A storm had rolled in for the morning. She smiled to herself. The weekend had been nice. She and Bridger sat on the deck of her boat Friday night waiting for the carnation to float past. She started to think Bridger was pulling her leg that they would be able to watch it, but it was a sweet gesture.

They sat and talked until one in the morning, watching the river as the moon rose and pleasure boats glided quietly past them, the engines throttled back.

When Bridger rose to leave, Hope thanked him for a wonderful evening. He leaned in and kissed her gently, chastely on the lips. She lifted herself on her toes, wanting more, hoping the kiss would deepen, but he put his index finger against her lips. She would have to wait, but there seemed to be a promise of more.

She wrapped her arms around herself as she watched Bridger walk down the dock to his boat. About halfway there he began to whistle, the notes ringing clear and haunting in the night. A bird called back to him and the wake from a passing boat lapped against hers. She stayed out on the deck for another hour just soaking in night on the river. Just before she turned in, she saw something float past in the moonlight. It was out toward the middle of the river, just a small thing. She fancied it was the carnation.

Saturday found her being lazy, reading a book and getting used to just existing on the little boat, working around the kitchen and doing laundry at the marina laundromat. Sunday was dedicated to shopping for food and some more clothes for work, then planning out the rest of the week for her classes. She went to the Cathead Diner by herself for dinner. Maeve and Jennifer were swamped, they were down a waitress. They were friendly, but too busy to sit and talk. After that she drove around the town, trying to get a feel for the place. She found her way down to the public beach and spent what was left of the day plopped in the sand watching evening fall over the ocean. Dolphins played in the surf and families gathered their children and sandcastle buckets and left for the night. Darkness fell on the beach and Hope still hadn't moved. Her life had changed so drastically, but it felt right. Sure, she was lonely, but everything she needed was here in Grey's Harbor. She would make friends and put down roots. It just felt right.

The rain started pounding down even harder. She was surprised just how loud it was in the little boat. She looked around her nervously. It was getting a little wild outside. Was the boat safe? Was it watertight above the water line? She glanced at the ceiling half expecting to see drips, but the little boat remained perfectly dry, cheerfully riding out the storm.

Hope took a fast shower in her little shower cell and dressed quickly for school. She pulled her new lunch bag out of the fridge checking to be sure she had put everything in it for her lunch. Satisfied, she put it down next to her briefcase. It was time to go, but the rain had not let up. Damn it. She didn't have an umbrella. That was the one thing that had been an issue. She'd just up and left everything when she filed for divorce. She wanted nothing from her marriage, but she realized that many of the things that were in her old house she took for granted. Like having an umbrella on the closet shelf.

No worries. She had a raincoat with a hood. Putting it on, she tucked her hair under the hood and pulled the drawstring tight. That should work. She gathered her briefcase and lunch, took a deep breath and stepped out of the little cabin into the weather.

As she hurried down the dock, a voice called to her from the neighboring boat.

Clarence.

"Hope come on aboard. I'll rub you down with a towel and dry you off. If you're a little chilly, I know how to make you warm. What do you say?"

"Thank you, Clarence, but I'll be fine. I need to get to work. Have a nice day."

"You, too. You just don't know what you're missing. Oh, and Hope, be careful, the dock gets slippery."

"Got it. Thanks." Hope didn't break stride as she hurried past Clarence's boat on the way down the dock to her car.

She glanced at Bridger's houseboat, but there was no sign of life, and the sailboat looked like it was sealed up tight. She felt sad about that. She didn't know what she was expecting, but it wasn't lifeless boats. *Where was Bridger, and where did he spend the night?* More importantly, why did she care?

Chris was by her mailbox when she stopped to see if she had anything in it and to pick up some paper in the teacher's workroom.

"How was the rest of your weekend?" he asked, moving close to her side.

"It was nice," she replied.

"Are you getting settled in and finding your way around? I'd say I'd be happy to help you do that, but I'm still figuring that out myself. If you want, we can discover our new home together."

The bell rang before she had a chance to answer and the halls were filled with noisy students.

Hope gave him a little wave and plunged into the current.

"So, don't groan too loudly, but I need to get a timed sample of your writing," Hope paused waiting for and getting the expected response. "To make it even worse, the prompt is an old-fashioned one that is trite and overused. Are you ready?"

The over achievers sat eagerly waiting, leaning forward slightly in their chairs, their pens already poised over a clean sheet of college-ruled paper. Most students sat casually in their seats awaiting the punishment that was to befall them. A couple slouched, disinterested but resigned to the task.

"The prompt is: What I did over my summer vacation."

The groan was even more audible now. Two students were off and running, writing furiously, worried that they wouldn't have enough time to produce an A-worthy five-paragraph composition.

A hand went up from an insolent looking blonde in the second row. Amanda.

"Yes, Amanda?"

"Seriously, is this really your prompt? Couldn't you find something more interesting, more contemporary and thought provoking?"

Hope smiled, anticipating this kind of response.

"Yes, I could, and I will. But the purpose of this is for you to write a narrative, and I want it to be about something you wouldn't have any trouble writing about. I don't want the subject to get in the way of your ability to write. I just want to see what your strengths and weaknesses are."

"Plus, you're nosy and want to know what we do in our private time," said a young man in the back-corner seat under his breath. Rusty Walsh.

"No, I'm not nosy, but I would like to get to know my students better," said Hope with a smile. She had taught in a large urban school district. These small-town kids didn't intimidate her in the least.

"Wait, you heard that?" a petite brunette asked, her face registering surprise.

"Yes, I did. I have pretty good hearing and the pre-requisite set of teacher eyes in the back of my head. Okay, you have thirty minutes to complete the five-paragraph essay. Do your best. I shouldn't have to say this, but please proofread it before you call it finished."

Most of the students went to work. Rusty stared at Hope, anger clouding his face. She just smiled and nodded at him, indicating he should start writing. Then she sat down at her desk in the front corner of the room and purposely avoided looking at Rusty, not rising to the bait of a stare down. She had too much experience to fall for that.

12

*T*he day was over before Hope knew it. On her way out of the school, several of her students called to her, wishing her a good night. Hope smiled to herself as she walked under the arching maple branches that made a green tunnel on the sidewalk. This was such a good place. Most of these kids didn't have the same kinds of issues some of her previous students had; homelessness, hunger, and gang affiliation. The last one was always a hard one for her. She understood the need for family and the gangs provided that for her students, but they were also full of danger. She missed those kids. When she married Gary, he insisted she stop teaching and stay at home as a trophy wife. They argued about it, and she won for a little while. Then, out of the blue, Hope was offered a teaching job at a small, prestigious private school. The pay wasn't the best, but the students were a dream. Gary pushed her to leave the gritty urban school that she loved to try this. He claimed he was concerned for her safety. It turned out he was really concerned about his image. She always wondered if he had pulled strings to get her there. She didn't doubt it.

She loved her students in the private school, too. But they came with their own set of problems. Privilege does not always equate success, but it certainly adds to the pressure. When she cut her ties with Gary, she discovered a layoff slip in mailbox.

She smiled to herself again. Things work out the way they are supposed to. She had a group of students who were diverse in income, ethnicity, and gifts. She had the perfect group of small-town students to teach and she was happy. Truly happy.

As she rounded the corner and entered the small drugstore on Main Street, she stepped aside to avoid the teenager who was on his way out. He saw her and scowled.

"Hello, Rusty," she said pleasantly.

He looked at her defiantly.

"I suppose you are going to say something inspiring or tell me to get my homework done on time," he growled.

"No, I was just going to say hello and have a nice evening," she didn't expect a polite response, so she wasn't disappointed. Rusty just shook his head and sulked down the steps to the sidewalk. He didn't look back.

"That Rusty Walsh can be a real asshole."

Hope looked up startled to see a young clerk looking at her with concern. She quickly searched the files in her brain, trying to put a name with the semi-familiar face. She was failing.

"I'm Sarah Wallins. I don't have you for English, but I'm taking your Creative Writing class next semester."

"Well, hello, Sarah. I'm pleased to meet you, and I look forward to having you in class."

"Thanks. I'm sorry Rusty was rude to you, but don't feel bad. He's rude to everyone."

"That's okay, Sarah. Usually when people are like that, they have something going on in their lives that makes them that way. Sometimes we just need to understand that they're going through some stuff and we need to give them space. You know what I mean?"

"Yeah, I do. No wonder Molly says you are a great teacher! She loves you."

"Molly Lerner? Long strawberry blonde hair, freckles?"

"Yep, that's her."

"Well, I am very glad she is happy with me as a teacher." Hope smiled at Sarah and moved out of the way as a customer came to the register with an armload of goods. Sarah turned her attention to the customer, and Hope walked away looking to pick up the things she needed for her medicine cabinet. Not only did she not have an umbrella, she couldn't treat a simple headache. Maybe she should have rethought leaving everything in the house and walking away.

No, it was better this way. She picked up a small basket and began to fill it with her needs.

"Headache already?" The voice came from behind her. Startled, she turned to see Chris standing there, looking at the contents of her basket. She was grateful she hadn't started down the feminine aisle yet.

"No, just stocking up. I discovered this morning I didn't have an umbrella, and I also realized that I didn't have a Band-Aid."

"Poor thing. Did you get hurt?"

Hope found his look of concern almost comical.

"No, just a paper cut." Hope reached up on the shelf and selected a box of adhesive strips, adding it to the basket.

"So, what do you say, would you like to join me for dinner tonight? I'm still getting my bearings, and I hate to eat alone." Chris put on his best lost puppy look.

Hope laughed and shrugged. Why not? She wondered briefly what Bridger would be doing for dinner.

"That would be nice. Where shall I meet you and what time?"

"I'd be happy to pick you up."

Hope thought quickly. She wasn't sure why she said she would meet him. It just came out of her mouth, but she was glad it did.

"Oh, I appreciate that, but I have some more errands to run and it would be easier just to meet you somewhere."

Hope looked back down into her basket, mentally running through her list so she missed the cloud that passed over Chris's face. By the time she looked up, his face was smiling again, accommodating.

68 | LARK GRIFFING

"Sure, I get that. Is pasta okay? I am hungry for some all you can eat breadsticks."

They agreed on a time and Chris said his goodbyes, moving toward the front of the store. Just before he left, he turned saying loudly, "I'm looking forward to tonight. See you then."

Sarah looked up from the register to see who Mr. Komat was talking to. When she realized it was Ms. Chandler, she grinned. She would have some juicy tidbits to tell Molly tonight while they were studying for their science quiz.

Hope saw the gears working in Sarah's head and she groaned inwardly. *Great*, she thought, *the rumor mill has begun.* She finished her shopping, topping the basket with a compact umbrella, and waited patiently in line for her turn to check out with Sarah.

Sarah quickly rang up her order, smiling broadly at Hope, thrilled that she had a front row seat to the show.

"Have a good night, Sarah," said Hope, knowing that mentioning the incident would just make it worse. *Thank God she wasn't refilling her birth control prescription today.*

"You, too, Ms. Chandler, You have a really good night, too," said Sarah giggling a little.

Hope forced herself to refrain from shooting Sarah her patented teacher look. She just kept a pleasant smile on her face and made her way out the door, stepping carefully down the set of ancient sandstone steps. She didn't see Chris sitting on the park bench across the street, watching her. She turned to head back down Maple. Chris rose and followed her. Keeping his distance.

13

*H*ope pulled into the popular Italian chain restaurant located by the mall and turned the key, shutting off the engine in her car. She looked at the bustling parking lot and sighed. She was now living in a small village on the coast, full of character and local color, but she was meeting Chris at a chain restaurant. Granted, the food was always good, consistent, but boring. Strike one against Chris.

As Hope exited her car, Chris appeared instantly by her side, startling her. She stumbled slightly as she tried to regain her composure. Chris reached out and cupped her elbow in his hand.

"Are you okay? Did you twist your ankle?" he asked, concern written all over his face.

"No, I'm fine. You just surprised me showing up like that. Where were you?" Hope asked, feeling a little uncomfortable.

"I'm sorry. I had just pulled in. When I was getting out, I recognized your car, so I walked on over here. I didn't mean to spook you."

"You know my car?"

"Hope, you parked next to me the other day. Don't you remember?"

"I guess."

"I'm kind of overly observant. It's the counselor in me. People tend to forget my job is being aware of nuances in people so that I can help them. It's especially helpful with students who are having trouble finding a voice. On the other hand, well-adjusted people might find it a bit disconcerting."

Hope relaxed, realizing he was right. His demeanor was just an occupational hazard.

"Shall we? Normally, I would prefer an established independent restaurant, but I haven't discovered a decent Italian place here in this mom and pop town. At least the food here is palatable, and the breadsticks are surprisingly good." Chris kept his hand on her elbow and guided her to the restaurant. He had secured call ahead seating, so their wait was short. The hostess led them to a corner out of the way, a detail for which Hope was appreciative. The rumors were already going to start to fly in a big way. She didn't want to add fuel to the fire.

"Cabernet?" Chris asked as he perused the wine list.

Hope would have preferred a solid rum drink but decided to play nice. She expected a glass, but Chris ordered a bottle. She had no intention of having more than one glass, and she suddenly felt very good about driving herself.

"So, what do you think of Grey's Harbor so far?" asked Chris, settling back in his chair swirling the wine in his glass, studying it, for what Hope had no idea. She was not a wine connoisseur.

"I love it, don't you?" Hope searched Chris's face, trying to read him.

"I do like it, but it is a little backwater for me, you know? This area here, around the mall and the subdivisions, are much more to my liking. The village part seems wrapped in the past, not progressive. I am concerned many of our students might be stuck here, unable to get out."

"Get out of what? This is a lovely town with an amazing history. From what I can see the people are proud of where they live."

"No, no, you are right," soothed Chris, "but I'm concerned that there isn't enough opportunity here. I feel like the families might encourage their children to stay and settle here instead of seeking out the great opportunities that are outside this protective bubble."

"I understand what you are saying, but there's nothing wrong with tradition and staying in a small town. If that's what you love and are content with, why not?"

"I agree, but don't you think a person should be encouraged to discover what is beyond the walls? Then they can decide what they want?"

"Well, I don't see walls around this town, but it is an interesting viewpoint." Hope remarked kindly.

Chris felt a moment of irritation. She was patronizing him. He didn't like that.

The waitress arrived at that moment, dispelling the mood. Hope ordered the fettuccini alfredo and Chris exclaimed that it was his favorite, too. His face took on the look of a conspirator who had just found a partner in crime.

Good grief, Hope thought, *it's just fettuccini alfredo.*

The waitress quickly brought the salad and breadsticks. After serving Hope, Chris dug in with gusto declaring the buttery bread perfection. Hope had to agree. She was starting to loosen up, the glass of wine she had started to sip easing away the tensions of the day. By the time dinner arrived, Chris and Hope were engaged in a stimulating conversation about guilt and its place in motivation.

Over dinner, the conversation moved to school, and Chris asked about Hope's students. Were there any who concerned her?

"I'm looked at as an outsider here," he remarked, "so the students are hesitant to come see me. Any referrals would be helpful."

Rusty Walsh immediately came to Hope's mind, remembering the surly attitude and the guarded looks. She kept her tongue, however.

"No, I think I'm able to handle them all right now. I'm just getting to know them, learning their writing styles. I've got a great group of kids."

Chris studied her, his eyes veiled.

"Hmmm. I thought you would have been experienced enough to catch Rusty Walsh's depression." He waited; his eyes steady on hers.

Hope's face colored slightly.

"It sounds like you don't need a referral there. You're already aware that he is sulky, but honestly, he hasn't given me any trouble, nor have I felt the need for a counselor to intervene on my behalf." She returned his gaze, not backing down. This wasn't her first rodeo.

"But you didn't think I should be consulted and brought in to help this student?"

"No, I didn't, and I don't. I'm still building trust with my students. None of my students have given me any indication that they are a danger to themselves or others. Some are eager to please, some couldn't care less, and others, like Rusty, are putting up a typical teenager front and putting me through my paces. I don't refer every kid who is sullen. I build a relationship with them first. Then, if I need help, I'll call out the entire army. I'm not there yet." She smiled to help soften the blow. After all, they were going to have to continue to work together.

Chris was immediately contrite.

"I'm sorry. I didn't mean to come off as aggressive. I just want to be there for all my students. Like I said, I'm an outsider. A lot of the village residents are unhappy with the fact that Gaylord Fornby hired me, an out of towner instead of a local. It's a tough place to be in."

Again, Hope's kind heart melted. She knew what it was like to be treated like an outsider. Several of her students had made that clear, but she was beginning to think she was winning the majority of them over, slowly but surely.

"I know. I'm sorry that it has been a hard start for you. I promise, I'll bring you in when and if the time is right. Then we will work as a team to make sure Rusty has the supports he needs. Fair?"

Chris grinned, suddenly happy, the mood lifting. He raised his glass, his third, to hers. Hope could only follow suit at risk of being rude.

The waitress asked if they wanted dessert. Chris raised a questioning eyebrow to her. Hope declined, declaring herself full. The evening had been somehow exhausting, and she was ready to head home.

"Please, go ahead and order dessert for yourself. I'll be happy to wait," said Hope, kindly.

Chris smiled tightly and declined, asking for the check.

"I don't suppose I could interest you in stopping on the way home for a drink, just to top off the evening?"

"No, I'm sorry Chris, but I'm a little tired. I have some work to do before I turn in for the evening, so I will need to say goodnight,"

"No, I understand. Let me walk you to your car." Chris led her out of the restaurant and through the parking lot to her vehicle, his hand resting lightly on the small of her back.

She pulled out her keys, and he gently took them from her, acting chivalrous as he unlocked her door and opened it for her. He held the keys up in the air as if he wanted her to beg for them. His eyes glittered.

Hope took a deep breath and held out her hand for them. Instead Chris took her hand in his and glanced around the parking lot. Hope's eyes followed his. Chris smiled slightly as he saw a tight group of students loitering by the door of the mall arcade. He and Hope had their attention. In an instant he bent down and pressed his lips to hers, literally stealing a kiss before Hope had a chance to react.

She turned her face as his lips slid to her cheek. She stepped back, anger rising, but she kept her face controlled. She was not going to make a scene in front of the students.

"I don't do that in public," she stated firmly, so that there was no mistake.

Chris had the decency to look sheepish, but his eyes took on a glint.

"In private then?"

Hope realized her mistake.

"Good night, Chris. Thank you for a lovely evening." She held out her hand again, leveling a cold look in his eyes. He actually squirmed like a student. *I've still got it*, she thought, thinking back to her urban school days and the times she had to face down a tough street-smart student.

Chris pressed her keys in her hand and told her good night. Then he had the audacity to turn from her and wave cheerfully to the tight group of students. Hope blew out her breath, exasperated, got in her car and closed the door a little more forcefully than necessary.

14

*A*t the last minute, Hope changed directions. She was on her way home but felt incredibly unsettled and remarkably alone. She drove past the diner and saw that there was still a steady stream of business. She continued down the road, not knowing where she was going, but she knew she was not ready to go to the boat. As she neared the river, she spotted the lights of the Mizzen Mast. Making a decision, she turned the car into the parking lot.

Izzy looked up as Hope entered the bar. She noted Hope was alone. That was good, because rumor had it Hope had spent the evening with the new counselor having dinner on the north end. She watched the woman walk hesitantly toward the bar. Izzy knew the walk. It was of someone who was not used to frequenting bars alone.

"Evening, Hope. What'll you have?"

Hope hesitated. She didn't want to drink, but she was in a bar.

"Decaf maybe?" Izzy raised a pierced eyebrow.

Hope smiled gratefully. Izzy was a smart lady.

"Grab a seat, I'll have it for you in a minute."

Hope scrambled up on the bar stool, never comfortable on them, and leaned on the bar with both elbows. Gosh, she was tired. The school day had gone well, but now she was exhausted. She shouldn't have stopped.

"What's eating you?" Izzy asked, setting down the cup of coffee on the bar and leaning on it herself. "Cream and sugar?"

"No, black. Thank you."

"I knew I might like you." Izzy nodded in approval.

Hope took a sip of the hot coffee and was surprised at how good it was.

"Next town over. Shifting Dunes Coffee Company. This is their decaf. Pretty good, but their dark roast will put hair on your chest."

"I'll have to try the dark roast sometime. That's my favorite roast." She took another sip appreciatively

"So, what's bothering you?" Izzy looked frankly at Hope, not being coy or even pretending not to pry.

"It shows? How?"

"You're not the type to wander into a bar alone."

"What makes you say that?"

"Honey, it's obvious."

"Shows that much, huh?"

"Sure does. Look, I think you're probably a strong woman, but I think you have had a man guiding you most of your life. I think now that you're here, in Grey's Harbor, you have the chance to come into your own. You just need to do it."

"And coming here by myself is the first step."

"Possibly."

Izzy poured herself a cup of coffee. She glanced around the quiet bar and then settled in to listen to Hope.

Hope just sat, quietly.

"So, your date with the good counselor didn't go so well?" Izzy said, slyly.

"What the hell? Already?"

"Honey, you're in a very small town."

Hope swirled the remains of coffee in her cup.

"It was fine. He just, I don't know."

"Sounds like he was moving faster than you were ready."

"Oh, for the love of God," Hope said, frustration rising.

"Don't let it bug you. You'll be the town entertainment for a while. You might as well get used to it. You're new and you're interesting. Just remember, you teach these people's kids. They won't be kind if you screw up. Understand?"

"I most certainly do. And I don't intend to screw up." Hope glanced around. "Why is it so quiet in here tonight?"

"It's Monday. Things won't heat up until after nine o'clock. That's when Pappy comes in."

"Pappy?"

Izzy smiled fondly, thinking of the old black gentleman who lived in a tiny ancient trailer on the river.

"Yes, Pappy. Just Pappy. He comes in on Monday nights after nine and sits over on that stool in the corner. Then he starts wailing on his harmonica. He doesn't talk to anyone. He doesn't take requests, and he doesn't stop playing for over an hour. He will accept a drink or two, thank you very much. He will also pick up an envelope at the end of the night. I always leave one on the bar. Folks slip money in there. It's a good relationship. When he's done, he nods his head, tips his hat, picks up his envelope and slips out the back door. That's it. That's Pappy."

Hope thought about that for a minute. It was a Monday night. She was bone-tired, but it was eight forty-five and she wasn't going to miss this.

"Come on. Let me pour you another cup and put you in a booth in the corner. You'll have a decent view and when you've had enough, you, too, can slip out the back."

Izzy warmed up Hope's cup and Hope followed her to the booth. They both sat down.

"Hope, this is a small town. People talk. Your business will never be your own. You need to always remember that. Lots of people hate that, especially outsiders. What they fail to understand is, if they manage to make it through the scrutiny and they roll with the punches, the villagers will begin to accept them. Once they accept them, they begin to love and protect them. Right now, you are just beginning the trial."

"Are you trying to tell me that Bridger already knows that I went out with Chris tonight?"

"Of course, he knows, but you don't have anything to apologize for. As far as I know, you two aren't exclusive. You've gone to dinner a couple of times and have enjoyed the deck of your boat. That's all the intel I've gotten."

"You've gotten all of it." Hope smiled ruefully.

"The real question is, has Clarence gotten to you yet?"

"You don't know?"

"Clarence is discreet."

"Bullshit" Hope retorted, laughing.

"Clarence is discreet because he is so open. If one person gets talked about, they'll all get talked about, so no one talks about Clarence."

Hope shook her head. Small towns are not as simple as they seemed.

Izzy rose to go back to the bar. The place was beginning to fill up. The atmosphere was completely different from Friday night. It was almost reverent and respectful.

Before Hope knew it, a stooped ancient black man wearing an old-fashioned soft baseball hat hitched onto the stool in the corner. Out of the corner of her eye, Hope saw Izzy slip an envelope on the end of the bar. Pappy nodded to her without looking at her. He slid a shiny harmonica out of his pocket and started pulling the saddest wail of blues Hope had ever heard from the tiny instrument. The music pulled at her soul, tearing at her heart. Tears sprung to her eyes as the sweet sounds rose and fell, unending.

Sweat poured from Pappy's brow, but he never stopped. The music was endless. The music was everything. No one in the bar spoke. It was like a church service, only the sermon was the sounds of the reeds pouring from the breath of an old black gentleman.

Hope sat mesmerized. Nothing mattered. Not her day. Not Chris. Not Bridger. And it was over too soon.

Pappy stood and bowed ever so slightly. He took an offered shot on the way out and slid the envelope into his pocket. There was a moment of silence, of respect as he left through the back door.

Hope left enough money on the table to cover her coffee and a tip and headed out, too. Izzy nodded to her as she left and Hope smiled back a wan smile.

When she got home, she swiped at her deck chairs with the broom, careful to dislodge the spiders without hurting them. Then she settled in to think about her evening. About Chris and his seemingly juvenile and coarse manner and about Pappy and his elegance and style.

Both kinds of people made up a place like Grey's Harbor. They were all part of the tapestry, but Hope had the distinct impression that the tapestry might have a flaw in the material. Her instinct was warning her that something wasn't quite right.

15

"Wow, you move fast," Pepper teased as Hope handed her a cup of coffee from the Cathead.

"That's cold. I bring you a dark roast with a shot of toffee and you give me grief. Seriously, how bad are the rumors?"

"Well, you've become the hottest topic in town," said Pepper, taking a cautious sip. "Damn, this stuff is good. Thanks."

"What do you mean I am the hottest topic in town?"

"Apparently you were the talk of the barber shop last night, and Manny said he would keep score." Pepper picked up a dry erase marker and started to write the day's outcomes on the white board.

"Wait, who is Manny, and what score?"

"Manny Wodarski. He's the barber and the owner of Manny's Barber shop. He has officially dubbed himself the scorekeeper, you know between you and Chris."

"But what's the score? Are you kidding me?"

"So, they are basically keeping track of Chris and his moves. You know, he didn't score last night."

"That's horrible. I thought this was small town USA. You know, wholesome and everything." Hope's heart was beating fast, her flushed face giving away her distress.

"Relax. It's just for fun. Besides, small town USA folks have sex, too."

"Not with the English teacher! This is awful."

"No, this isn't awful. When the bell rings and all your students come into your room and look at you, wondering the same thing, that's when it gets awful," Pepper commiserated.

"Oh, no. They get weirded out just running into their teacher in a restaurant or the grocery store. They don't think we come out of our cells. Now they are going to be thinking about me having sex with the guidance counselor. Oh, no…" Hope groaned.

"Now what's wrong?" Pepper asked concerned, taking another sip.

"We start reading a new unit today."

"I'm afraid to ask."

"*The Scarlet Letter*," said Hope miserably.

Pepper burst out giggling then tried to hide it when she saw the look on Hope's face. It didn't work. Try as she might, she couldn't suppress her laughter.

"What's so funny?" Chris asked as he poked his head into Pepper's room.

"Girl talk," said Pepper breezily trying to keep Chris's attention off Hope so he couldn't see the flush on her cheeks.

"Hey, Hope. Did you hear the town thinks we're an item?" He wagged his eyebrows at her.

Hope groaned and excused herself from the room.

"Was it something I said?" asked Chris.

Pepper just rolled her eyes and finished writing on the board.

"Did you need anything, Chris?" she asked, trying to keep the irritation out of her voice.

"Yes," he cleared his throat, putting on his professional persona. "Please send me Brian Trend. I need to speak with him in my office."

"Of course, I will send him down right after attendance."

*H*ope sank into the chair at the table nearest the window. She thought about not coming down for lunch at all but rather eating in her room, but then she thought better of it. Hiding was probably not the way to go.

Pepper came in and dropped some coins in the soda machine.

"Need one, kiddo?"

"No, I'm good. She lifted her thermos filled with iced tea.

"Did you make it through the morning? Were your students merciful?"

"Actually, it wasn't so bad. A little giggling, and Rusty was grumpier than usual, but they were good."

"They like you. That's why. You're doing a great job here, Hope. The students think you're great and the administration is happy. Just keep doing what you're doing, and everything will work out just fine. Keep your head up and ride this wave until the end."

"How long do you think it will take?"

"The truth?"

Hope nodded miserably.

"Until you shut him down or he scores. It's as simple as that."

Hope sunk her teeth into her ham sandwich and Pepper turned her attention to her phone when Mr. Fender entered the room.

"Good afternoon, ladies," he said cheerfully.

They returned his greeting and watched as he approached their table.

"Ms. Chandler, it has come to my attention that you are the topic of the day."

Hope's face burned bright red. Suddenly the mouthful of sandwich turned to sawdust in her throat.

"I'm sorry, sir," she stammered.

Mr. Fender held up his hand to stop her.

"No worries. This is the curse of a small town. All I ask is that you are discreet with your relationships and that you keep everything professional here at school."

"John, seriously, and in front of me?" Pepper scolded him.

"I was going to add that I was just quoting from the board president and that I didn't think any of this even needed to be mentioned. I think you are the utmost professional, Ms. Chandler. Please let me know if you need anything or have any difficulty, and I will be happy to assist."

He bowed to both of them and wished them a good day.

Hope dropped her head to the table and slowly banged her forehead against it three or four times.

Pepper reached over and absently stroked the top of Hope's head while she continued to catch up on the news feed on her phone.

*It was worse when she got home. As she walked by Clarence's boat, he was sunning himself in a lounger on his deck wearing a skimpy speedo. A martini sat beside him. Hope groaned inwardly; an intoxicated Clarence is not what she needed right now.

"Hope, dear, I am crushed. You turned me down for some inexperienced child? You deserve smooth moves, not a bumbling idiot. Experience, my dear, is everything. If you're interested, I have a bit of time now. Not as much as you are worthy of, but it would be the start of something beautiful, I promise." He lifted his glass as an invitation.

Instead of feeling irritated, Hope found herself bursting into laughter. Clarence smiled.

"Can I take that for a yes?" His elderly face beamed.

"Um, no thank you Clarence, but you did help put things in perspective. You are a dear." She stepped onto his boat, leaned over, and gave the suave gentleman a kiss on the cheek. "You're truly a gem, my friend."

"Be careful, you're playing with fire." Bridger's voice called out behind her. He was carrying a white paper bag and a couple of Island Goatfish IPA's.

Hope's heart skipped a beat, then guilt washed through her.

"These are for me," Bridger gestured toward the beer in his hands.

"I figure you have had a day, and a Hemingway Special is the only thing that'll help."

Hope grinned at him.

"Now you're talking. See you later, Clarence."

"You could see a lot more of me later if you choose, my dear." Clarence teased, "but I can see you are occupied with another young one. At least he is top shelf compared to the bottom bracket you entertained last night. Life is too short not to taste the top shelf delights."

Bridger handed Hope the white paper bag and then took her hand as she moved from Clarence's boat back to the dock. The white bag emitted amazing aromas, tantalizing Asian cuisine teased her as she remembered the sandwich she ended up throwing away at lunch.

"I hope you like pepper steak and sweet and sour pork."

"I do. Please tell me there is wonton soup in there."

"Of course. I don't do anything half-assed."

"I can vouch for that," Clarence called after them. "I could tell you stories about Bridger's ass."

"Clarence, I'm going to raise your dock rent."

"Touché," Clarence said as he rose to ready himself for his evening visitor.

16

*B*ridger wiped down the small bistro table on the deck of the little houseboat while Hope busied herself in the kitchen. She emerged with table settings for two and a rum drink for one.

"Bad day, huh?" said Bridger sympathetically.

She was grateful he wasn't displaying normal male territory marking.

"Yeah, not my best." She took a sip of her drink and sighed setting it down on the table.

"I hope I am not too forward inviting myself for dinner."

"Not when you bring dinner. Be as forward as you want, but can it hold on for just a few more minutes? The oven is on low if you want to put the food in there to keep it warm. I'll only be a few minutes."

"Take your time. I'll just settle down here and sip my beer. Clarence will provide me with a bit of entertainment soon."

Hope disappeared into the cabin, kicking off her wedge heels the minute she stepped in. Once in her bedroom she slipped off her dress. She looked longingly toward the shower. It would feel so good.

She heard Bridger come inside and the telltale sound of the oven door opening. Good, dinner would stay warm. It would only take a minute.

She slipped into the shower cell and drowned herself in a steamy escape.

True to her word, she kept it quick. A few minutes later she emerged, her long damp hair combed straight down her back. She slipped on her old Cleveland Indians shirt and a pair of boxy terrycloth shorts. She decided barefoot was the style for the evening. After putting away her dirty school clothes, she made her way back into the kitchen to pull dinner out of the oven, but Bridger was standing there, beating her to it.

She tossed him an oven mitt, while she took some serving spoons out of the drawer. Together they made their way back to the deck.

"God, you smell amazing," said Bridger, as he pulled up short behind her.

"Thanks," she said, blushing slightly. "I couldn't resist a shower, sorry if I took too long."

"Not at all. You look a little more relaxed and that was the point. Sit down and let's eat this stuff." Bridger pulled out her chair and went to sit himself when he heard his name being called. He turned and looked down the deck to see Clara Cotter heading their way.

"Shit," he said under his breath.

"What's wrong? Who's that?"

"That's Clara Cotter, Ralph Cotter's daughter."

"Why does that name sound familiar?"

"Because she's the person who thought she was going to get your job. Her daddy is the one who's been making noises all around town about how an outsider doesn't understand our culture." He stopped speaking as Clara came up to Hope's boat.

"Good evening, Bridger," said Clara, dripping with sweetness. She flashed a frosty smile at Hope, the smile freezing on her face as she looked Hope up and down.

Suddenly it dawned on Hope how this looked, freshly showered, the two of them dining on her deck. *Damn it. This was not good.*

Bridger tried to smooth the awkward moment.

"Clara, have you met Hope Chandler? Hope this is Clara Cotter."

"We haven't met, but I have certainly heard all about her." Clara said, her voice heavy with contempt.

"Please to meet you," Hope said sweetly, trying hard to be polite and not transparent.

"What brings you here this evening, Clara? Did you come to visit Clarence?" Bridger said slyly.

Clara gasped, her mouth working like a fish out of water, open, close, open.

Hope put her hand over her mouth to stop herself from laughing.

"Of course not. That's absurd. Seriously, Bridger. How could you..."

"Calm down, Clara. It was a joke. What can I do for you?"

Clara took a deep breath, attempting to gain composure and the upper hand.

"Daddy sent me down here to see if we can count on you, or rather Cadigan Marina, on your normal donation sponsorship for this year's Oyster Festival?"

"Of course. We always do that. Just send the paperwork to the office as usual."

"Well that's just the problem, Bridger. We sent the paperwork three weeks ago, and we haven't received a response. Daddy thought perhaps you had decided not to be one of our premier sponsors. After all, he had heard that you might have run into some financial, um, embarrassment." She raised her eyes brows, now completely in charge.

Hope looked down at the table, not wanting to be a witness to this exchange.

"I can assure you Clara. I am not financially embarrassed. I don't know how this rumor started but doesn't have any merit. I'll check with my mom to see if she received the paperwork and just hasn't gotten around to it. Please tell your dad that we are always proud to be a premier sponsor, this year and every year."

"Well, I'm glad that things are okay, and I'll tell Daddy. The thing is, Bridger, more often than not, there is a kernel of truth behind every rumor." She smiled wickedly at Hope.

Hope calmly returned the gaze and decided it was time to take the bull by the horns.

"Clara, would you care to join us for dinner? I'm sure there is plenty, and I would love to get to know you. Heaven knows I am new here. It's hard being an out of towner, moving, getting a new job, and not knowing anyone. I'm sure you can be sympathetic to that. I'd cherish any friendships I can nurture." Hope gestured to an empty chair.

Flustered by this tactic, Clara was momentarily at a loss. Luckily for her, the cell phone in her purse chirped allowing her to regroup.

"Thank you for your kind offer," she said, dripping southern etiquette, but I really must be getting back. I have an oyster festival to organize."

Clara said goodbye warmly to Bridger and stepped off Hope's boat, catching her toe as she moved to the dock. She landed awkwardly, like a pelican coming in for a landing, but she recovered without being physically hurt. Her dignity, on the other hand, suffered. She stalked away with as much aplomb as possible.

"So, how long before the entire town figures we slept together, and I showered after the dirty deed?"

"I would guess right about now," said Bridger as he gestured to Clara's retreating figure, the phone pressed to her ear, her left-hand gesturing wildly.

"I think I need another drink," said Hope.

"Go ahead and make it, and I'll dish this food up. Then let's eat, I'm starving."

*H*ope wanted a third Hemingway special, but thought better of it. It was a school night, after all. On the other hand, it was still early. Maybe it wouldn't hurt.

"What's troubling that pretty head of yours?" Bridger asked lazily as he cracked open another beer and took a long draw. Hope slapped a mosquito that was drawing blood from her elbow.

"I am contemplating one more drink. I'm wondering if that's an intelligent choice. Probably not. But then, obviously I am becoming known for poor choices."

Bridger looked at her carefully. She didn't sound bitter.

"Do you want me to try to make it for you?" Bridger asked, wondering just how picky she would be about the quality of her drink.

"Sure, give it a shot. Thanks." She relaxed back in her chair watching an egret fishing in the reeds along the shore.

Bridger got up and made his way to the galley. He had no idea what he was doing, and he knew Hope knew it. He checked his phone and found a recipe. The ingredients were still on the counter, so he figured it was a no brainer.

He proudly emerged from the cabin, drink in hand and stopped short when he saw Hope. The sun was low in the sky, casting the world in a warm pink wash. Hope's skin glowed tan and her face was relaxed, eyes closed. Her hair, now dry, cascaded down her shoulders, tumbled over her arms, and hung over the back of the chair. He wanted to scoop that hair up into his palms and run his fingers through it while kissing Hope's neck and the hollow of her throat. He had feelings stirring that he had buried years ago. He wasn't interested in a relationship, but this woman was driving him crazy. He moved toward her, the ice tinkling as it touched the side of the glass. He wanted to take one of those ice cubes and run it from her throat, down between her breasts and then…

Hope opened her eyes. Bridger was looking at her like he was hungry, and she was a sandwich. She had the craziest desire to ask him if he had had enough to eat, but she thought better of it.

"Let's see how you did." She held out a hand, the tips of her fingers touching his as she took the glass. Electricity ran through both of them. Neither of them moved as they looked in each other's eyes.

Bridger was the first to break.

"If we're not careful, we're going to really give this town something to talk about," he said in a husky voice.

Hope smiled at him. It was tempting. So tempting.

Bridger read her thoughts.

"It's not that I don't want to Hope, but the timing, it's just not right."

"I know," she whispered and patted the chair next to her.

Once again, they spent the evening watching the river flow past on the way to the sea and watching Clarence welcome ladies into his floating Casanova suite.

17

*I*t was early evening. The sun was still hot, and the air was still. Heavy humidity dripped with the hint of thunderstorms to come. Bridger was sitting on the deck of his houseboat staring at the computer screen of his laptop, trying to make sense of what he was looking at.

It looked good. The marina accounts were solid, but there didn't seem to be any disbursements. He scrolled through the numbers. Deposits were there, but he wasn't surprised. He often made the deposits because his mom wasn't fond of driving.

"Hey, Bridger."

Ryker Wynn hailed him from the dock. Bridger looked up startled. He didn't hear Ryker come up the dock.

"Hey, Ryker. Come aboard."

Bridger stood and welcomed his friend, shaking his hand and slapping his back at the same time.

"How's the cabin coming?" Bridger asked.

"Pretty well. We just finished sheeting the roof." Ryker glanced at the sky.

"No rain in sight yet," said Bridger, "but you know it's coming. You can feel it in the air. How's Jennifer?"

"She's good. She's on her way over to work the dinner shift at the diner."

"So, you're alone tonight and looking for someone to snag a beer off of is my guess."

"Well, if you are offering." Ryker grinned. "I'll spring for pizza delivery."

"That's a deal I won't pass up." Bridger closed his laptop and headed into the cabin to get a couple of beers.

"Double extra-large half sausage and mushroom, half pepperoni and onion?"

"You know me so well," Bridger came out and batted his eyelashes at Ryker as he handed him a Sperm Whale Ale.

"I always feel weird drinking this stuff. Like maybe it compromises my manhood."

"It's just a name, my friend. Drink up and embrace the label."

Thirty minutes later, a hot cheesy pizza between them, Ryker and Bridger dug in.

"Man, I don't know what you have against mushrooms," Ryker said to Bridger, his eyes closed in mock ecstasy.

"Bridger doesn't like mushrooms? What's wrong with him?"

Hope overheard the two of them as she walked toward her boat, her briefcase and lunch bag in one arm, a load of groceries in another.

"There is a lot wrong with our boy," Ryker laughed.

Bridger jumped up to help Hope. She waved him away with an awkward arm.

"I've got this. No worries, but thanks." She started down the dock toward her boat.

"Hope, join us for pizza. Ryker ordered a double extra-large. He keeps thinking we're still the young men we used to be. He does this all the time and we end up with a bunch of leftover pizza."

"I don't want to interrupt boy's night." Hope said, hesitating slightly.

"No interruption at all," Ryker assured her. "This wasn't a planned boy's night. Please join us."

Hope realized they were sincere.

"Give me two minutes and I'll be down. Do we need anything?"

"Nope, unless you want something other than beer."

Hope nodded. She had to stop herself from skipping down the dock to her boat. She hadn't been looking forward to eating her microwave dinner for one.

Five minutes later, wearing a soft, gauzy sundress that tickled her bare feet, Hope walked back down the deck toward Bridger's boat carrying a plastic container of brownies.

"Damn," Ryker said, watching Hope walk toward them. "You've got a good-looking woman at your fingertips who obviously likes you. I suggest you don't wait too long to make your move, or you'll lose her to that weak-chinned guidance counselor. Which would be a crime. The town has you on the losing end of this game. You know that, don't you?"

"Why?"

"Because everyone knows you don't date anymore."

Bridger shot his friend a warning glance.

"Don't worry. I'm not going to ride your ass, but Bridger, it's been years since you and Pepper were an item. I'm not going to give you shit about that whole thing. You know I respect you, but you've got something special here. I'd hate to see you lose this." Ryker popped a piece of pizza in his mouth, watching amused as his friend jumped up to help Hope onto his boat, despite the fact that she was perfectly capable of doing it herself.

"Pepperoni and onion, or sausage mushroom," Ryker asked as Bridger handed Hope a paper plate.

"Yes, please." She said and smiled.

Ryker nodded approval and dished two slices of pizza onto Hope's plate. Bridger handed her a beer and Hope settled into a chair.

"Oh my, this is delicious. Is there anything this town can't provide?"

"What, you're surprised this sleepy, backwater coastal town has good pizza?"

"Well, frankly, yes," Hope admitted.

"Okay, the truth. We didn't have good pizza until about fifteen years ago. That's when Tony Conti and Danny Marino moved here from New York. They're a couple. They opened Harbor New York and introduced the village to openly gay and New York style. The rest is history," Bridger said, helping himself to another slice.

"Well, thank goodness for Tony and Danny. I was worried when I left the Cleveland area that I was leaving behind good pizza."

"Why would Cleveland, Ohio have good pizza?" Ryker asked, curiously.

"Well, we have an amazing restaurant scene, and we have Little Italy."

"Cleveland? For real?"

"For real. I was afraid I'd have trouble settling into this quiet town after having all the amenities I had there, but I love this. I love the quiet. I love the community, and best of all you guys have really good food here."

"Wait until the Oyster Festival. It's an amazing food fest. We don't allow outside vendors in. The food booths are local families, restaurants, and churches. Each brings their specialties, and of course, there are oysters prepared every way imaginable."

Hope wrinkled her nose, not sure about the oysters.

"What, not a fan of oysters?" teased Bridger.

"I'm not sure. I remember trying them when I was young. To be frank, it was like swallowing a ball of snot."

Ryker burst out laughing, beer shooting out his nose.

"Nice, Ryker. Now that's a gift." Bridger absently handed Ryker a napkin.

"Give them another try, Hope. If they're prepared correctly, they're delicious."

She reached for another piece of pizza and chewed it thoughtfully.

"Does Harbor New York have a pizza stand?" she asked.

"Yep, and they make a smoked oyster pizza that's amazing," said Ryker.

"Of course, they do. When is this festival that everyone is talking about?"

"Second weekend in October, so not too far away," Bridger said.

Ryker stared at him, nodding slightly, encouraging.

Bridger sighed.

Hope waited.

Ryker grinned.

"I can show you around if you want, let you know the best booths to sample the oysters," Bridger finally said.

"I'd like that," Hope said with an encouraging smile, as she licked a spot of sauce from her finger.

Bridger watched the tip of her tongue flick out and snag the stray dollop of sauce.

Ryker didn't miss the look on Bridger's face. He took a quick drink to cover up the smirk.

Hope looked between the two of them, wondering what she'd missed.

"Excuse me, Bridger…"

"Hey, Dom, what's going on?"

"I'm sorry to interrupt, sir." The older man held his hat in his hands, twisting it slightly. He looked nervous.

Hope's heart went out to the elderly man. Why was he so stressed in front of Bridger? What was going on?

"Dom, you're not interrupting. Hope this is Dom Costa. He works at the marina for me. Dom, this is Hope Chandler."

"Pleased to meet you, Dom," Hope said, warmly.

"The pleasure is all mine," Dom said, his eyes shining kindly. "Bridger, I didn't know what to do. I would have called you, but I thought I'd better tell you in person." Dom was visibly shaken.

Ryker stood up and offered Dom his chair, excusing himself to go get another beer. Dom didn't sit. Hope followed Ryker, but they were not out of earshot.

"Go ahead, Dom. Tell me what's wrong."

"It's Mrs. Cadigan."

"Dom, what's wrong with Mom?" Bridger asked, standing up suddenly, concern filling his voice. Ryker moved out of the cabin to stand next to Bridger, Hope by his side.

"She called this evening," Dom said haltingly, "She asked for Mathias. I didn't know what to say. I didn't know what to do, so I said he wasn't here right now. I didn't know…" Dom squeezed his hat tighter. "Then she said she just wanted to know when he would be home for dinner. She asked about you, too, so I told her I would find you and you would call her back."

Hope looked up at Ryker, questions in her eyes. He shook his head ever so slightly, watching Bridger carefully.

"You did fine, Dom. Thank you. I appreciate you coming over here and telling me in person. I'll check on my mom."

"Bridger, I hope Mrs. Cadigan's okay. She's such a nice lady. Maybe she just misses Mathias and is a little confused." He shrugged helplessly.

"Thank you, Dom. I'll let you know. Can you lock up for me tonight?"

"Absolutely. You don't worry about a thing. I'll take care of everything. Please give Mrs. Cadigan my best."

With that Dom rose and bowed slightly.

"It was a pleasure, Ms. Chandler, Ryker," and he left the boat, walking quickly back toward the marina building.

"Bridger are you okay?" asked Ryker. "Do you need me to come with you to check on your mom?"

"No, thanks. I've got this. This might explain a few things, though." said Bridger, his mind working a mile a minute.

"Go take care of your mom. I can get this cleaned up," said Hope as she bent to pick up the abandoned paper plates.

"You don't need to do that," said Bridger as he patted his pockets for his keys and wallet.

"Go Bridger, we'll take care of everything here. Call us if you need anything."

"Okay, thanks guys." Ryker placed his hand on Bridger's back as he stepped off the boat. Bridger turned and looked back, catching Hope's eyes.

"Sorry the evening is ending this way, Hope."

"Don't be silly. My prayers are with you and your mom." She stepped forward and lightly kissed Bridger on the cheek, giving his shoulder a squeeze. "Drive carefully. You won't do your mom any good if you get yourself hurt going over there."

"You're a smart woman, Hope Chandler." He brushed her lips with his and turned, leaving her standing there with a worried look on her face.

"Well, that just sucks," said Ryker.

"Yeah, it doesn't sound good. I take it this Mathias is not around?"

"Mathias Cadigan is Bridger's dad. Was. He died when Bridger was a junior in high school."

"Okay, that's not a good sign. Has Bridger's mom shown signs of dementia?"

"Not that I know of, but there has been talk in the town that Bridger might have run into some financial issues. There are several businesses who haven't had their invoices paid." Ryker stopped short, realizing he was sharing gossip about his best friend.

"It's okay, Ryker. I know you don't carry tales about your friends. You're just concerned. Just the other day, Clara Cotter came by to mention something about the sponsorship for the Oyster Festival. Bridger seemed surprised she would ask."

"Clara Cotter is one of the people who is doing the talking, saying that Bridger can't pay his commitments. The thing is, Bridger's mom runs the office end of the marina business. She's done it for years. As an ex-librarian, she is an organization freak. The business has always been an efficient machine, Bridger's mom handling the office, his dad the marina. When his dad died, Bridger stepped up and took over the marina end. He had already started building custom wooden boats as a hobby, so he just fell into his career. He handled the marina and high school at the same time. He had thought about going to college, to learn what he could to help with his boat building dream, but that was dashed when his dad died. So, he taught himself. He and his dad built the houseboat you live in."

"I love that boat. At first, I was nervous, because it looks hand-made, but it is wonderful."

"Bridger builds amazing boats. He almost stopped doing it."

"Why?"

"That's a story for someone else to tell. Not my place." Ryker took a swallow of his remaining beer.

Hope waited patiently. She was a pro at waiting someone out.

"Hope, Bridger's life has been touched by tragedy. Some of it is just bad luck, like his dad having a heart attack at a young age. Nothing anyone can do about something like that, but other things, they can be bad luck, too, but if you can find a person to blame, that somehow makes it easier. If you can blame yourself, then that becomes a tragedy."

"Bridger blames himself?"

"Yes, he does. He doesn't have a reason to, but he still does. That's all I'm going to say about it but know this; Bridger is a great guy. He just may take a while to, you know, form a bond." Ryker shrugged, helplessly.

"So, what you're saying is if I am interested in Bridger, I need to give him time. He doesn't just jump in the sack with any available female." Ryker blushed at Hope's words. "Well, neither do I. Contrary to the town rumors, I am not easy. I intend to date. I intend to get to know people, but I don't give away my heart on a whim. If and when I ever do, it's going to take an amazing man who I can trust with all my heart and all my soul. Truthfully, I don't see this happening soon. Now are you done eating pizza, or shall we sit and salvage what's left of the evening, because quite frankly, I am not leaving this boat until Bridger comes back and I know that he is okay."

"Then I guess you and I are settling in for the long haul. Are those brownies?"

"They are." Hope opened the package and offered them to Ryker. She helped herself to another piece of pizza.

Ryker laughed

"What? It's good. I love pizza."

"I know what you mean. I can eat that stuff until I'm ready to throw up because I've eaten so much."

They settled in to wait for news from their friend.

18

Two hours later, Jennifer joined them on the boat. She had a chicken dinner in an ovenproof container which she put in Bridger's oven on low. Ryker offered her the last piece of pepperoni onion.

"I'm not hungry, but I won't turn down Harbor New York. Hey, are those brownies?"

Hope passed the container over to Jennifer as she settled in to wait, too.

The sun had long set. The lights on the docks twinkled merrily, and a slight breeze picked up. Clouds were moving in from the west, covering the stars, obscuring the moon.

"Why do I feel like something bad is about to happen?" asked Jennifer, glancing anxiously around.

"Just a storm rolling in, honey," Ryker soothed her. He pulled her chair close and casually dropped an arm around her shoulder. She snuggled in close and sighed.

"I love storms," said Hope, "just not super violent ones. We used to get some bad ones back in Cleveland. Do you get tornados here?"

"We do, but not often. Sometimes they spin off of hurricanes. A hurricane will get you to sit up and take notice," Ryker remarked, lightly rubbing Jennifer's back. Hope watched Jennifer try to relax.

"I take it you don't like storms," Hope asked her.

"No, I really don't."

"Jenny had a pretty bad experience earlier this summer. A bad storm dropped a tree on the house she was living in. She got pinned down. "

"Oh, no, Jennifer, I'm sorry. I didn't realize. Thank goodness you're okay." Hope reached out and touched Jennifer's arm, trying to make a soothing connection.

Jennifer smiled.

"You know, I didn't think I would be able to walk away from that situation, but I did. You know what they say, what doesn't kill you only makes you stronger. Ryker was a big help in that department." Jennifer turned shining eyes up to search the man's face. He looked at her tenderly. Hope's heart pinged. She thought she had that once.

She was mistaken.

Headlights shone down the dock as a truck pulled into the marina and parked.

"Bridger's back," Ryker announced.

They waited until their friend walked up the dock and boarded the boat.

"You guys didn't have to wait. Hi, Jennifer."

"Of course, we did," said Hope.

"How's your mom, buddy?" Ryker asked as he twisted off the cap of a bottled water and handed it to his friend.

"Thanks. They admitted her. The want to keep her for observation and run some tests, but they're pretty sure it is some form of dementia. I can't believe I missed it."

"Don't beat yourself up," Hope offered. "My grandmother had dementia. We didn't know for a long time. She was good at hiding her confusion. We learned that people who are very intelligent often can hide their condition for quite some time. Sometimes people close to them cover for them without even knowing it. Assuring the person that it's normal forgetfulness."

"I think that's exactly what has happened."

"Did your nephew say anything?" asked Ryker.

"I texted him, but he hasn't texted back. Typical teenager. He never mentioned anything to me, but I'll talk with him tomorrow. What is that amazing smell?" Bridger asked suddenly aware of the scent of the chicken dinner.

Jennifer jumped up and brought the food out of the cabin.

"Ryker said you didn't eat much of the pizza, so I brought you a fried chicken plate." She fussed around Bridger, setting out a napkin and silver ware.

Bridger caught her hand.

"Thank you, Jennifer. That's kind of you. Please sit, you don't have to wait on me, but seriously, this is awesome." He picked up a fork and dug into the mashed potatoes and gravy.

Jennifer beamed and sat back down next to Ryker. Hope watched the whole exchange. There was a story there. Bridger and Ryker were very careful with Jennifer, Ryker always reaching a hand out, calming her. Hope got the feeling that there was once a frightened bird there who was now finding her wings. Hope made a mental note to get to know Jennifer better. She got the feeling that Jennifer could use some female friends whom she could count on.

They sat with Bridger as he ate, talking quietly, offering support and help.

"This explains the mix up with all the invoices. I'm sure you've heard rumors about my impeding financial doom," Bridger said wryly.

Jennifer glanced up at Ryker then looked down.

"A lot of talk at the diner?" Bridger asked gently.

"Some," Jennifer said softly. "I didn't pay much attention to it."

"Well, I've heard talk. A bunch of people are saying that Cadigan Marina wasn't paying their bills. It's actually one of the reasons I came out tonight, to talk with you about it."

"And volunteered to spring for pizza?" Bridger asked, watching his friends face.

"Hell, no. It was my turn. Actually, I came out ahead because last time it was pizza and cannoli.'"

"True," Bridger remarked, grinning in spite of himself. "So, now I have to go over everything with a fine-tooth comb, figure out where Mom's been stashing the invoices and squaring away all the accounts."

"Bridger," Hope said, hesitating.

"Yeah?" He raised his eyebrow at Hope, waiting for her to go on.

"I've learned that this town knows everybody's business instantly. My guess is the county knows your mom's been admitted. Don't you think they'll figure out what happened and resubmit the invoices? And hopefully not take advantage of that?"

"You're right, usually everyone knows everything, but Dom won't talk about this to anyone. My nephew certainly won't, and the staff at the hospital know to keep their mouths shut, but you're right. Word will get out, and the folks around here will figure it out and let me know how to get squared away. I'm more worried about outside accounts. I order from all over the country, and I have some international accounts. It'll take a while to figure out this mess."

"I'll help."

Everyone turned to look at Jennifer.

"That's kind of you, but..." Bridger began to protest.

Hope put her hand on his arm, stopping him. She nodded to Jennifer.

"So, Maeve told me that she was going to need to cut my hours. Susie's husband got hurt, and Susie really needs to work more hours. I'm okay with that because I can get along, but I like to stay busy. I'm not good at calculus, but I can do basic accounting. Would you like me to try to help in the office? You don't have to pay me." Jennifer looked steadily in Bridger's eyes.

Ryker swelled with pride. Not long ago, Jennifer wouldn't have looked any man straight in the eyes.

"I would like that," Bridger said. "I think Mom would like that, too. Once she gets over her stubborn streak. I'm warning you; she won't like it at first, but she's a good person."

"Bridger, I'm kind of good at working on staying on a person's good side and knowing when to lie low, if you know what I mean."

A look passed between Ryker and Bridger, a flash of anger they shared, but they quickly put it away.

"You won't need to worry about that, Jen," Bridger said, using the nickname only Ryker used. "You'll be safe at the house and with my mom. She's a sweet woman who is going to have a hard time accepting the fact that she is getting forgetful and won't be able to be in charge anymore."

"I know Bridger. I'll be fine. So, you'll let me?"

"No, I won't let you. I'll hire you. Don't argue with me," Bridger said holding up his hand as Jennifer started to protest. "Besides, contrary to popular belief, the marina can afford it."

19

"*R*usty, what are your thoughts about Hester, and why she won't reveal who the father of her child is?"

Rusty scowled and sunk deeper into his seat.

"There isn't a right or wrong answer here. I just want to know what you think." Hope gently prodded the sulking teen. Most of the other students watched Hope with interest, a few turned toward Rusty. Every couple days Hope tried to engage him, but he wouldn't have any of it.

Hope sensed a movement in her doorway.

Chris Komat was standing there watching the exchange. Hope smiled at Rusty and turned from him, letting him off the hook.

"Carla, your thoughts?"

Carla, of course, went into a long explanation of why Hester did what she did, and how it is relevant to students today. That last bit she did for brownie points. Hope knew that would happen. She also knew it would be enough to make Chris move away from her door.

"Thank you for your insight, Carla, I appreciate your ideas. Okay, for the last ten minutes, I would like you guys to get a head start on tonight's homework. If you hustle, you won't have to do anything at home. I know a bunch of you are working on your floats for the parade coming up next weekend, so get cracking."

Hope turned toward Rusty, casually walking down the aisle toward his seat. All of the other students had their heads bent working earnestly. Rusty didn't open his notebook but stared at Hope as she approached him.

She bent down toward him and whispered.

"Please stay after class for a minute. I'd like to have a word with you." She did it quickly and quietly. None of the other students paid attention, but she was careful to be sure Rusty didn't miss her demeanor. She wasn't happy and she wanted to clear the air.

When the bell rang to dismiss class, the students gathered their books and moved to leave the room. Rusty was leading the pack. Hope was surprised. Not that he was trying to get out of the room without talking with her, but because she had never seen him move that fast.

"Rusty, a minute please."

Rusty kept walking.

Hope hated to do it, but she knew that the time had come to assert her authority.

"I asked you to please stay back for a moment, Rusty Walsh." There was no mistaking the tone of her voice. Several students faltered, glancing nervously to make sure she wasn't speaking to them. Relief and sympathy showed on their faces when they realized they were not being summoned.

Rusty kept walking.

"Dude, she was talking to you. Don't be an ass."

Hope hid the smile that was creeping to her lips as Allen Conway stepped up to her aid.

Rusty reluctantly stopped, then turned and came back into the room. Hope settled a pleasant look on her face.

"Rusty, obviously there is something going on here. You're not happy in this class or with me. How can I help make this a more pleasant experience for you?"

"You can't," Rusty said, holding her gaze with his cold blue eyes. They looked vaguely familiar, throwing her for a second.

She recovered.

"Okay, maybe I can't, but the bottom line is you have to take this class and pass it to graduate. I can do what I can to make this as painless as possible, but I need you to give a little. Can you do that?'

He continued to stare at her.

Hope was a little unnerved. He was a tough case. Usually she could get them to soften up.

"I wonder if it would help to talk with your parent or guardian. I have left several messages, but no one has called back."

She waited to see what the minor threat would produce.

"Why don't you mind your own business? I sit through your damn class. I don't skip. So just leave me alone."

Rusty stormed off, his boots echoing off the now empty hallway walls.

"Well, that didn't go well," she said to nobody.

"Maybe I can help."

Chris appeared from behind her half-opened door.

"Were you there the whole time?" Hope asked, feeling somehow violated.

"No. I just came out of Tony's room. Tell you what, I need to talk with Rusty about his science grade anyhow, so I'll see if I can get him to open up to me about what he doesn't seem to like about English. I'll let you know what happens." He winked at her, assuring her that he would swoop in and save the day.

Hope could only smile and thank him.

At lunch, Hope ate alone because Pepper wasn't at school and had a substitute teacher for the day. Hope ended her lunch early and headed back to her room to grade papers.

When the final bell rang for the day, she gathered her things and walked to her car. She was feeling out of sorts, so she decided to treat herself to a malt at the Cathead. Instead of turning for home, she made her way into town.

Already feeling a little more cheerful with the vision of one of Maeve's malts dancing in her head, Hope parked in front of the diner and put a smile on her face. She got out of her car determined not to let the encounter with Rusty ruin her day. It had been weighing heavily on her mind, but she wasn't going to let it mess with her evening.

It was such a nice day, Hope opted to sit at one of the small bistro tables in front of the diner. Maeve had scattered about pots with brightly blooming flowers and had installed black and white striped awnings that rolled out and provided shade and some rudimentary rain protection. It was an utterly delightful set up and only added to the charm of the historic part of downtown.

"Hey, Hope, what can I get you tonight? I know you want a double chocolate malt, right?"

"Absolutely, and Maeve, I'm torn between the burger and the fried chicken plate."

"It depends. Comfort food or a sinful burger?"

"Comfort food."

"Then chicken it is. Hey, are you okay?"

"Yep, just one of those days at work."

"The juvenile delinquents giving you trouble?" Maeve asked with a grin.

"Something like that."

"If you need to talk…"

"I can't, but thanks. Student confidentiality and all." Hope smiled apologetically.

"Don't apologize, honey. That says a lot. It tells me you won't carry tales about your students. You're a good teacher. Let me get this order in and bring you that malt." Maeve patted her shoulder and went back into the diner.

Hope leaned back in her chair, closing her eyes, trying to let the tension of the day drain from her shoulders.

"Mind if I join you?"

Hope sat up and shaded her eyes to see who had interrupted her meditating. It was Chris.

"No, please, be my guest," she said graciously.

Chris grinned and settled himself in a chair.

"Bad day?" he asked. "I mean even more after the exchange with Rusty?"

"No, not really," she said, not feeling like rehashing her day.

"Good. I spoke with Rusty."

"Already?" Hope sat up straighter in her seat. Apparently, Chris was a man of his word. She didn't really expect it to happen this fast, so she was pleasantly surprised.

"Yeah. He's got a bunch of stuff going on, but I think he actually likes you."

"Well, that's good to know, but he doesn't show it very well," said Hope feeling a bit relieved. She wasn't accustomed to her students not warming up to her.

"No, I mean he really likes you…a lot," Chris said, meaningfully.

"He told you that?"

"No, not in so many words, but I am a trained counselor. I have experience in reading between the lines and young adult behaviors and clues."

"And you think he has a crush on me?" said Hope, incredulously.

"No, not really a crush. That's kind of juvenile. I think he has some feelings that he is really not sure how to resolve."

Chris stopped talking as Maeve approached with Hope's malt.

"Hello, are you joining Hope for dinner?" Maeve asked, her tone lacking its usual warmth, but only those who knew her well would realize it.

Chris cocked his eyebrow at Hope, questioning.

She nodded and he grinned, his face lighting. *Rusty isn't the only one,* thought Hope. She was surprised she didn't really feel flattered.

"Yes, I believe I am. What did you order, Hope?"

Chris ordered the same and settled back to wait for his malt.

"Please, go ahead. Don't let it melt," he said generously to Hope. "Mine will be here soon enough."

"I would, but it is still too thick to get through the straw." She waited politely until Maeve brought Chris his malt and together, they tackled the thick, chocolatey goodness.

20

*C*hris leaned back in his chair, satisfied.

"That was a reasonable chicken dinner," he remarked, wiping his lips delicately with his napkin. He carefully cleaned his fingers before he placed his napkin precisely folded by his place.

Hope hid her smile at the ritual he was performing. *He was a little OCD for a counselor,* she thought.

"I thought the chicken was amazing. I loved the seasoning."

"Thank you," Maeve spoke up behind her as she bussed a table. "That recipe was my grandmother's, and she said it had been handed down for generations. Probably an original Grey recipe, and if not, no one would ever admit it."

"Well, don't change it because I absolutely love it. The mashed potatoes and gravy were wonderful, too. You were right, this was the perfect comfort meal dinner, but I am going to have to take a long walk to work off what I just ate."

"I'd be happy to take a stroll with you," Chris offered, and he reached for the checks Maeve had dropped at the table.

"I can get my own," Hope said, firmly, reaching for her wallet in her purse.

Maeve watched with interest as did Bridger who had just come out of the barber shop across the street.

"No, I insist," said Chris and he gently removed the check from Hope's hand.

Bridger thought she looked a little embarrassed, but he didn't know why. He wished he was closer. *Were they on a date?*

Maeve looked up to see Bridger watching. She smiled at him but shook her head ever so slightly. He started across the street toward the diner. Chris looked up as he handed some cash to Maeve and caught sight of Bridger. He scowled slightly.

"Hi, Hope, Chris," Bridger said lightly as he stepped up on the sidewalk. He greeted Maeve with a kiss on the cheek.

"Hi Bridger," Hope replied. She wanted to ask about his mom but didn't feel the time was right.

"Hello, Bridger. I'd ask you to join us but Hope and I were just going to take a stroll down to the beach. We need to walk off the excellent dinner Maeve served us."

Hope frowned slightly. For a minute she thought he said it in a condescending way, but then she realized she was just feeling awkward. *She shouldn't. She wasn't tied to anyone or anything. But still...*

Bridger was grinning.

Damn him. He was enjoying her discomfort.

Maeve looked at Bridger and shook her head. He was playing a dangerous game here.

"Bridger, are you going to have something to eat? Ryker and Tank are inside."

"Sure, I could use a burger. See you guys later," he said to Hope and Chris and turned his back following Maeve inside.

"Ready?" Chris asked as he stood and waited to pull out Hope's chair for her.

"Sure, I guess so." She gathered her purse and they set off down the street toward the beach, glancing back at the diner as she left, not sure what she was looking for.

The air was warm, and evening was falling. Summer was coming to a close, and there were subtle reminders everywhere that fall was on its way. As they reached the end of Main Street and turned toward the beach Hope was surprised to feel a bit of a chill in the breeze off the ocean. She thought about her little boat and the upcoming winter. She sure hoped that it would be warm.

"Are you cold?" Chris asked, noticing her shiver.

"No not really. I just was surprised at the temperature change after we got out from behind the buildings. The ocean breeze has a bit of a bite to it. Oh look, they're getting ready for the Oyster Festival." Hope pointed to the temporary grandstand that had been erected on the beach.

"It should be interesting with all the small town local amateur musicians," Chris said, dryly.

"What's wrong with local musicians?" Hope asked remembering the night they danced at the Mizzen Mast. "You didn't seem to have any trouble dancing to a high school garage band."

"The company made it palatable."

"Well, I thought it was fun and charming. I love the small town feel and the fact that locals enjoy each other's talents."

"I do, too, but sometimes I miss the cosmopolitan amenities of a big city."

"I do miss some things, like the theater district back home."

"I didn't know you were from New York," Chris said, his brow furrowing slightly.

"I'm not."

"I'm confused. Theater district?"

"Cleveland, Ohio has a fabulous theater district."

"Seriously. Cleveland?"

"Um, yes, we have an amazing theater district and a world class symphony, thank you very much," Hope said, her back up a little.

"Easy, sorry." Chris held his hands up to appease her. "I guess I am naive. So, this oyster festival, do you eat oysters?"

"I'm not fond of them, but I'm going to give it a go again and see if I've changed my mind. Bridger tells me that I just haven't had them prepared correctly. He promised to show me the best booths to sample from."

"Oh, you're going to the festival with Bridger?"

"Yes, he said he would show me around," said Hope firmly, trying not to sound apologetic.

"I see. Well, I guess I'll have to figure out the oyster scene on my own," Chris smiled, but Hope sensed that it was not as sincere as he was trying to make it.

Men, she thought.

They walked to the ocean edge and she slipped off her sandals. She walked in wet sand enjoying the tickle of the ocean as it lapped her toes.

"You're going to get your shoes wet," she teased Chris as he refused to remove his shoes. "Just slide 'em off and roll up your trousers. It feels great."

Chris looked at her and stiffly bent over, pulling off his shoes and socks and carefully cuffing his pants. Hope had to bite her lip not to laugh out loud. He looked like he was doing something so incredibly distasteful. Like he had to swallow fish oil or something. He started to walk next to her, his shoulders hunching up to his ears. She was feeling free and easy, the tension leaving her body as the ocean lapped her toes. He looked like a miserable kid. She remembered him fastidiously wiping his mouth and hands of the chicken grease at dinner and realized that he was completely out of his element. He really hated what he was doing right now. It was sweet that he was doing it for her, but she felt badly that he didn't enjoy this simple pleasure. This man was extremely uptight, especially for a guidance counselor. Yet he seemed kind, and the fact that he was trying so hard was a little endearing.

"Why are you smiling?" Chris asked.

"I just think it's sweet that you are doing that."

"What?"

"Going barefoot when it is obvious that you don't really like it. I just think its sweet," Hope said, and smiled kindly, trying to put him at ease.

He relaxed a little and grinned at her, his face lighting up in a boyish way.

"Thanks. It would be better if I were in my swim trunks. It would just feel, more right, you know?"

Hope nodded. Yeah, she knew. Her ex-husband was like that. He would never take his shoes off and walk the beach in his power suit. Those two things didn't mix. *Oh,* she thought, *what they were missing,* and she wiggled her toes in the sea foam that caressed her feet.

"I hate to cut this short, but I need to get home. I have a bunch of grading to do," Hope said apologetically as she turned to make her way back.

"No problem, I have a few things I need to do myself tonight. I did enjoy this evening and the company," Chris said, meaningfully.

"So, did I, Oh, Chris, look!"

Hope grabbed Chris's hand and turned him to look out to the sea, pointing to a pod of dolphins playing in the waves.

Chris didn't look out at the water but looked instead at Hope and the joy on her face. He squeezed her hand.

"Beautiful," he whispered.

"Aren't they?" she echoed, unaware he never even saw them.

They stood there for a few minutes as the dolphins continued on their way frolicking up the coastline.

Suddenly, Hope was aware that Chris was still holding her hand. She didn't want him to feel bad, or awkward, after all, she was the one who grabbed his, but she didn't want to continue to hold it as they walked back to the car. But she didn't want to be unkind either.

The opportunity presented itself as she discovered a delicate pink shell, lit by the evening sun. It was perfect. She casually dropped his hand as she bent to pick it up. She admired the curves and the beautiful shine of mother of pearl.

"Isn't it amazing that an animal made this perfect shell? It's hard to wrap my head around that." She held the shell up to the sky and let the setting sun shine through it. She marveled at its translucence. "I must sound crazy."

"No, you don't. You sound wonderful." Chris cupped her chin in his hand and turned her to look at him. "You see the wonder in every-thing, in a shell and in your students. You care, and that makes you really special. I think you are really, really special Hope." He leaned in and kissed her forehead, smart enough to know he might be moving way too fast after the other evening, but he was unable to stop himself. He had to kiss her, even if it was only a chaste kiss on the forehead.

She backed up and smiled nervously.

The mood broken.

Chris took charge.

"Do you have anything to dry your feet with before you get in your car? I might have something." He trailed off helplessly.

"No worries," she answered lightly. They're almost dry and the sand will brush right off. How about you? Are your feet almost dry? Will you be able to stick your socks back on?"

She knew darn well that would make him crazy. He grimaced and shrugged. As they reached the steps to the sidewalk Hope leaned over gracefully and gently brushed her feet. The fine sand fell to the ground leaving her feet dry and salty. She slipped her feet in her sandals.

"Good as new. Your turn. Do you need me to steady you?" she asked as she offered her arm.

Chris awkwardly brushed his feet and pulled on his socks one at a time. He leaned on her gently, just to keep his balance. Hope bit the inside of her cheek almost hard enough to draw blood. She had to stop herself from laughing at the image of Chris, his lips drawn against his teeth in a distasteful grimace, his entire demeanor in abject misery.

She glanced up to see Bridger, Ryker, and Tank sitting outside the Cathead Diner talking to Maeve and Jennifer. She felt her lips turn up in a smile as her eyes met his.

Chris straightened in time to see her soft smile. When he realized it wasn't for him, he felt a white-hot stab of anger sear through his brain. It was over in a second, and he worked to settle his face into a pleasant visage.

Bridger raised a glass to the two of them and nodded.

Once his shoes were on, Chris reached for Hope's hand with the excuse to help her up the steps, and he kept his grip on it as they strolled down the sidewalk toward the diner and their respective cars.

Hope was aware of the tension between the two men. She decided not the create a scene and allowed Chris to claim her hand until she reached her car. There, she told him goodnight firmly, stepping back slightly so as not to invite a kiss.

"Thanks again for dinner. You really didn't need to pick up the check. I'll see you tomorrow in school."

"Absolutely. I will see you tomorrow, at lunch for sure." He waited until she got into her car and closed her door, looking over the roof of her vehicle at Bridger. Chris waved at the group, a triumphant smile on his face. As far as he was concerned, he won.

Hope pulled away slowly, waving casually at the group in front of the diner.

Bridger nodded to her, not glancing at Chris.

As Chris drove away, Tank reached over and slapped Bridger's shoulder.

"Score another one for Chris. It looks like he is way up in the game."

"I have to agree," chimed in Ryker glancing up at Maeve to get her read on the situation.

"Nope," said Bridger, "that boy just lost points, and he doesn't even know it."

21

"Hope, this is lunch. You know, where you relax and talk to your best friend?" Pepper dropped down in the chair across from Hope and stared at the stack of papers between them.

"I know. I should know better than to assign a five-paragraph essay before the weekend. I was thinking that this way the kids wouldn't have any work to do during the Oyster Festival."

"Yeah, but it looks like you just punished yourself. Smooth move," Pepper teased. "So, before he comes in here, how's it going with Chris?"

Pepper shot Hope a sly grin before she bit into her sandwich.

"First of all, nothing is going on between Chris and me. Second, he was already in here and got called out for a student crisis."

"That's too bad. I'll miss our third lunch partner," Pepper lied, rolling her eyes.

"You don't like him very, much do you?" Hope said as she skimmed the first essay while munching on a carrot stick.

"It's not that I don't like him, it's just that there is something off about him. I can't put my finger on it."

"It's called being uptight. He's from New York. The big city. He isn't local and laid back, so he sticks out like a sore thumb and looks awkward. I kinda feel sorry for him."

"Sorry enough that the whole town has decided you'll be engaged soon?"

"What?" Hope looked up from essay number two, circling a misplaced modifier with her hot pink pen.

"Just kidding, but they're ready to award him more points when he shows up at the Oyster Festival with you on his arm."

"Well, that's going to upset the townies."

"Why?"

"Because I'm going to the festival with Bridger."

"Oh really?" Pepper looked steadily at her friend.

"Oh, Pepper, I'm sorry. Is it okay with you? I mean with your history. I don't know what happened, but,"

Pepper held up her hand interrupting Hope.

"Honey, we were over before we even started. I think you guys would make a great couple, it's just that the rumor mill doesn't have that happening. Have you guys been hanging out?"

"Just a couple of evenings on the deck, sharing a beverage and talking. That's it. It's not like we're dating. It's not like I'm dating anyone."

Hope put a comment and grade at the top of the paper and flipped it to the back of the stack. She started to read the next paper, but stopped, her face turning pale.

"Hope, what's wrong? What is it?" Pepper reached across the table and gently took the paper from Hope's hand. It looked like a letter, not a composition.

"No, it's okay. Just a student trying to get under my skin." Hope took the paper back before Pepper had a chance to read all of it.

"By the sounds of it, the student has a thing for you. Have you talked to Chris or Fender about this?"

"No, yes, well, I've talked to Chris about the student, but this is the first time something like this has happened. It's weird and creepy." She folded the paper and slipped it in her tote bag, then gathered the rest of the papers and shoved them in.

"Done grading?" Pepper asked, amused.

"Yes, done for now, done for the day, and done for most of the weekend. I'll look at them again Sunday night. It's Friday, and I am ready for some fun and sun. The weather looks like it's going to hold out, don't you think?"

Pepper knew Hope was trying to steer the conversation away from the disturbing letter, so she graciously allowed it to happen, but she was going to keep a close eye on her friend. The letter creeped her out, too. Nothing like that had ever happened in this school as far as she knew. She wondered which student would have done that, but knew it wasn't her place to interfere.

"Here, start the weekend with a cookie. My Nana makes the best chocolate chip cookies in the universe."

Hope popped one in her mouth and nodded in agreement.

"Ooooh, I love your Nana."

"Yep, Nana Anna has the best baked goods in the world."

"Wait, like the Anna in Anna's Bakery? Downtown next to the barbershop? With the powdered sugar donuts that the old men eat while sitting on the bench in front of the barber shop, dropping powdered sugar all down their fronts? That Anna is your Nana? I feel like I am in a weird little nursery rhyme."

Pepper laughed and handed Hope the white paper bakery bag.

"Take the rest. I'll end up with more tomorrow. Nana wants me to stop by and help her make Moravian Molasses cookies for the Oyster Festival. I help her every year."

"Moravian Molasses cookies sound like they are wonderful. I will be by to get a dozen or so."

"I'll have Nana save a dozen back. She usually sells out early. Oops, there's the bell. Just a couple more classes and we're free."

They threw away their trash and gathered their belongings. Hope had all but forgotten about the letter tucked in her tote.

*T*he afternoon classes passed quickly, the students in high spirits. Hope indulged the festival talk as the kids excitedly made plans, where to meet, who was on what float, where the party on the beach was going to take place that no adults were supposed to know about. Hope pretended not to hear as she conferenced with individual students about their writing. The last bell of the day was accompanied by a collective 'whoop' from the students as they rushed to start their weekend.

Hope collected the huge stack of compositions that needed to be graded, stuffing them in her teacher tote, then locked up her classroom. Pepper met her in the hall, her arms completely devoid of any weekend grading. She winked at Hope.

"It's all in the planning, my dear. Never, ever have grading to do during oyster festival." She laughed gleefully at the look on Hope's face.

"Live and learn," she sighed.

"Just don't let the grading get in the way of your time with Bridger," Pepper teased, then snapped her mouth shut as they passed Chris in the hall. His face held a sour look.

"Have a great weekend Chris," Hope said as she passed him.

"You, too," he muttered, but he didn't sound sincere.

Pepper rolled her eyes and waved at a few other faculty members and staff, calling out good wishes for the weekend.

"I'll probably run into you at the festival. I'll be helping Nana at her booth, so be sure to stop by, and I won't forget to save you some of the molasses cookies."

"Thanks. I'll see you there," said Hope as she pushed through the doors of the school.

22

*H*ope dropped the tote of papers on the dinette bench and made her way into her bedroom, casting off her school clothes. She liked dressing professionally for school, but she couldn't wait to shed the clothes when she got home. She slid on a pair of faded jeans and an Ohio University hoodie, catching her hair into a ponytail as she made her way into the tiny kitchen. She quickly sautéed some chicken strips and tossed them in her homemade buffalo sauce. Filling a bowl with salad greens and sliced celery, she arranged the chicken strips on top. She carried her salad and a glass of ice water out to the bistro table on the deck, then stepped back in to retrieve the canvas bag of compositions. She was determined to make a big dent in the pile today instead of waiting until Sunday like she had told Pepper. She hated putting things off, knowing full well something would come up and she would be sorry one way or the other.

Eating absently, she bent to her task, circling spelling errors and grammar mistakes with her hot pink pen and making encouraging comments on the top.

*B*ridger hung up the phone and leaned back in his deck chair. He had been going over the accounts and had found some discrepancies from the numerous emails his suppliers had billed him and the monies his mom had going out of the accounts. He had decided he was going to take Jennifer up on her offer to help with the office. He just had to convince his mom. He sighed. He really didn't want to have to do this, but his mom's memory was failing, and he couldn't allow the business to suffer. The doctor seemed to think she was still fine living on her own with occasional help, but the day to day attention to detail that the business required was too much.

He gazed down the dock, watching Hope. Her hair was caught up in a ponytail and she was twisting some strands around her fingers as she worked. Occasionally she lifted her fork to her mouth. His stomach growled. He hadn't eaten anything, and he was getting hungry and cranky.

He watched her as she dropped her pen on the table, shaking her head. She leaned back in her chair and stretched like a cat, her hands clasped, her arms reaching for the sky and then tipping behind her.

He wanted to run his hands up the sides of that gently arched torso. Then take that ponytail down and run his hands through her hair as he ravaged her mouth.

Damn, he was hungry, and not just for food.

Hope turned toward him, her eyes searching. She saw him and a smile lit up her face. That turned the fire in his belly up a notch. She waved a lazy wave.

He waved back.

They grinned at each other.

Bridger got up.

Hope beckoned him to her, waving her hand.

He groaned. He had to behave.

He wasn't going to lose.

He slowly made his way off the boat and sauntered down the dock, not looking like he was in any particular hurry. Inside he wanted to run to her. *God, she looked amazing.*

"Hey," she said, smiling that wonderful, girl-next-door smile.

"Hey," he said.

"Come on aboard," she invited.

"I'm sorry, I didn't mean to interrupt your dinner." Then, much to his embarrassment, his stomach growled, loudly.

Hope laughed.

"Let me guess, you haven't eaten anything."

"No," Bridger admitted. "I haven't had a chance to eat all day. I did have some coffee this morning."

"You have to be starving."

If she only knew.

His eyes lit up.

She cocked her head to the side, one eyebrow lifted in a question.

"Yeah, I kinda am."

"I can probably scare up something to make you a salad or a sandwich," Hope offered, getting up from her chair.

He put out a hand to stop her, gently closing his fingers around her wrists.

Both of them felt the searing shock of electricity.

Hope looked at him, her eyes large and luminous, her lips parted slightly

"Oh," she whispered.

"Oh, yeah," he said.

They stood there for a minute, looking at each other, each of them feeling a warmth spreading through them.

She took a small step forward.

His hand slid from her wrist up to her elbow, cupping it gently.

She shivered, imagining his hand cupping her breast in the same way.

Bridger looked amused for a second, like he knew what she was thinking, then his eyes darkened.

He moved toward her and waited.

She leaned in, a soft mewl escaping her lips.

That was it.

Bridger was undone.

He circled her slender body with his arms and crushed her into him, his lips bending to hers.

The kiss was not chaste.

This kiss was not subtle.

The kiss was demanding.

Searching.

Learning.

Hope's body responded releasing a wild desire she had never known. She gasped and reached up to the back of his head, twining his hair between her fingers, forcing him to crush her mouth.

Bridger's hands slid to her ass, cupping it, hitching it close to his pelvis. She could feel his desire and it made her crazy.

His hands rubbed her ass and slid down to the back of her thighs, then he brought them back up to her face, holding it tenderly in his hands.

Slow down, buddy, he thought. *Don't blow this.*

Hope felt the shift.

His kisses became lighter, teasing, promising.

She wanted more.

He knew it.

It wasn't going to happen.

Not now.

Not yet.

"I thought you were hungry," she teased in a husky voice as Bridger reluctantly pulled away. Hope was surprised at how disappointed she felt.

Oh, darling, I am famished, but I've been on a diet, he thought to himself.

"I am. Wanna go get a steak? My guess is the rabbit food really didn't fill you."

The mood was broken, but she didn't mind. She figured it was going to come back with a vengeance. And soon.

"Sure, where?"

"Come on, I'll take you."

"It'll take me a minute. I have to put these papers away and put on something respectable."

"Um, better not. Don't change. In fact, you might be too dressed up."

Hope stared at him a minute then looked down at her faded jeans and oversized college sweatshirt. Then she grinned.

"I've a feeling this is gonna be good. Hang on." She gathered her papers and went inside. In just a few minutes she emerged with her phone tucked in her pocket and a pair of slip-ons on her tanned feet.

"Good thinking on the shoes."

"Let me guess. I'm going to stick to the floor."

"Probably."

"Then that means we aren't going to Izzy's or Maeve's place."

"Oh no. Nothing even nearing that respectable. Are you ready?"

"Always. Your truck?"

"Nope."

"My car?"

"Nope."

She looked at him quizzically.

He took her hand in his and led her off her boat. As they walked down the dock, Clarence gave a low whistle. He had just stepped out of his cabin wearing a tight baby blue speedo with a white towel around his neck. He had two martinis in his hands.

"Good evening, Clarence," Hope said, trying hard to unsee what just assaulted her eyes.

"Good evening, my dear. Bridger."

Bridger nodded, "Evening Clarence."

"Hope, my dear. I really wish you wouldn't waste your time on him. It should be obvious after tonight that he can't finish what he starts."

Hope's face colored brightly, realizing Clarence must have enjoyed a full view of the passionate kiss she had received a few minutes ago.

"Behave," Bridger warned as they passed by. He slipped an arm around Hope's waist. "I'm sorry if you're embarrassed."

"It's okay. I forget he's always lurking. I'll have to remember."

"I could switch your boat to a closer slip, but that means you would be closer to me. I'm not opposed to that idea, but I'm afraid your reputation would be in question. The gossip line would have a heyday."

Hope nodded, then grinned.

"I should take Clarence up on the offer. That would throw a wrench in all of their speculation."

Bridger stopped and looked at Hope to see if she was serious. She looked at him steadily, a grin playing at her lips.

She wouldn't. Would she?

Hope burst out laughing.

"Oh my. The look on your face."

It was Bridger's turn to blush.

23

"Hop in." Bridger gestured to the speedboat tied up at the fourth slip.

"In the boat? I thought we were going to get a steak."

"We are, now hop in."

"How many boats do you own?"

"Well, this isn't technically mine."

"We're stealing a boat?"

Bridger looked at her steadily.

"Somehow, I get the weird feeling that you'd like that."

"Well, it would be exciting," Hope teased.

Once again, the fire in Bridger's belly stirred. *Damn, this woman.*

"The boat belongs to the marina, the business."

"But you own the marina, so it's your boat."

"Wrong, the Cadigan family owns the marina, so it's the marina's boat."

"Okay, which boats are yours?"

"Well, you know the sailboat, and the houseboat I live in, wait, no that belongs to the marina, your houseboat, the racing skiff, the wooden kayak, the restored Lyman…"

"Stop, I don't even know what some of those are. So, you own a bunch of boats. But this one is the marina's, and we're stealing it for the evening."

"Sure, we're stealing it for the evening." Bridger smiled at her indulgently.

"I like it," she said as she stepped in and settled herself on a seat.

"Um, you can't sit down yet."

"Why not, aren't we going?"

"Yes, but you're going to help me get the boat out of the slip." Bridger grinned at her, knowing she didn't like the fact that she had no idea what to do.

"I'm going to loop the rope over these uprights and you're going to hold it taught. Then I'm going to untie the boat and start the engines. When I tell you to, flip the rope off the upright. Easy."

She looked at him doubtfully but stepped into position. He expertly lassoed the uprights and handed her both ends. She held onto them for dear life. When Bridger untied the boat, it gently moved sideways in the slip. She gripped tighter and pulled so hard the boat crashed into the dock.

"Oh no, did I hurt it?"

"No, ma'am, that's why we have bumpers. And you can relax a little. She isn't really going anywhere."

He started the engine and the boat purred beneath her. She gripped even tighter.

"Okay, Hope, you can flip the rope over."

She tried to do it in a smooth move but failed miserably. The rope came up over one upright but stayed on the other, and the slack flopped in the water.

"Well, damn it," she swore.

"No need to stress, just pull it off the other and we'll be on our way."

Awkwardly, she worked the rope over the last upright and coiled up the dripping line. Bridger reached out and took it from her.

"Now, just pull the bumpers up over the side into the boat." He gestured around the boat and Hope did as she was told as he guided the boat into the river and headed upstream against the current.

Once Hope was satisfied that the bumpers were in the boat and their lines were neatly stowed, she looked up at Bridger for approval. What she saw was a man with his jaw taut, looking at her hungrily. She realized she had been bent over giving him a nice view of her jean clad ass. She liked what it seemed to do to him.

"Anything else you need," she asked sweetly.

"Don't," he warned.

"Don't what?"

"You know what, now come over here, sit down, and take the wheel before I toss the anchor over and finish what we started earlier."

Hope's heart jumped at the thought of him up against her, naked, in the middle of the river, the sun low in the sky. She could lose her teaching license acting on thoughts like that.

"Wait," she shook herself. "What do you mean take the wheel."

"You're going to take us upriver."

"I've never driven a boat before."

"It's easy, just keep her between the white lines."

Hope looked past the bow of the boat.

"I don't see any..."

Bridger grinned at her.

"You asshole," she said, realizing she was incredibly gullible.

"Yes, I can really be an asshole, but not tonight. Come on up here."

She made her way to the seat. Bridger throttled back the engine and they switched places. Once again, Hope held on with a death grip.

"Relax. It's easy. This river is wide, there are no waves to contend with, and there isn't anything to hit. Just take us upriver."

Hope started to relax as she got the feel of the boat. Bridger was right, it was easy. Bridger slowly throttled open the engine, and soon they were flying. The wind picked up her hair, whipping her ponytail around. It was exhilarating. She turned to tell Bridger that she loved it, but her hands turned the wheel, too. The boat was quick to respond.

Hope panicked, but Bridger calmly reached over and got them back on course.

"It's just like a car. It'll go where you turn the wheel, and if it's going fast things are going to happen fast."

"No kidding," she said. "What are those?" she asked pointing to the stern at some metal mesh things that looked like collapsed baskets piled in the bottom of the boat.

"Crab traps."

"Seriously, can we catch some?"

"I don't have any bait with me, so not tonight, but we can do that. You wanted to go fishing, too. We can do that whenever you want."

"I'm ready when you are."

"Okay, maybe Sunday?"

"Sure. Are we still going to the Oyster Festival tomorrow?"

"Yep, unless you plan on standing me up."

"No, sir. Do you want to drive now?" Hope asked.

"Are you done?"

"Truthfully, I want to be selfish. I want to sit back and watch the riverbank and the scenery. I don't feel comfortable doing that when I am driving."

They traded places again and Hope settled back into her seat. She watched the side of the river. It was so peaceful.

Within a few minutes the river made a bend and a building came into view along the bank. There was a large deck decorated with lights and colorful advertising banner.

"Wait, that's Izzy's place, The Mizzen Mast, isn't it?" exclaimed Hope.

"Yep,"

"You said we weren't going to eat there."

"We're not. Izzy makes great food, but we are going for the finest steak along this river. We have a bit of a ways to go yet."

Bridger slowed the boat as they approached Izzy's place. He tooted the horn and he and Hope waved as a woman straightened up from wiping down a table.

Izzy.

Bridger throttled back and cruised up close to the small dock below the deck.

"Where're you guys headed tonight?" Izzy asked in her slow drawl while sizing up the situation.

"Gotta pass you up, Iz. I've got a hankering for a steak."

"Ah," she said, a dreamy look on her face. "Enjoy and give Hank my best."

"Will do, have a good night, Izzy."

"You, too. Hope, it's good to see you."

"Thanks, Izzy. Have a good night."

Bridger banked the boat away from the dock and opened the throttle more. They sped past the edges of town then the riverbank closed again with trees and bushes. Occasional small docks jutted out into the water where the bank was cleared of trees, and modest houses could be seen set back on the hill above the bank.

They continued on this way until they came to a larger dock where several boats were tied up. Loud, mournful country music floated down through the trees, and the sound of raucous laughter could be heard skipping across the water. Bridger edged the boat around to the side of the dock, away from the other boats, and he tossed Hope the rope.

"When I tell you, try to loop the line over the uprights, just opposite of what you did when we left the marina. But before you do, flip the bumpers over the side, please."

Understanding now the purpose, Hope quickly dropped the bumpers to protect the side of the boat, and she managed to catch the upright with one toss of the rope. Bridger finished gliding along the dock, and Hope held steady on the rope until Bridger tied the bow and stern to the dock cleats.

After making sure everything was secure, Bridger hopped up onto the deck and reached for Hope's hand, helping her to scramble to the slippery floating wood.

Unlike Izzy's place, there were no cheerful lights or decorations. There was no festive deck. Only a set of steep wooden stairs leading up the embankment away from the dock. Vines crept up the railings and mosquitoes whined in Hope's ears. She swatted them away and looked at Bridger, concern on her face.

"Where exactly are you taking me?"

"Hank's"

"Hank's what?"

"Just Hank's."

Just then her toe slipped on the moist wood and she misstepped, falling forward. Bridger caught her gracefully around the waist, pulling her close to him. His strong biceps wrapped around her and she breathed deeply his scent.

"You okay?" he asked, his lips against her hair.

"I'm very okay," she said as she reveled in the strength of this man. They stood there a minute, Bridger still protecting her, not wanting to let go. Hope let him.

He planted tiny kisses against the top of her head as he breathed out and then in again, smelling her sweetness. It was too much.

He cupped her right cheek in his hand, ever so gently and explored her face with kisses, her eyelids, her forehead, her nose.

Her lips.

She parted them for him. She opened herself to his tongue, closing her eyes and forgetting they were standing on a stairway leading to God knows where. She surrendered herself to his mouth, not caring who saw or what they would think.

At the last minute, Bridger stopped himself from reaching up under her sweatshirt and palming her breast with this left hand. It almost happened. His fingertips almost brushing her nipple, but he stopped.

Not now.

Not here.

She opened her mouth more, urging him to go deeper with his tongue.

He obliged.

A door banged above them.

Reluctantly, Bridger pulled away.

Hope reached up to pat her messed up ponytail in place.

An enormous black, furry dog came bounding down the stairs,

toenails scraping against the wood, and he hurled himself toward them, baying loudly.

Hope gasped in fear as she pressed herself against Bridger, trusting him to protect her.

"Oh my God, what?"

Bridger tightened one arm around Hope's shoulders, steadying her against him. He braced himself for the onslaught.

The dog launched himself at the couple.

Bridger caught the dog around the chest with the other arm, absorbing the blow as the furry beast made contact with them.

"Okay, Ed, get down. Sit!"

The dog slathered Bridger's face with a huge sloppy tongue, some of the spit straying to land on Hope's nose.

"ED, ENOUGH!" Bridger commanded

Ed whined, squirmed, and then sat with his front legs on one step, his butt two steps above.

"Ed? Who the hell names a dog Ed? And are you sure this is a dog? He looks like a freaking bear."

"Hope, this is Ed. Ed, Hope."

Ed proffered his paw and nearly fell on his face. He'd forgotten his butt was so much higher than his front.

Hope laughed despite her recent scare.

"Pleased to meet you, Ed."

The dog's face broke into a wide, panting grin, complete with lines of drool that reached from his black, flappy stuff to the decking below.

"Ed, have some manners," Bridger scolded. Ed hung his head in shame.

"Bridger, don't be mean to this poor dog."

"Poor dog, a minute ago he was a terrifying beast."

"That was a minute ago."

Again, the sound of a wooden screen door slamming and a voice called out from above.

"Ed, come on buddy. Bridger, is that you down there?"

"Hey, Hank. Yeah, it's me."

"I figured. Ed doesn't act a fool for just anybody. Who's that you got with you?"

"I brought a friend. Her name is Hope."

"She the one the folks in Grey's Harbor figure is going to end up with that guidance counselor guy?"

Hope's jaw dropped open.

"Yep, she's the one."

Ed stood up and awkwardly tried to turn on the stairs, reconciling the fact that his ass was where his head should be. He gave up and leaned against Bridger's legs, skipping his back legs down the two steps. He took a minute, using Bridger as a crutch to untangle the mess he had made of his legs. Once he accomplished it, he looked back at the couple with a comic grin.

Hope burst out laughing.

"She laughing at me?" the voice asked, the hurt tone undeniable.

"No, Hank, she's laughing at your fool dog."

"So, is the guidance counselor going to win?"

"We'll see," Hope's voice floated sweetly up the stairs.

"Did you come for a steak?" asked the disembodied voice in the trees.

"Yes, sir. I figured Hope needed to know what a steak should taste like."

"Well, it should at least score you a few points. Come on, Ed, let them come on up. Get up here, boy."

"Is he talking to you, or the dog?" Hope asked Bridger,

"Not sure, but it's never a good idea to make Hank wait. Are you okay to walk up the stairs?"

"Are you asking if you left me weak in the knees?"

"No, I wasn't, but are you?"

"Maybe a little," she admitted.

And the ember flared again.

"You're a tease. You know that? I just wanted to be sure the dog didn't hurt you."

"No, I'm fine. Are you going to feed me or what?"

Clasping her hand firmly in his, Bridger led Hope up the long flight of stairs, Ed, the giant Newfoundland, leading the way, his graceful sweep of a tail happily waving from side to side.

When they reached the top of the stairs, Bridger opened an old wooden screen door which had seen better days. At one time it had probably been painted white, but now it was a weathered gray with just a few remaining flecks of its former self. The screen was old and had several patches sewn onto the screen with long stitches of wire.

They stepped into a dimly lit room. Hope's impression of the place was of all dark wood and trophy fish hung on the walls. A large fireplace graced the far end of the room, but despite the graceful stonework, the fireplace did not lend a feeling of quaintness but necessity. A fire was blazing, taking the evening damp chill out of the air.

A few wooden tables were scattered about the large open space, all with mismatched chairs around them. The table in front of the fireplace was occupied by six men, all in work clothes. Fisherman coming off of a day working the sea or the river. None of them looked up from their poker hands to acknowledge the newcomers but a voice came from the general direction.

"Hey, Bridger."

"Hey," he answered back as he led Hope to another table in the back corner. The music had stopped and a middle-aged man wearing a stocking cap pulled down to his ears, gray straggles of hair hanging down his back, dropped quarters in the juke box and made his selection. The music started to play and one of the card players groaned.

"Damn it, Max, why ya gotta play the same damn songs over and over again. Give it a rest."

Max shuffled away from the juke box and made his way back to the bar and to his half-finished beer sweating on the coaster. He hitched himself up on the stool and nodded to Bridger before he bowed his head and stared into the amber liquid.

A smallish man with a pronounced limp made his way over to Bridger's table. He was wearing faded jeans and a Creedence Clearwater Revival t-shirt. His baseball hat proclaimed him a Vietnam Veteran.

"So are you both here for steak, or is the lady looking for a salad. If so, I can't help you. I don't have salad."

"No, sir, I'd like a steak, and I'd like it medium rare. That is, if you know how to do it really medium rare. If you're not sure, I'll order it rare, cause it'll probably come out the right way then."

Bridger's eyes crinkled and his lips twitched in the corners.

Hank stared at Hope.

Hope stared back.

Hank's Adam's apple jiggled.

Bridger watched the exchange and waited.

Silence.

The poker boys stopped talking.

"You're getting applesauce and a baked potato with it. Butter, no damn sour cream and you'll have broccoli on the side." He rubbed his gray stubble with his open palm.

"Can I assume the applesauce is without cinnamon?"

"Got a problem with that?"

"Not at all. It's what I prefer."

Again, they stared.

"Holy shit, Bridger, you got a good one. Ain't no way some New York counselor is going to handle her. Hell, you might have your hands full yourself. Hello, ma'am. Name's Hank. Pleased to meet you."

"Hello, Hank," Hope said warmly and reached for the old man's hand, catching the calloused skin in her soft, warm hands.

Bridger's heart melted.

24

*H*ank placed two drafts in front of Hope and Bridger. He didn't ask what they were having, and they didn't question him. She longed for something with rum in it, but decided she was going to roll with it tonight.

"Are you okay with the beer?" Bridger asked, quick to pick up her feelings.

"Sure. It's fine."

"I can get you something else if you'd rather."

"No, thanks, but I'd rather experience this the way Hank intends."

Bridger smiled at her and reached for her hand across the table.

"You are a kind person. I really appreciate that."

She smiled at him, relishing the comfort of his big hand closed on her tiny one.

She felt safe.

She glanced around the bar, looking at the men who were there. No women were present. The men were rough looking, but nothing but respectful to her. They were hard-working blue-collar men, comfortable in a place that was devoid of any urban cosmopolitan trappings.

Her ex-husband would have hated it. He wouldn't have even set foot in the place. If the truth be told, she wouldn't have done so in the past either. Not that she was opposed to it, but rather she hadn't had the opportunity. But she felt comfortable. The men reminded her of her grandfather, a man she lost when she was very young. She just remembered his work clothes, always with a peculiar smell, sweat and pipe tobacco, and his big, rough hands. He was a pipe fitter, a hard-working man, who had a strong sense of what was right and wrong, and he adored his granddaughter. He died when she was around eight or nine. She didn't exactly remember. She didn't know then what killed him, only that he had been very sick. She remembered the word cancer being whispered about, and then he was gone.

This place brought the memories of him flooding back. The smell, the work shirts, the leather lace up boots, all remnants of the man her grandfather had been.

"What are you thinking?" Bridger asked, lifting his glass to her before drinking.

"Thinking about my grandfather. He would have fit in here." She sipped her beer. It was cold and good. Score a point for Hank.

"I take it the memories of him are good?"

"Very. It's just sad that he died when I was young. I would've liked to have had the opportunity to get to know him now."

"Yeah, it sucks when kids are robbed of their grandparents."

"You, too?"

"I never knew my mom's parents. They died before I was born. My dad's parents lived with us. Grandpa ran the marina. It was a smaller operation back then. Most of the business came from the boat repair operation, the rest from summer boat rentals and docking for the fishing boats. Grandpa was the one who actually got me started boat building, although he didn't live long enough to see my first boat finished." Bridger stopped to take a sip of his beer.

Hope waited him out, matching his sip with one of her own,

"He started me building models when I was really little. I wanted to build model airplanes, so he bought me airplane model kits. We would sit in the basement together working with those tiny pieces. His hands were so big, his fingers so large, it was amazing to see him handle such delicate parts. Then, one day, he bought me a model of a boat. It was a model made of all wooden pieces; some so small only tweezers would do to pick up the parts. Together we built that boat, hour after painstaking hour. It took months to finish it, but when it was done, it was a thing of beauty."

"Oh, I wish I could see it."

"You can. It's at my mom's on the mantle. I'll show you some time."

"I would love that."

She looked so earnest, so truthful, and he knew that he was falling hopelessly in love with her.

"Did you and your grandpa build more?"

"Many more. Gramps would sometimes have to push me out the door to get me to go fishing with my friends. He would say too much time with grandpa is not a good thing. Then, one day, a shipment arrived at the house. It was a full-size wooden boat kit."

"No way. They make those?"

"Sure. Basically, they have everything you need to build your own boat, all kinds of boats. So, he bought me a kayak kit and together we started to build it."

"Oh no. That's when he died, isn't it?"

"Yeah. He and my grandmother were coming home from a VFW chicken dinner. The car went off the road, hitting a tree. They were both killed instantly."

"Oh, Bridger, I'm sorry. That's horrible. You lost your father when you were young, too. Didn't you?" Hope said, kindly.

"I did. And a sister." Bridger's eyes were studying his beer.

Hope knew better than to push. She sensed his pain, raw and unresolved.

Just then Hank approached the table, steaks sizzling on cast iron skillets. Hope's eyes grew big at the sight of the giant steaks, perfectly seared with a ball of herb butter melting into the crust. Her mouth started watering and her stomach growled in anticipation. The aroma of garlic and grilled meat swirled into her nostrils as Hank placed the steak in front of her.

"Don't sit around chit chatting letting the damn steak get cold. Get to it," he said gruffly, and he plunked Bridger's in front of him. Hank went back into the kitchen, and returned with the baked potatoes, broccoli, and applesauce.

Hope cut into the meat. It was cooked perfectly. Spearing a piece with her fork, she popped it into her mouth.

Hope swooned.

Never had she tasted a steak like this.

Nothing could have prepared her for this moment.

It was epic.

Bridger grinned at her from across the table.

Hank's cranky face lit up in a smile, all the creases and wrinkles moving northward in pleasure.

Reticent Hank whooped and he and Bridger high-fived.

The other customers looked up from their card game and turned their attention on Hope.

"A virgin, Hank?" asked a rough looking, middle-aged man in a flannel shirt, his mouth cracked into a smile barely visible through his grizzled beard.

Bridger's face instantly became aggressive.

"It's okay, Bridger. I'm not offended."

Hank looked over at the man who already looked chastened from the look Bridger threw him, but now looked positively petrified at Hank's visage.

"Mind your manners, Tom."

"My apologies, ma'am. I didn't mean any disrespect. It's just, Hank's steaks are manna from heaven."

"Tom, I can't argue with you. Until today, I didn't know what steak was supposed to taste like, but my eyes have been opened. This is incredible."

Hank beamed like a woman at the church bazaar who sold out of her baked goods before any other. He fussed around the table for a minute, then resumed his previous cantankerous persona and limped back to the bar.

"So, you like the steak?" Bridger asked, still grinning like a maniac.

"Shhh."

"What do you mean shhhh?"

"I'm in a special place right now. I need to be alone." Hope closed her eyes and ate another bite. "My goodness, what does he do to make it taste like this?"

"Not a clue. I don't question, I just make sure I never piss him off."

"No kidding. I want to be his friend for life."

$\mathcal{H}$ope patted her mouth with her napkin, removing any trace of grease. She groaned; her belly full. Bridger did the same, finishing the last swig of his beer.

"I couldn't eat another bite," Hope admitted, trying not to belch.

"I bet you can," Hank said, as he approached the table holding a single plate with two forks flanking a chocolate delicacy.

"Anna's?" asked Bridger.

"Anna's," affirmed Hank.

"Okay, you twisted my arm. Let me guess, something made by Pepper's Nana Anna?" asked Hope

"Yep," said Hank, "What ya got here is a chocolate brownie of sorts, filled with pecans, topped with a pecan bourbon sauce, topped with freshly-made whipped cream and drizzled with the finest chocolate sauce in the world."

"And who's chocolate sauce would that be?" asked Hope, suspicious that she already knew the answer.

"That would be mine," said Hank, completely devoid of modesty.

The concoction was warm, sticky and delicious.

"Okay, now I couldn't eat another bite," said Hope as she scraped the rest of the chocolate sauce off her side of the plate.

"I have to admit, I've hit my limit, too. I'm impressed you kept up with me."

"So, you don't look down on women who can keep up with a man when it comes to packing away chow?"

"Not at all. I find it refreshing."

Bridger paid the bill and Hank stopped by the table to say goodbye to Hope. She took his offered hand, then leaned in and planted a kiss on his cheek. The men in the bar cheered, and Hank colored furiously.

"Get out of here, you two, before I throw you out. You've worn out your welcome." Hank turned and limped back to the kitchen, a faint smile playing on his lips.

25

The day of the festival dawned warm and sunny with the promise of a perfect day. The parade kicked off at ten with the high school marching band leading the way, followed by the mayor, then all the different clubs and organizations. Boy Scouts, Cub Scouts, 4-h groups all joined the parade with their homemade floats, all somehow paying homage to the oyster. The oyster king and queen drove by sitting on top of the back seat of an antique convertible, waving and smiling, the queen wearing a crown of oyster shells. Bringing up the rear of the parade was a brigade of children, all riding their decorated bikes, following the others in a disorganized wonderful mess of wheels, training wheels, and big wheels decked out with trailing crepe paper.

Hope stood next to Bridger, delighted with the small town, home-made efforts. Once the parade was over, they walked over to Anna's booth. Pepper was there, and she saw them coming. By the time they arrived, she had had a bag of Moravian Molasses cookies ready.

"Hey, Hope, Bridger." She planted a kiss Hope's cheek and hugged Bridger warmly. Hope was happy to see what Pepper had claimed earlier was true. There was no awkwardness between her two friends.

"What did you think of the parade, Hope?" Pepper asked her as she released her hold on Bridger.

"I loved it! So many of my students went by, in the band, on the floats. I've never experienced this kind of small-town parade, and I think it is the best thing ever!"

"I don't know any different, and I still think it is pretty cool. Your students will not forget that you came out to see them."

"I wouldn't have missed them for the world."

Bridger and Hope wandered through the craft booths and youth group games of chance, while munching on the bagful of freshly baked cookies. Several of her students saw her and waved or said hello while shyly casting a sideways glance at Bridger and giggling furiously as they passed by.

"Ready for some oysters?"

"I guess," Hope said hesitantly, "but these cookies are good, too."

"Don't worry, I told you I would steer you in the right direction. The Methodist church makes the best fried oysters."

"Fried?"

"Sure, we're going to start easy."

He led her over to a festive booth decorated in cloth buntings printed with oyster shells.

"Ms. Chandler! Are you going to try our fried oysters?" asked Shelly, the freckled-faced, strawberry blonde student from her second period class.

"I guess so."

Shelley's sidekick Connie giggled, trying to hide the smile behind her hand.

"Haven't you ever had fried oysters?" Connie asked, her eyes wide, not quite believing it was possible.

"Nope, never. So, you guys had better make it good, or I might be ruined on oysters forever," Hope teased.

Shelley rose to the occasion, which Hope knew she would. An A-student, Shelley liked a challenge. She shook her head at Connie when Connie reached for a paper basket already filled with the fried delicacy

Slipping a pair of food service gloves on her hands, she grabbed a handful of raw oysters from the cooler in the back of the booth. She expertly dipped them in buttermilk and dredged them in the church's secret seasoned cornmeal. Then she dropped them one by one in the hot peanut oil. They sputtered furiously. After a few minutes, Shelley scooped them out and flipped them into their own cardboard basket. Connie dropped a container of cocktail sauce in next to the steaming oysters and handed them over to her teacher. The two friends watched Hope anxiously.

"Oh yeah, be careful they're hot, Ms. Chandler."

"Thanks for the warning, Connie."

Bridger paid for the oysters and reached over to snag a big crispy morsel. He danced it between his fingers while blowing on it to cool it down. Then he dipped it in the cocktail sauce and popped it in his mouth. He nodded to the girls.

"Perfect."

They beamed at Bridger and giggled self-consciously. Then they turned their attention on Hope.

It was now or never.

Hope looked over the basket and picked out a small one.

"You should probably taste it without the cocktail sauce," Shelley suggested. "You know, so you can get the full flavor of just the oyster. Then, try it with the sauce. I eat mine without any sauce. That's the way I like them."

Hope blew on the oyster stalling for time. All she could think of was the time Gary made her eat oysters on the half shell. They were at a formal fundraiser and all of his friends were slurping them down, making jokes about being especially potent that evening. Hope tried to avoid it, but Gary made it painfully obvious he would be very unhappy if she didn't join the eating orgy. Watching the techniques of the others, she gave it a go. She tipped the shell and slipped the glob of oyster and liqueur into her mouth. Instead of sliding down her throat, it stuck there, a mass of mucus-like, fishy tasting offal.

"Are you okay, Ms. Chandler?" Connie asked, her face filled with concern.

"I am fine, just waiting for it to cool." Hope smiled brightly at them. They didn't look convinced.

"I promise, Hope. It's going to be fine. You are going to love them."

You're being silly, she told herself, then she popped the oyster in her mouth.

The breading was crunchy and slightly spicy, and the oyster tasted like the sea. It was delightful.

"I knew she would love them," Connie squealed and high-fived Shelley.

"They're delicious. You guys were right. I shouldn't have doubted you. Extra credit to the two of you for encouraging someone to try something new."

Both of the girls blushed and started giggling again. They said their goodbyes to their teacher as they turned their attention to their next customer and Bridger and Hope wandered away munching on the crispy seafood.

They stopped at a game of chance run by a group of 4-h kids. It was a giant wooden board divided into small squares. Some squares were blank, others had dots of blue or yellow. For a dollar, a player received ten dimes to toss on the board. A blank square was worthless. A yellow square doubled your money and a blue square won you a stuffed sea animal.

Bridger lost three dollars.

Hope handed over a dollar. She was determined to win the stuffed spotted eagle ray.

Bridger watched, amused at the determination on Hope's face. She tossed her first dime. It landed on its edge and rolled off the table. Hope's lower lip pushed out in a pout.

Bridger wanted to bite that lip.

He noticed a movement behind the adjacent booth.

It was Chris. The guidance counselor was watching Hope intently. Bridger angled himself so he could watch Chris without being obvious and still see Hope.

She tossed her second coin. A blank square.

Third, fourth, fifth. Nothing.

Chris watched her.

Bridger watched Chris

Sixth. The coin landed flat on the board, the momentum pulling it forward, skidding across the smooth surface through a blank square, a yellow square, landing on a blue.

Hope won.

She squealed and jumped in the air, clapping her hands with glee. Forgetting where she was, she whirled and caught Bridger by surprise, wrapping her arms around him in a joyful hug. He obliged, surrounding her in his strong arms. Over Hope's head he saw Chris's face darken. Bridger flexed his biceps as he pulled Hope a little closer.

"That boy is not happy," a voice behind Bridger said.

Bridger released Hope and she went about the business of picking out her prize. Bridger turned and shook Ryker's hand and gave Jennifer a kiss on the cheek.

"No, I don't think he is," Bridger agreed.

"And Hope is going to have to deal with the increased gossip that is going to result from that very public hug," said Jennifer, laughing at the thought of tomorrow's diner discussions.

"I really don't care," announced Hope as she returned to them, hugging her eagle ray, its black fur body sprinkled with stark white spots. "I think you're all juvenile anyway." She smiled to let them know she was just teasing.

"Quite possibly," agreed Ryker, "but it makes for an interesting day. Are you guys hanging here all day, or leaving and coming back tonight?"

Hope looked at Bridger, questioning him with her eyes.

"I don't think we made any definite plans, but I know I want to be here so Hope can watch the oyster shucking contest this evening. Plus, Heartbreak is playing tonight in the main tent. They're really good, and I thought Hope would enjoy it."

"I'll enjoy anything. Will there be dancing?" she asked, hopefully.

"Yep, and hootin' and hollerin'."

"I'm in," Hope said.

While they were talking, Bridger noticed Chris edging his way closer until Bridger was certain Chris could overhear their plans. Bridger took Hope's hand in his and began to steer the group away from the booths of chance.

"I could use a lemonade," Bridger said. Ryker slid his eyes from Bridger to Chris and back to Bridger. Silent communication passed between them.

"Jennifer, lemonade?" Ryker followed Bridger's lead, holding Jennifer's hand and the group walked across the grounds to the Girl Scout lemonade booth.

"The reason I asked if you were staying or coming back later is, I promised to take Jennifer out in the boat today. Carly Marshal mentioned seeing a couple of whales hanging out about a mile off the lighthouse. You guys want to come?"

"Oh, Bridger, can we?" Hope asked her eyes shining.

"Sure, if you want, but Hope, the chances of seeing a whale is slim. It's early in the season to catch sight of them. Usually we see them a month from now, but it's always a good day to take the boat out."

"I'm glad you guys are going to come. It'll be fun. Before we go can we grab an oyster Po' Boy?" Jennifer asked as she watched an elderly couple walk by carefully trying to take a bite of their sandwiches without losing the filling.

"Those look good," agreed Hope.

"Oh, so now you like oysters," Bridger teased.

They each ordered a sandwich from the adjacent booth and then made plans to meet at the docks in twenty minutes. After some discussion, they decided to take Bridger's boat because it was larger and faster. That fact lent itself to some good ribbing between the friends.

Bridger guided the boat out of the channel and out of the no wake zone. He opened the throttle and the boat leapt forward. Hope and Jennifer sat in the stern enjoying the bright October sun while Ryker and Bridger scanned the horizon for a sight-ing. They followed the coast north, the historic lighthouse growing closer.

Once they were parallel with Grey's Light, they turned the bow for open water. Carly Marshall and her husband ran a fishing charter out of Cadigan Marina, and she told Ryker she had spotted a pod of humpbacks yesterday even though it was way too early for them.

They spent the next hour crisscrossing the area, keeping their eyes out for the classic hump out of the water. Dolphins played in the wake from the bow, leading the boat for a while before disappearing.

Finding nothing, Bridger throttled back and baited a couple of fishing rods. He remembered that Hope had said she wanted to fish, so they spent the next couple of lazy hours fishing. Hope's pole finally showed activity after she loudly pouted about never catching anything.

Bridger coached her as she worked the line, the pole bending under the strain of the fish.

"What is it?" she asked, excitedly, hanging onto the pole for dear life.

"Not a clue. It could be anything from a mackerel, tuna, or a shark."

"Shark?" Hope squeaked. "No, I don't want to catch a shark!" She looked panicked for a minute.

"It'll be fine, just hang on to that pole." he cautioned.

Hope grimly turned her attention back to the job at hand. Jennifer shouted encouragement while Ryker readied a long handle net. Bridger stayed by her side as she worked the fish closer and closer to the boat.

"Yep, shark," said Ryker as he leaned over the boat.

Hope squealed nervously.

"It's okay, just keep hauling it in. Your arms tired?" he asked, looking at her kindly.

"A little," she admitted.

"Here he comes," Ryker announced as he leaned over and scooped the fish into the net, drawing it aboard.

"I caught a fish!" Hope yelled, letting the heavens know of her accomplishment.

"You caught a black-tipped shark," Bridger said proudly, holding the fish up for Hope. "He's not terribly big, but he put up a good fight."

They got a quick picture of Hope with the shark, then cut it free and sent it back into its watery home.

"That was so much fun," Hope said, her eyes shining. "I'm sorry we didn't see any whales, Jennifer."

"It's okay. I really didn't expect to see any, especially now, but I had a lot of fun."

"Are you girls ready to go back, get cleaned up and eat more oysters?" asked Bridger.

"Yep, and you promised dancing, right?"

"Absolutely." Bridger turned the boat and headed back to the marina.

26

"*H*ope, are you about ready?" Bridger called from the dock. The patio door was open, and Bridger could see Hope's shadowy figure through the screen.

"Almost. Come on board and make yourself at home. I'll be out in a minute. There's a pitcher of iced tea on the table and some glasses. Help yourself."

Bridger stepped into the boat and made his way over to the table. He helped himself to a glass of tea, then had a seat. There was a stack of papers in front of him, narrow lined with chicken scratches all over them. He was glad he wasn't a teacher. It would give him a headache trying to decipher the terrible handwriting on that top composition.

He leaned back in the chair and sipped his tea, waiting for Hope to come out. The evening was still warm, a gem for this time in October. A light breeze was coming off the ocean.

Hope slid open the screen door and stepped out. Her hair was down around her sun-kissed shoulders, which were currently mostly bare expect for some slim spaghetti straps that held up a deep blue sundress. A pewter seashell pendant nestled in the hollow of her throat, and silver thin bangles sparkled on her wrist. Bridger looked into her eyes, which were framed by a light sweep of mascara. A touch of soft pink lip gloss graced her lips.

He was going to mess up that lip gloss.

"God, you're beautiful," he whispered as he moved toward her.

She blushed shyly.

"Thank you. You look pretty good yourself. Where the heck did you get those shorts?"

Bridger looked down at the khaki shorts sprinkled with oyster shells. His deep blue shirt set off the watercolor edges of the printed shells.

It was his turn to blush.

"My mom got them for me. I like her sense of humor."

"So do I," she said, and she moved toward Bridger and into his waiting arms.

Then he did what he had previously intended. He thoroughly messed up her lip gloss. Once he was certain that he had done an exceptional job on her lips, he moved to her throat, where that shell was pressing against her skin.

She tilted her head back, giving him permission to explore every part of her neck.

Damn, she wanted more, and he wanted to take it. He brought his hand up to her breast and rubbed her nipple between his fingers. The fabric was thin, and he discovered that she was not wearing a bra.

That made things infinitely more interesting.

She moaned and leaned into his hand, moving her fingers up to his hair. She took control of his head and brought his lips back to hers, opening her mouth for him to explore.

If she wasn't careful, this was going to escalate. Her loins decided that was okay. Her brain was cautioning her, but he was so strong, so there, so real. She was thinking about skipping the festival.

A gust of air lifted her hair and flipped up the hem of her skirt. Bridger's other hand took advantage of the opening and he ran his palm up the back of her thigh, cupping her ass. He felt her lace panties under his fingers and he about came undone.

Another gust of wind lifted all of the papers off of the table, scattering them across the deck.

"Oh, no," Hope exclaimed, pulling back reluctantly, frantically.

She bent to gather up her students' papers.

"I hope none went overboard." She sounded so distressed. Bridger moved quickly to the rail and looked.

"I don't see anything in the water." He bent to pick up a few more papers that were caught up against the side of the boat near the decking. He straightened them carefully, making a neat pile to hand back to Hope.

What he saw on top cooled his blood quickly.

"Hope, what's this?" he asked.

"What?" Not looking up, straightening her own pile.

"This paper. It looks like a letter. I didn't mean to read it, but Hope, it's kind of threatening, in a weird way."

Hope flashed back to Friday in the teacher's lounge.

"Let me see, please." She reached out to take the paper from Bridger, and he handed it to her reluctantly. He really didn't want her to have it. He felt like he needed to protect her from it.

"It's like this guy likes you, but he also threatens you."

She glanced it over. It was the same paper she saw before and had stuffed into her tote.

"Yeah, it's kind of strange. I've never had something like this happen before. I have a student who is very hostile towards me. He doesn't participate in class, and he does the minimum amount of work. What he does do is actually quite insightful. Anyhow, Chris has spoken to him, and he said that the student's hostility springs from the fact that he actually might be infatuated with me. Chris is working with him and his issues."

"Do you think Chris can do any good with this student? I don't like this. Who is this kid, anyway?"

"Sorry, Bridger. I can't tell you that. I have to protect my students. You understand, don't you?"

"I do understand, but I don't have to like it," he growled.

"Thank you for respecting me. Don't worry. We've got this. I'm sure Chris can handle the emotional side of this young man, and I can handle the academic issues. I promise."

To make him feel better she took him in her arms and kissed him again. She looked into his eyes and whispered to him, her lips against his.

"It's okay. I promise. Now, are we going to eat more oysters? You know what they say about oysters."

He was rock hard in an instant.

*H*ope took the stack of papers inside and then locked up the boat. Throwing a light sweater over her arm, she took Bridger's hand and he helped her off the boat. They met Clarence stepping down off of his boat, too.

"Good evening, Clarence. Are you heading over to the festival?" Hope inquired.

"Yes, my dear. I wouldn't miss it for the world. I am fairly certain my dance card is full, but I am sure I can find time for you. Come look me up in the big tent. I will lean you against me and we can sway to the music while you discover the magic of my oysters."

"Clarence," Bridger warned, but Hope just laughed and wound her hand through Clarence's crooked elbow, finding herself escorted down the dock by two handsome gentleman, one sporting oyster shorts and the other in white patent leather shoes, matching belt, silky shirt opened to his navel, revealing several gold chains swinging against his hairy chest. Hope felt very special indeed.

They said their goodbyes to Clarence as he climbed into his white convertible and sped off waving in the rearview mirror. Hope and Bridger followed in his truck.

Hope was surprised at the transformation at the festival. Hundreds of lights had been strung overhead, lighting the park and the beach with a festive twinkle. The sun was setting, and several volleyball games were underway under bright temporary lights. Music was everywhere, from small tents set on the perimeter to the large tent with the dance floor set up inside. Food booths were doing a booming business and the games of chance had long lines. It was a lot busier than the lazy morning venue Hope had experienced earlier.

"Okay, you've had your oysters fried, so it's time to move on to a higher level. Let's head over to the volunteer fire department's booth for some Oysters Rockefeller."

"Ooh la la," Hope teased. She was looking forward to the next taste of oyster since the last two experiences were positive.

"These guys can really cook," said Bridger as they approached the booth.

"Hey, Bridger. I see you get to escort the English teacher tonight. Toby figured it would be the guidance counselor." A large man with a handlebar mustache wearing an apron that said, 'keep your panties on,' smiled at Bridger while he waved a pair of stainless-steel tongs.

"Randy, you're an ass," said Bridger good naturally,

"That I am, my friend. That I am. I'm assuming an order of Rockefeller for you and the lady?"

"Yep, we're going to share. She has a lot to sample this evening."

"Now Bridger, you know you might as well just stop here, because these are the best."

"I'll be the judge of that," Hope spoke up.

"I am not intimidated," Randy quipped. "Just because I got D's in English doesn't mean I'm not a helluva cook."

"Sounds like you might be concerned about your grade?" Hope mused out loud.

"Not a chance." He handed her a plate with two oysters broiled to perfection. "Hi, I'm Randy. Be careful, they're hot."

"Pleased to meet you, Randy. I'm Hope." She balanced the plate and offered her hand. Randy shook it solemnly, then waited for her to take a bite.

She tasted the oyster and a huge grin split her face.

"This is amazing. Holy cow. Do you cook like this at the station? Can I be a fireman...person...whatever?"

"We're volunteers, so we don't live at the station. If there's a fire, we all get a call on our phones and we grab our gear and head out."

"Gotcha, so no hope of eating this stuff other than here."

"No, but if you give me a good grade, I'll share the recipe." Randy looked at her earnestly.

"You have a 110% A. I will expect the recipe on my desk sometime next week," she teased.

Bridger stood back and smiled, watching Hope win over the locals of Grey's Harbor. Not an easy feat for an outsider.

They made their way around the festival, eating roasted corn from the Boy Scouts, who stripped the husks back and twisted them into a handle, then dipped the ears in a coffee can of melted butter before handing them over. They also worked their way through the booths sampling a myriad of oyster delights. Hope really enjoyed the slice of oyster pizza that Tony Conti and Danny Marino from Harbor New York served up. She had buffalo fried oysters, smoked oysters wrapped in bacon, and pieces of crusty bread dipped in a cheesy oyster gratin. When she didn't think she could eat another bite, they ran into Ryker, Jennifer, Tank and Maeve. Tank announced it was time for oyster and Bloody Mary shooters.

"I don't know about that." Hope looked nervously up at Bridger.

"Don't worry, Hope. I can't do raw oysters either, and I grew up here," admitted Jennifer.

"I'm in," Maeve chimed in.

They made their way to a large tent that was roped off all the way around. They had to show their ID's to enter. Hope was flattered until she saw them card Clarence. Bridger burst out laughing when he saw her face fall.

They moved their way up to the makeshift bar and found a space to huddle together. It was elbow to elbow in there. Hope found herself pressed up against Bridger, unable to move away. He rested an arm around her, with a questioning look.

"You okay?"

"Yeah, just a little crowded and self-conscious. You know how these people talk, and we've already given them a lot to talk about."

"You might as well give up on it, darlin'," Tank advised. "You're still the best entertainment they've had in some time."

Bridger, Tank, Ryker, and Maeve each ordered a shooter. The bartender set down a wide mouth short glass filled with a Bloody Mary. Balanced on the rim was a large oyster shell filled with the requisite raw oyster.

Hope felt her throat close at the memory.

Bridger looked at her in amusement.

"Cheers," shouted Tank, and the four of them tilted their oysters back into their mouths and followed with the Bloody Mary shot.

Hope shuddered.

"Delicious," Maeve exclaimed. "And now, we dance!"

The friends fought their way out of the tent and headed to the large entertainment tent where the Heartbreaks were already well into their first set.

The next hour was a sweaty, dizzy blur. Hope danced with Bridger and Tank. At one point she was sashaying around the tent with Clarence, who swung her into him, slid his leg between hers and tilted her forward, leaving her straddling his leg with hers dangling help-lessly behind her, her breasts pressed up against his chest. He carefully landed her back on her feet, then whispered in her ear.

"Thank you, my dear." He spun her into Bridger's arms and found a new lady waiting to be whisked away.

"What the hell just happened to me?" Hope asked, trying to regain her composure.

"You've been Clarenced," Maeve said wryly. "It's happened to all of us at some point or other. The old pervert always manages to get some kind of feel from every woman in town. He's a harmless, old man who's lonely and who gives a lot of lonely women a bright spot in their day. All of us tolerate him because he really is very sweet. In fact, we love him and wouldn't want him any other way. If he bothers you, all you have to do is tell him and he will turn into a perfect gentleman. There are several women in town who don't appreciate his advances. He leaves them alone."

"I do like him. He just took me by surprise. I'll be right back." Hope excused herself to head over to the port a potty. When she returned, she had lost Bridger and the rest of the group.

The band slowed things down, and Hope found herself face to face with Chris. He reached out and took her in his arms to slow dance. Hope smiled graciously, but looked over his shoulder, searching the crowd for Bridger.

"Hope, did you hear what I said?" asked Chris, forcing her attention back on him.

"I'm sorry, I was distracted for a moment. What was that?"

"I wanted to let you know that we are all set next week for that Inservice. We'll leave after school on Thursday. It should take us a little over an hour to get there. Then there are two sessions, A and B on engaging the reluctant student, dinner, then the last session on alternative assessment for the challenging student. After that we can head home."

He was a good dancer, and as he talked, he maneuvered her effortlessly around the floor. Hope kept her attention politely on Chris, resisting the urge to once again look for Bridger. She wouldn't have been able to see him even if she tried. Chris expertly kept turning her away, so Bridger wouldn't be in her line of sight.

"I figured we could share a car, and I would be happy to drive." He smiled at her, giddy with the thought of her in the car next to him, alone with him. He wouldn't have to compete with that small town, crass oaf she kept hanging around.

"That would be fine, thank you." The music stopped and Hope stepped away from Chris. "And thank you for the dance."

"There you are." Bridger's voice was in her ear and his hand on her elbow. "Hello, Chris."

"Bridger."

"Thank you again, Chris. I'll see you on Monday." She smiled at the man kindly, then turned to walk with Bridger back over to the others. As she walked, she could feel the eyes of the locals. Her face began to color. Damn, dancing with Chris would just add fuel to the fire. She was thinking that she was beginning to get tired of this.

Chris watched her walk away with Bridger, a fire burning in his heart. He didn't like losing, especially to someone so inferior. He decided he was done watching Hope with Bridger. He walked out of the tent while Bridger and Hope fast danced with their friends.

It was time for the band to take a break, so they all made their way back to the adult beverage tent. This time, Hope had a Bloody Mary minus the oyster. It was spicy and good. They munched on an order of oyster ceviche served with plantain chips, then had another round of Bloody Mary's just to be social.

They announced the final round of the oyster shucking contest, so everyone moved out of the tents to watch four men compete for the title. Hope was astounded at the speed and skill these men had with a knife.

After the winner was awarded the giant oyster shell belt, the bands started tuning up again. They finished up with their food and drinks and headed back to the big tent. Hope was beginning to think this just might be the most fun she'd had since she was a kid.

The band started again, and Bridger asked Hope if she was done or if she wanted to dance. It was another slow dance and she wanted nothing more than to be in Bridger's arms. She smiled and nodded, joining him as Maeve and Tank moved together next to them, Ryker and Jennifer following suit.

The band was good, and she was enjoying swaying to the music, held close by Bridger when she became aware of a note that was at odds with the music. This tone was harsh and penetrating. Everyone stopped dancing and men were reaching into their pockets, pulling out their cell phones. The sound was on a lot of the men's phones.

Everything stopped.

"Bridger, what?"

"Hang on," he said listening to his phone. Hope noticed Tank and Ryker were doing the same, as well as a dozen or so other men on the dance floor.

"Fire phone," hissed Maeve.

Hope's heart sank. Somewhere there was a fire. Someone was in trouble. Her thoughts went immediately to her students. She wondered if any of them would be affected.

"Pappy's place, down on the river. Damn it. It's just a trailer, there won't be anything left." Bridger said. "Maeve?"

"I'll take Jennifer and Hope home, no worries. You guys go. Be careful."

"Bridger, please be careful." Hope's eyes were large with worry. She didn't know anything about being a volunteer fireman, but she had a feeling there was potential to be seriously hurt.

Bridger stopped and turned toward Hope. He gave her a quick kiss on the cheek, then spun on his heels and hurried out of the tent, following Ryker and Tank.

People milled around for a minute or two after the men left. The band started to play again, but the festive atmosphere was gone. The band toned it down, providing background music while people found tables and sat down in groups, talking together, a community drawn together in concern for a neighbor.

ridger, Ryker, and Tank made their way down the dock towards Hope's boat. The girls could see the slumped shoulders and slow walk. The news couldn't be good.

Maeve got up and went into Hope's kitchenette, pulling three mugs out of the cupboard and pouring strong, hot coffee into them. By the time the men reached the boat, she had the coffee outside waiting for them.

"Hey," said Maeve, reaching out to Tank as he crossed over the gunwale. Tank touched the tips of Maeve's fingers then took the steaming mug from her.

"Thanks," he said. His eyes were tired and sad.

"Bridger?" Hope asked, searching his face. She saw past the strain, exhaustion and the soot, and saw something else. Not just pain, but anger.

It was Ryker who spoke first.

"The trailer was gone before we even left the festival. It must have gone up like a dried-out Christmas tree."

"Pappy?" Maeve asked.

Tank shook his head.

Bridger slammed his fist down on the table, surprising all of them, sloshing the remaining cups of coffee sitting there.

"It was torched. Someone torched the place. Pappy didn't have a chance."

"What do you mean someone torched the place?" Jennifer asked, horrified.

Ryker moved closer to her, dropping an arm around her shoulder. She was gaining strength, but underneath was still the fragile woman who had been abused and raped for years.

"Who would have done something like that? I don't understand," Hope said, not believing something like this could happen in Grey's Harbor.

"Any idea, Bridger?" asked Maeve.

"No, the Fire Marshall was called. He's there now."

"Are they sure it's arson? Are you sure it's not an accident or something?" Jennifer asked in a small voice.

"Positive. This guy wants us to know it was intentionally set."

"Bridger, are you sure Pappy was there? Maybe he was out or something." Hope's voice was rising, bordering on hysteria.

Bridger moved to her quickly and wrapped his arms around her.

"I'm sorry, honey. He was in there."

"Bridger found the body, Hope," Tank said, taking a sip of the coffee. "Maeve, someone has to tell Izzy, unless the word has already gotten to her."

"Come with me?" she asked Tank. "Please?"

"Of course. Thanks for the coffee, ladies. Bridger, you good? Ryker?" Tank's look of concern for his friends was touching, and a contrast to the tough guy exterior he always presented the world.

"I'm good," said Bridger, as he shook Tank's hand. "Tell Izzy I'm here for her if she needs me."

"You got it." Tank shook Ryker's hand and all the girls hugged before Maeve and Tank left the boat. Bridger sank into a chair and lifted a mug of coffee to his lips.

"God, that's good. Thanks Hope." He reached for her hand, wanting her contact, her warmth, her inherent goodness.

Ryker picked up the other mug, waiting for Jennifer to get settled in a seat before he sat down himself.

"I don't know what to do," said Jennifer. "I feel so helpless."

"Did Pappy have any family?" asked Hope.

"No, as far as anyone knows, Pappy is, was a loner. I'd heard he had a wife, but I guess she died years ago, and as far as I know, he didn't have any children."

"How awful to be so alone," Jennifer mused. "I used to think I wanted to be completely alone, but now I know that I really need people around me." She looked up at Ryker and smiled shyly.

"Yeah, well, Pappy wasn't completely alone. He had..." Bridger was interrupted by his phone.

"Bridger, it's Izzy. Hohner. Did you see Hohner out there?"

"I'm on it, Iz. I just remembered he had that old hound, and I don't remember seeing any...sign of the dog. I'll head back out there now and see what I can find. Don't worry, Iz. If Hohner's out there, I'll find him and make sure he's okay. Are you okay, honey?"

"No, but I'm going to be. Don't worry, Bridger. I won't go off the deep end. Pappy would be disappointed in me if I did. Please just go and find Hohner."

"Hohner? Like the harmonica?" Hope asked, a sad smile playing on her lips. She was getting up and heading into the cabin. "Jennifer, do you need a sweatshirt or something? It's cooling down."

"You guys coming with me?" Bridger asked.

"Of course. You aren't doing this alone. We'll find him."

"If there's anything left to find," said Ryker, warning them that this could be a gruesome quest.

"Ryker, this is a crime scene we're going to. How are we going to handle that?"

"Don't know, but we'll figure it out on the way. Do you have flashlights in your truck?"

"Yeah, but let's stop by the houseboat and pick up a couple more."

The four left Hope's boat and headed down the dock, determined to find Pappy's dog and bring him some sort of comfort.

28

*L*ong before Bridger's truck approached Pappy's property, Hope could smell the fire. The acrid smoke still filled the night air. She wrinkled her nose as imagined images filled her head. She couldn't even fathom the idea of dying in a fire.

Bridger parked the truck along the road in front of the devastated trailer. As they all piled out of the truck, a man approached them.

"What are you doing back out here?" the man asked Bridger.

"Tom is the fire marshal," Bridger explained to the girls. "Tom, this is Hope, and Jennifer. They came out here with Ryker and me to see if we could find Pappy's dog. You didn't see anything, did you?"

"If you're asking if I found remains of a dog, no I didn't."

Hope breathed an audible sigh of relief.

"That doesn't necessarily mean good news, ma'am. If the dog was in that trailer when it burned, he wouldn't have had much of a chance. The trailer went fast. He could have been badly burned and crawled away."

Hope nodded her understanding. Jennifer just looked sick, the moon accenting her pale face and wide eyes.

"Do you mind if we look around? If the dog is still alive, we'd like to find him and take care of him."

"No, Bridger, I don't mind at all. I'm pretty much done here. Just don't go sifting through the remains of the trailer. I'll come back tomorrow in the daylight to wrap things up, but I pretty much have what I need."

"So, you agree with us? It was arson?" Ryker asked.

"No doubt. The perp threw a Molotov cocktail with a chemical detonator against the trailer. Pappy had the windows open. The curtains caught fire and the accelerant splattered inside the trailer. The device he used made a particularly hot fire and Pappy's trailer was no match for it."

"Did Pappy die of smoke inhalation?" Jennifer asked hopefully.

"I'm sorry to say, probably not. He was sitting in his recliner near the open window. My guess is the accelerant also splattered on him, engulfing him in flames." The Fire Marshall looked at the girls' faces and remembered he wasn't talking to professionals here. "I'm sorry. That probably sounded cold and unfeeling."

"No, you're doing your job and we appreciate the information and your straightforwardness. Thank you," Hope said kindly. "Just please do what you can to catch this guy and punish him for what he did to Pappy." Tears sprung to her eyes.

"Believe me, ma'am. I'll move heaven and earth to bring him to justice. You can count on that. Now I'm heading home. Please be careful out here and stay away from the trailer. Good night, all."

Tom walked to his truck and backed out of the driveway. As he did, his headlights revealed the utter devastation before them. In the moonlight it had looked like a jumble of debris. In the headlights, it looked like a tragedy.

As Tom backed onto the road, his headlights swept the woods, briefly lighting the underbrush.

"Bridger, what's that?" Hope said pointing to a spot at the edge of the woods.

"I'm not sure. What did you see?"

"It looked like eyes lit up. Let's go check, it might be Hohner." Hope started jogging toward the spot.

"Hey, slow down, hero." Bridger said, catching her arm. "It might

not be Hohner. We have all kinds of wild animals out here, and if it is
Hohner, he may be frightened and that will make him aggressive."

"You're right. I wasn't thinking," Hope said, chastised.

"Your heart is in the right place, honey. I just don't want you hurt
while trying to help. Got it?"

"Yep, got it."

"Um, Bridger? Just what kind of wild animals do we have out
here?" asked Jennifer, nervously.

"I'll protect you," Ryker claimed, dropping his arm around her
shoulders.

"No seriously. When I was a kid living out here, I don't remember
any wild animals to speak of, other than a couple of deer." Jennifer
glanced around at the dark shadows surrounding them.

"Norm Chadoury spotted a black bear last month tearing apart a
rotted log along the riverbank. He had gone upriver to do some fishing. We also have had coyotes and bobcats make a good comeback,"
Ryker said.

"I was thinking more along the line of raccoons or skunks,"
laughed Bridger.

"Yeah, I don't want to walk up to a skunk thinking it might be a
dog," laughed Hope.

Bridger switched on his flashlight and Ryker did the same as they
swept the edge of the forest with the strong beams.

There. Another flash of eyes.

"Hohner?" Bridger said softly.

The eyes didn't move.

The group carefully walked toward the eyes.

"Hey buddy, it's okay," Hope called soothingly as they approached
the eyes. "We just want to help. Hey, Hohner."

As they got closer, the beam revealed a shape with the eyes.

Then they all heard the sound of a tail thumping against dry
leaves.

The dog's ears were down, flat to his head. His tail thumped feebly.
He was covered with soot, and he didn't stand to greet them, but he
stretched his nose out and licked Hope's outstretched hand.

Hope's compassion won over any good sense as she dropped to her knees and reached to check out the dog.

"Hope be careful. If he's hurt, he might bite out of fear and pain."

"Hush, Bridger. It's fine. He's hurt and he knows I'm going to help him. Do you have a blanket or a tarp in that truck? If so, would you get it for me, please?"

"Damn, Bridger. She really is a teacher. She can bark orders with the best of them."

Bridger smiled, proud of the way she handled herself. He liked her take charge attitude and her lack of concern for herself when another was in need. He stood for a moment, watching this woman. He was falling in love with her, and he didn't know what he was going to do about it.

"Bridger? The blanket?" Hope looked over her shoulder at him, her eyebrow raised.

Ryker looked at his friend.

"Let me help you with that tarp, buddy. Jennifer, are you okay with Hope?"

"Of course, Ryker. I'm fine."

Bridger and Ryker walked toward the truck leaving the girls with the dog, Hope talking softly to him as he licked her fingers.

"My friend, you've got it bad, don't you?" Ryker said as Bridger dropped the tailgate and folded back the tonneau cover.

"Got what bad?"

"You're in love with Hope."

"What makes you say that?" Bridger asked, not looking back at his friend. He reached in the bed deeper and came up with a small gray tarp.

"It is written all over your face, my friend. You might need to step it up, because the town still has the good counselor winning the game."

Bridger's face darkened with Ryker's words. Not a chance, he thought.

"Come on, let's get back to the girls."

As they turned and started back, the quiet night was pierced with the cry of a dog, a snarl and the snap of jaws.

"Hope!" Bridger cried out, and broke into a run, Ryker hot on his heels behind him. Within seconds Bridger had dropped to her side. The dog, frightened by the frenzied activity tried to stand, but couldn't. Getting more agitated, he lifted his lip in a snarl of fear.

"Bridger, relax. I'm fine."

"What happened. I heard him snarl and snap."

"Yes, he did. But he didn't bite me. He was just telling me he hurts." Calmly she settled a hand back on the big bloodhound's head, gently stroking his ears. The dog heaved a sigh and relaxed again, whimpering softly.

When Hope pulled her hands away, Bridger could see they were covered with soot. He searched her face to see if she was lying, if she was indeed hurt, but hiding it from him. All he saw was a woman full of compassion with a smudge of soot under her right eye.

He reached out with his thumb and tenderly wiped the smudge away. Hope looked at him and smiled. Jennifer and Ryker glanced at each other, Ryker shaking his head and Jennifer grinning from ear to ear. "They've got it bad," Ryker mouthed to Jennifer. She nodded her head in agreement.

"I'm pretty sure his shoulder is hurt. He was really unhappy when I ran my hands over it. I was looking for injuries. I didn't get past his shoulder. I'd like to try again, but not if you're going to get all wound up and scare him more if he snaps again."

"Hope, I don't want you hurt."

"I know. Just trust me, okay?" Hope looked back at Bridger.

"I trust you. I don't trust an injured dog. Hang on a second." He crouched down next to Hope, positioning himself near the dog's head. "Hey, Hohner, buddy. You had a bad night, didn't you?" Bridger's voice was soft and soothing. The dog's tail thumped, thumped, thumped against the leaves. "I know. It's going to be okay. We've got you." Bridger moved his hand up to the dog's ears and began scratching them gently. The dog moaned and licked Bridger's wrist.

"Okay, Hope, go ahead. Slowly and carefully."

"I will, I just want to see if I can find anything else bad before we try to move him, although we can't see the side he's lying on. Bridger, he might react if something else hurts, but I don't think he will bite me, so don't overreact okay?"

Ryker about choked with Hope's words. If there was anything Bridger hated was someone suggesting he might overreact.

Bridger's eyes narrowed into a squint, but he held his tongue. He also held his hands at the ready. There was no way this dog was going to bite Hope. He would see to it.

Hope ran her hands lightly over the dog's body, avoiding his shoulder. The dog tensed at first, but relaxed as he realized she wasn't hurting him. When she reached down to check his paws, he jerked.

Bridger's hands tightened on the dog's head.

Hope looked at Bridger reproachfully.

The three took a moment, then relaxed again.

Ryker stooped down with them and shined the flashlight on the dog's paws.

"I think they look burnt," said Ryker, shaking his head. "That has to hurt. How are we going to move him, Bridger? We can't risk anyone getting bitten."

Bridger thought for a moment and looked into the dog's eyes. The dog looked back.

"I think it's going to be okay."

Bridger spread the tarp on the ground then patted it with his hand, encouraging the dog to move himself onto it. After a few moments, the dog sighed and crawled his way to the tarp, whimpering with each movement. Hope couldn't stop herself. She ran her hands along his back, gently pushing to help his momentum. The dog looked back at her gratefully.

Bridger wrapped the tarp tightly around the dog, then he and Ryker picked up the ends of the dog burrito and carried it to the truck.

Hohner tried to be stoic, but occasionally he let out a pitiful whimper. Bridger and Ryker loaded the dog into the back of the truck. Hope stepped up on the bumper to ride in the back with the dog.

"Um, no. You are not riding back here."

"Um, yep, I am," Hope fired back sweetly.

"Not a good plan," Bridger said, firmly.

"I disagree. It's a perfect plan," Hope said

"Bridger, I'll ride back here with Hope and the dog. I'm strong enough to make sure the dog doesn't slide around if you have to hit the brakes hard."

Hope hid a smile, knowing Ryker was giving a reason to have to ride back there with her, appeasing both her and Bridger and the same time.

"I guess that will work. Hope, it'll be cold back there."

"She can have this other sweatshirt." Jennifer offered. "I'll be warm enough in the cab."

"Bridger is there a vet we can take Hohner to at this hour?" asked Hope, realizing they didn't have a plan.

"I'll call Ingrid. She'll be happy to help."

When everyone got settled, Bridger pulled onto the road and headed slowly back in town. It was bittersweet. They had found Hohner, but Hohner was now an orphan, and an injured one at that.

29

*I*t was one o'clock in the morning when Bridger pulled into the marina, the tires crunching on the gravel driveway. He put the truck in park and looked over at Hope, her head against the window, sound asleep. He hated to wake her.

He switched off the truck and she stirred.

"Hmmm," she uttered.

"Hmmm, what?" Bridger said softly.

"Hmmm, it's late and I'm hungry. I don't think I got my fill of oysters tonight." She looked up at him and smiled.

He looked exhausted. There was soot on his face where it had escaped the swipes of his hands when they wiped off the sweat. His hair was standing up, and his shirt was probably destined for the trash. The last few feet to the vet's office gave Bridger's shirt a spray of steaming vomit from an apologetic dog. Hope tried to wipe it off with a tissue, but it was a lost cause.

"I need a shower," Bridger admitted, sniffing himself delicately.

"Do you have any food in any one of your boats?" Hope asked. "I'll be happy to whip something up while you get cleaned up. I'm guessing you're hungry, too."

His stomach growled in response.

They walked over to Bridger's houseboat, and he helped her aboard.

"Help yourself to anything you find in the kitchen. I don't care what you make, I'll eat it."

"Sounds like a plan," said Hope as she poked her head into the medium sized refrigerator. This boat was a lot bigger than hers, and the kitchen was well stocked.

"Okay, I'll be right back." Bridger turned and walked down a short hall, stripping his shirt off as he went. Hope watched the smooth muscles rippling across his back as his shirt came off over his head.

It lit a fire in her.

Those oysters really work, she thought.

She heard the shower start, and she decided she'd better busy herself in the kitchen so she wouldn't think about Bridger in the shower, his body naked, glistening.

Stop it, she told herself. Fleetingly she thought about joining him. *Where did that come from? Oysters. Definitely the oysters.*

She found some ham in the deli drawer and some onions and green peppers in the hydrator. A quick check told her he had plenty of eggs and cheese. Omelets were in order.

She set herself to the chore of chopping the ingredients, trying to keep her mind off of Bridger and his lack of clothing in the next room.

Bridger stepped under the steaming water. He sighed. He was tired and mentally exhausted. Finding Pappy burned like that haunted him. He would never forget that image as long as he lived.

He worked the lather up with the bar of homemade soap his mother insisted he use, made with local honey and milk. It smelled good, he admitted to himself as he soaped his body. The act brought up the image of Hope, crouched next to the injured dog, her eyes filled with compassion. Well, that brought him to attention. She was in the next room. He groaned, thinking of her joining him in the shower. What he would do to her there, all lathered up with honey smelling soap. *Note to self, don't take a girl to eat oysters unless you can finish the job*, he thought.

He quickly finished showering, trying to keep his mind off of the stunning beauty in his kitchen. The beautiful girl who really had no idea just how pretty she was. He loved that about her. He loved just about everything about her. *Except her tendency to be a little snippy. Telling him not to overreact. Seriously?* he thought.

He toweled himself off, then wrapped the towel around his lower half. He ran a brush through his hair then opened the door of the steamy bathroom. The smell of sautéing peppers and onions hit him hard. He was starving.

Hope looked around to see Bridger standing in the hall, his hair wet, shoulders still glistening with dampness, a towel wrapped low and slung around his lips.

Oh shit, she thought. *I can't.*

Oh, but I can.

She turned the burner off under the skillet and walked very deliberately over to Bridger, who was watching her, hunger written all over his face. The peppers and onions were forgotten. In front of him, Hope. His Hope.

He reached his arms around her, crushing her against him. She found his lips with hers and kissed him with urgency. All of the pain and sadness of the evening swelling inside her. Bridger felt it as it joined his own. He wanted her, needed her.

She stripped the sweatshirt over her head forgetting that she was still braless but didn't care. She wanted and needed him, too.

Skin to skin, they kissed, explored, discovered, until he lifted her into his arms and carried her to his bedroom, the omelets forgotten.

30

"Well, that was unexpected," said Bridger as he stroked Hope's hair, her head nestled on his shoulder.

"It was the oysters," Hope quipped, smiling in the dark.

"Hmmm," Bridger murmured, wondering how much truth was in her teasing.

"Speaking of oysters, I'm still hungry. Are you?"

Hope leaned up on her elbow, peering down at Bridger's face. The dock light providing a little glow through a slight opening in the curtain.

Bridger's stomach growled, answering Hope's question.

"Omelets on the way," Hope said, kissing Bridger's nose playfully.

She got out of bed and spun around looking for her clothes.

"It's like Hansel and Gretel," she laughed as she followed the path of clothing, putting the pieces on as she went.

Bridger caught sight of her bare ass as she bent down the pick up her panties. She was perfect.

He was not.

What was he doing?

Although she didn't seem the worse for wear.

In minutes, he could smell the peppers and onions heating up again. The sizzle and aroma of ham alerted him that it wouldn't be long before Hope had the food ready. Bridger pulled on his pants and padded out to the kitchen to see if he could help.

He paused in the hall, watching Hope efficiently breaking eggs in a bowl, then whisking them together. With each turn of the whisk, her butt moved along with the rhythm. She was adorable.

Bridger pulled a larger skillet out of the cupboard and handed it to Hope.

"Thanks. You read my mind." She flipped on another burner, added a hunk of butter to the skillet and placed it on the heat.

Bridger set the table and pulled the orange juice out of the fridge, while Hope added the eggs to the skillet, skillfully rotating it, and lifting the edges of the cooked eggs to let the raw egg flow underneath. She loaded the filling into the center and added a handful of cheese.

"Now the hard part." She bit her lower lip and held it between her teeth as she rolled the giant omelet out of the pan onto a plate, expertly encapsulating the filling in the egg. Quickly she garnished it with shredded cheese, then cut it in half, putting the other half on the other plate.

"Voila!" she announced, rather proud of herself.

"Voila, indeed. Thank you. This looks fantastic."

Bridger poured the orange juice and they both sat down to eat.

Bridger wolfed down the omelet in record time. Hope kept pace for about half the time. She started to slow down about the same time she walked her big toe up to the top of Bridger's foot. Despite her outward calm appearance, she still needed contact.

"You okay?" Bridger asked her, concern in his eyes.

"Yeah."

"Honey, are you okay with what we did tonight?" His heart started to harden around the edges, preparing itself for pain.

"Oh, Bridger, yes, of course. No, don't think that I did something I didn't want to do. Please," Hope saw the expression he had set on his face, unconsciously readying himself. "I'm just overwhelmed with the whole thing. Pappy is dead. We don't know if Hohner is going to make it. Life is so damn short. I just feel...lost."

Bridger moved from the chair and took her in his arms. She looked so small and fragile, not what he was used to seeing with Hope.

"But Bridger, as much as I would like to stay here with you tonight. As much as I would like to have you hold me all night, I am not interested in the walk of shame to my boat in the daylight. Do you understand that? Not that I am ashamed to be with you, it's just..."

"Shhh. Of course, I understand that. You're already the subject of way too much conversation. We don't need to add fuel to the fire. When you're ready, I'll walk you down there."

"I can go by myself."

"Of course, you can, but would you please let me walk you?"

"Only if you finish my omelet for me."

"Don't you want it? I thought you were hungry."

"I was, but now, I'm done. I just can't eat more."

Bridger downed the remaining omelet in two bites and went looking for his shoes. Once he found them, he helped Hope clean up in the kitchen.

"Ready?" he asked.

"No, but yeah." She smiled at him again and kissed him deeply, making certain he knew that she was really okay with what happened between them.

*T*he moon had set, and the night was very dark. The tiny dock lights lit their way as they quietly made their way to Hope's boat. Hope glanced at Clarence's boat as she passed half expecting a voice to tease her about her evening's activities. It didn't happen.

Hope was grateful.

Hope stepped onto her boat and Bridger followed, walking her to her door like a gentleman. He was all set to kiss her goodnight in a satisfying and thorough manner when something caught his eye.

It was a piece of paper folded in half and shoved in the crack between the door and the jamb.

"What's this?" Bridger asked as he pulled it out.

"I don't know," Hope said. She reached for it and Bridger reluctantly handed it over. He had a bad feeling about it.

Hope paled as she read it.

"What the hell?" she whispered.

Bridger took the paper. It was another note.

You haven't been paying attention to me.
I deserve it more than the other.
I can give you more.
Just because you think I am not present doesn't mean I don't know
what is going on.

"Hope, this is not good. You need to call the police," Bridger said, his jaw tense, the muscles pulsating with anger

"No, I don't want to do that to a student. Not yet. I'm sure he is just troubled and young. It's not like he is going to hurt me or anything. He's just crying out for attention."

"That's fine if he cries out for attention at school. It's not okay that he knows where you live, comes aboard your boat, and leaves creepy letters."

"Bridger," Hope said, laying a calming hand on his arm, "everyone knows where I live. This is Grey's Harbor, after all."

"Hope, I can't leave you here alone after this," Bridger said, pacing the deck and crumpling the note in his hand.

"Of course, you can. Bridger, the door locks. The note has already been delivered. Nothing else is going to happen."

"Hope, this guy came to your boat after we left to look for Hohner. He didn't know you were going to do that. That tells me he came here and left a note thinking you were in the boat. That's mighty ballsy. Don't you think?"

"Okay, but he left the note and didn't come in. The door isn't broken. It's still locked. He just delivered a message. I'll talk to Chris about it on Monday and he can work with the student some more. Okay?"

The mention of Chris made Bridger's blood boil. He knew he had to control it. *It wasn't Hope's fault that she had other suitors, but damn that guy.* He swallowed to control his emotions.

"Okay, if you think Chris can help. But Hope, if this escalates any more, you need to call the police. You understand?"

Bridger realized his mistake the minute he made it. He watched Hope's back stiffen.

"I mean, please, call the police. For me?"

Hope softened. She realized he was just worried about her.

"Okay, if I think it's escalating, I'll bring in the authorities. Now, both of us need to get some sleep. I'll be fine. I promise." She lifted her chin making it known she expected him to kiss her.

He obliged.

"Good night, Hope. Sleep well."

"You, too, Bridger. Thank you for everything, for tonight, for being there and for being you. You're a pretty special guy. Promise you'll call me the minute you hear from Ingrid?"

"You're pretty special too, for a girl and all."

Hope swatted him lightly and unlocked the door. She stepped inside. Bridger followed.

"Um, remember we said goodnight and all?"

"Ummm, yeah, but I want to check the cabin, just for my peace of mind."

Hope stepped aside and allowed Bridger to quickly go through the boat. When he was satisfied, he kissed her again and made her lock the door behind him.

"Call me with news of Hohner. Don't forget," Hope called after him.

He gave her the okay sign and stepped up onto the dock. He hated leaving her. It didn't feel right, but he knew he couldn't push it. Hope wouldn't take kindly to him not trusting her professionally. Against his better judgement, he walked back down the dock to his boat.

here was an incessant sound. A buzzing. A mosquito or fly, maybe. Hope swatted half-heartedly in her sleep.

Again, the damn buzzing.

It stopped.

Hope rolled over twisting the sheets in her hand so she could hold them against her cheek, a holdout from her toddler days. She snuggled down against the pillow.

So tired.

Buzz. Buzz.

"Oh, hell," she shouted, flinging the sheets off her, jumping up to confront the fly.

Buzz, buzz, buzz.

Her phone.

On vibrate.

Shaking her head to try to clear the fog, she snatched up the phone.

Three missed calls.

Bridger.

Footsteps on the dock outside. On her boat deck.

Hope sighed.

Now knocking on her door. Make that pounding.

Bridger.

She stumbled out of the bedroom and down the hall. She could see Bridger's muscular body, tense, filling the patio door.

She put on her brightest smile and waved.

He did not look amused.

What time is it, she thought to herself, glancing into the kitchen as she made her way to the door.

Eleven o'clock. Holy cow, no wonder he was worried.

She slid open the door.

"Good morning, sunshine," she greeted him.

He did not look sunshiny.

"Did you bring me breakfast?" She tried on her sweetest smile.

Nope, nothing.

"Oh no, Hohner." Immediately she was sobered.

It was Bridger's turn to look chagrined.

"No, honey, not Hohner. He's hanging in there. I just got worried when you didn't answer your phone."

"Worried? Or maybe a little crazy?" Hope asked, reproach in her voice.

"Hope, you can't expect a man like me to walk away from the woman he loves after she gets a note like you got last night."

Hope stilled.

Bridger realized what he'd said.

The silence stretched on forever.

"Well, that's not quite how that was supposed to go," Bridger growled.

"You can take it back. It's okay. I know it wasn't thought out. It was said in the heat of the moment. I vote we just rewind and move on. You are not responsible for words spoken out of concern," Hope babbled on, trying to be reasonable.

"I don't want to take it back," Bridger said softly. "It's just not how I wanted to say it or when."

"I understand."

"It's just too early for me to have shared that with you. I'm sorry." Now it was his turn to falter for words.

"I understand," she said again. "Please, don't worry. I'm not going to say I love you back just because I'm supposed to, but I am going to cherish it, because it means something special to me. Bridger look at me. It really does mean something special."

She reached up and wound her hands in his hair and went to kiss him.

Then stopped.

"What's wrong?" asked Bridger bewildered and thrown off kilter.

"Morning breath," she whispered, mortified, her hands over her mouth.

"Me?" Bridger's face colored a deep crimson.

"No, me, you goof." She scurried off to the bathroom while Bridger stepped in and closed the screen door. He could hear her splashing and brushing furiously.

"That's better," she said, as she walked out of the tiny bathroom.

She stepped up to Bridger and kissed him.

He pulled her close with his strong arms and hugged her to him, wanting to protect her forever.

She recognized it and reveled in the strength in his arms. She knew he would go to the ends of the earth to keep her safe. She knew it in her heart and soul. She hoped she would never have to call on him to do it. She knew her adversary wouldn't have a chance.

"So, I make you an omelet in the wee hours of the morning and you don't bring me breakfast," she teased.

"No, I didn't, but do you want to take a ride with me and go pick up Hohner?"

"Absolutely. When do we have to leave? This second?"

"I'm guessing you want a shower."

"Pretty please, a quick one," she looked at him under his lashes. "Unless you want to make it longer," she teased.

He did, but he wasn't going to. She pretended to pout then flounced off throwing instructions back over her shoulder.

"Then make yourself useful and brew a pot of coffee. I'm in

desperate need." She hopped into the shower and quickly took care of business. She started laughing imagining the two of them in the tiny stall. *Bridger was right. Not a good plan.*

When she stepped out, the boat was filled with the heady aroma of brewing coffee and the nutty smell of toast. Cinnamon toast.

Oh joy. The man was brilliant.

She tossed her hair up on her head and pulled on a pair of jeans and a fresh sweatshirt claiming Cleveland was not the mistake on the lake. Slipping her feet into her Birks, she made her way into the kitchen.

"Breakfast is served. Have I redeemed myself on all counts?" Bridger asked, putting on an air of deep concern.

"Yes, on all counts. So, have you already tried to have someone join you in that shower, because I realized the error in my thoughts as I shaved my legs this morning." Hope was amused to see the color rise on Bridger's face. "Never mind, you don't need to answer that."

She gave him a light kiss and followed Bridger out to the deck where he sat a plate of cinnamon toast in front of both chairs.

"So, Hohner is going to be okay?" Hope asked, munching on the toast.

"He has some serious healing to do, but Ingrid says he should make it as long as he doesn't give up."

"Give up? What do you mean give up?" Hope looked at Bridger in horror.

"Ingrid said the dog is seriously depressed. He knows Pappy is gone. He's pining for him. Ingrid thinks he might just decide to join him. Dogs will do that you know. They have been known to die from a broken heart."

"What are we going to do? I would take him Bridger, but would it be good for him to be alone all day? I would love a dog, but I want to be fair to him."

"I know. I wouldn't mind a dog either, but I know the perfect person for him." Bridger reached across the table and absently wiped the crumbs from the corner of Hope's mouth then traced her lips with his thumb. He was touched with her genuine concern for the old dog.

He was beginning to think it was a mistake not joining her in the shower.

She grabbed a napkin and patted her lips. Then took Bridger's hand, holding it in hers on the table as she picked up her second piece of toast. It was delicious as was the coffee.

"So, who is the perfect person, and have they already agreed to take care of him?"

"No, but she will." Bridger said with confidence. "She has a great talent for fixing people who are broken." His eyes shifted; a faraway look filled with pain replaced his normal confident spark.

Hope's heart broke when she saw it.

"Bridger," she said softly, getting him to look at her. "Did she fix you?"

He looked out over her head, to the river and beyond to the sea. He had told her he loved her. He didn't mean to. He wasn't ready. He wasn't ready to share with her everything, and wasn't that what love was? He was trapped and didn't know what to do about it.

Hope waited, not pushing. She knew better. She waited for him to come to her.

"Yes," he said, still not looking at her. "She saved me."

"Izzy?"

Bridger looked at her, startled out of his reverie.

"How did you know?"

"I didn't. I guessed. Izzy seems like an old soul who's been hurt. She's like the bird with a broken wing who actually healed, and healed strong and brave, but still, there is a tiny broken part inside. You, Bridger, have a huge broken part inside, but you work really hard to hide it. I won't push, but at some point, you have to share that with me. At some point, if you want us to move forward, I need to share that pain and help you heal. I need to be the one who finishes what Izzy started."

Bridger's jaw worked as his mind struggled to make sense of what this wise woman in front of him was saying. She was right, and he knew it.

"It's because you're a teacher, huh? Is that why you are so smart?"

"Probably," she said. She recognized that Bridger had had enough and needed time to work through his feelings. She had all the time in the world.

*I*ngrid gave them instructions on how to care for Hohner's wounds and how to administer his pain medication. Then they loaded the dog into the seat of Bridger's truck.

"Are we taking him to Izzy's now?" Hope asked as they pulled away from the veterinarian's office.

"No, the bar is too busy, and Izzy won't be able to give Hohner attention. I will stop over tonight, late. I hope you don't mind that I plan on going alone." He waited for her to be angry.

"That's a good idea," Hope agreed, pleasantly

Bridger let out an audible sigh of relief making Hope laugh.

"Bridger, the first order of business in our relationship is you have to trust me." She lightly touched his arm. He glanced at her briefly then put his eyes back on the road. "With everything." She poked his arm, making her point clear.

"I know. Can I take some time with that?"

"I would expect you to. It's called growing, and it doesn't happen overnight."

The truck hit a bump and Hohner let out a small whimper. Hope unbuckled her seat belt and turned, bending over the back of the front seat.

"What the hell are you doing?" Bridger asked, keeping his eyes on the road.

"Taking care of a sad, hurt dog. You just keep the truck on the road and do your job and let me do mine." With that she slid over the front seat and settled in the back seat, Hohner's large head on her lap.

She stroked his ears and murmured to him, trying to put him at ease. He licked her hand lethargically and stared at the back of the seat, the picture of abject misery.

"She's right, you know," Hope said over the seat to Bridger.

"Who's right about what?" Bridger asked.

"This dog's heart is completely broken. I'm afraid he won't heal."

"Yeah, well that's what I thought about me. Give Izzy a chance."

"I hope she's a miracle worker."

"She is," he said grimly. "She really is."

32

*I*t was dark when Bridger pulled into the concrete driveway. The neighborhood had seen better days, sidewalks heaved and split, weeds springing up between the cracks.

Izzy's place was neat and clean. Still old, the house having weathered more than one kind of storm, but Izzy was holding together the old homestead the best she could.

Izzy held everything together the best she could, which was better than most.

Bridger lifted the dog out of the back of the truck and set him on his unsteady feet. Hohner hated to be carried. Bridger had figured that out a couple of hours ago, so he let the dog limp, finding his own way to manage his pain.

Bridger knew better than to ring the bell. Izzy wouldn't be inside. He made his way slowly around to the back of the house, toward an ancient back porch. He heard the creak of old metal chains on eyebolts. Izzy was where he expected her, sitting in the dark in the old porch swing.

"Bridger," Izzy called out softly as he approached the step which led to the low porch. It was an odd thing, a porch on the back of the house. It would have been at home on the front, but there was already one there, too. Whoever had designed the house understood the value of porches, for shade and protection from the extreme storms that blew off the ocean.

The back porch was Izzy's favorite place, and she and Bridger had spent many, many hours there, holding each other up. Giving each other strength.

"Hey, Izzy. How're you doing?"

"Okay, you?"

"Hanging in there. Do I need to worry about you?"

"Haven't fallen off the wagon yet, but Pappy made that kind hard, ya know."

"Yeah, I do know. I'm so sorry, Iz. I know he was a good friend to you."

"Yes, he was. He and his music will be missed." She sighed and sipped her drink, the ice clinking in her glass. "Want something to drink, Bridger? I've got ice water if you want it," she said pointedly.

"No, but thanks. I brought Hohner."

"I see him beyond the steps. He's not ready to come up here."

"He's hurt pretty badly. The steps might be stopping him."

"No, Bridger. He's not ready. Leave him be."

"Okay. Here are the instructions for him and his meds."

"Hmmm. I wonder if you can mix the meds with alcohol?" she mused.

"What the hell, Iz?"

She snorted a harsh laugh.

"Bridger, the dog is an alcoholic of sorts. Pappy always complained that he had to share his beer with 'the damn dog.'" Her eyes filled with tears.

Bridger didn't miss a trick but turned his face away so she could have her private moment.

"Well, he may have to go cold turkey, Iz, but you know all about that, so I know you can handle it."

"Yep. I do."

"So, I'll leave you to the dog then. If he dies, Iz, it won't be your fault. I think you're the only one who has hopes of saving him, but if you can't..."

"I know, Bridger. Don't worry. I'll be fine. You, on the other hand are struggling with something. What gives?"

Bridger stood for a minute, considering.

Izzy waited him out like she had done so many times in the past.

"Oh, Iz, I opened my damn mouth at the wrong time."

"Hope?"

"Yeah, Hope."

"She's good people, Bridger. Why not take a chance? Trust her."

"Do you?"

"I don't know her well enough yet, but my gut says yes. More to the point, your heart is saying yes. Everyone else can see it, so you might as well face up to that fact."

"I did, Iz. It was too soon."

"Oh Lord, you told her you loved her? You? You actually went there?"

"Yes," he said miserably.

"God, there's hope for you yet. But now it means you have to do what goes along with that. You have to trust her and open up to her."

"She pretty much said the same thing."

"Yeah, she's a smart lady. Give it time, Bridger. Take it slow, but just like this dog, you've got to find a lifeline. I think Hope's throwing you a rope, you've just got to grab it and hold on for dear life."

She paused and took a sip of her water. Then she looked off the porch at the dog, still standing, unsure of what to do. He needed that lifeline desperately, but she wasn't sure he was going to grab hold.

Damn, she was surrounded by broken people and dogs who needed her. It was hard enough to keep her own world together, much less the worlds of others, but that is what she did. She seemed to always fix the broken.

33

*J*t was Monday morning, just shy of the first period bell, and Hope was still trying to get into her teacher persona. The weekend had been hard, and she was tired. Bridger had stopped back after he dropped Hohner at Izzy's. He was honest with her. He didn't hold out much hope. They had each had a Hemingway Special and Bridger bid her goodnight. She went to bed right after that but couldn't sleep, her mind turning over all the events of the weekend, the Oyster Festival, the notes, the fire, and Bridger.

The bell rang, startling Hope out of her reverie. Students started filing into her room talking excitedly about their weekends. Some whispered secrets, others bragged conquests. It was all typical high school stuff.

Hope tried to say hello to every one of her students as they came in, but she didn't interrupt conversations. She made certain she spoke with the loners, most of whom would light up at the greeting and flash a smile.

Rusty was one of the last to come in. Hope was careful to keep her demeanor neutral, not threatening or overly attentive.

"Good morning, Rusty. Did you have a good weekend?"

"It was fine," he grunted, passing her, not looking at her.

He didn't look at her.

He hardly acknowledged her. It wasn't as if he avoided eye contact, he just didn't seem to give a hoot one way or the other. Strange reaction for someone who was infatuated. But on the other hand, Chris said he had a lot of issues. He didn't elaborate, but if Rusty had mental issues, she didn't want to push him too hard.

*H*ope walked with Pepper to lunch. Pepper chattered about all of the gossip from the weekend, including what folks were saying about Hope. It seemed that they still held out for Chris, not rooting for the home team. Pepper said she thought Bridger had clinched it until Hope slow danced with Chris. That threw everyone into a tizzy. The word was Hope was just smart enough to be nice to her landlord, but the odds were on Chris.

Pepper snapped her mouth shut as they entered the teacher's lounge. Chris was already there, looking with distaste at his entree.

"What's wrong?" Hope asked kindly.

"You just can't get good Chinese food outside of New York City," he groused as he half-heartedly poked at his Kung Pao Chicken.

"I don't know," Pepper said, a little testy at his remark, "I think our dining scene in Grey's Harbor is pretty good, and we don't have to deal with rude New Yorkers."

Chris stared at her, and Hope was little taken aback by Pepper's remark. Normally, Pepper was very polite and kind.

"I'm sure it's hard to get used to different places when you always had your favorites," Hope said, helpfully.

Chris smiled at her.

"Thanks, Hope. I knew you'd understand. After all, you came from an urban environment, too, with lots of top chefs."

She stared at him for a second before she covered. Now he was singing the praises of Cleveland's culinary scene when he had doubted it earlier.

Pepper looked at him slyly.

"I didn't know you were up to date on Cleveland cuisine." She took a bite of her ham sandwich, curious as to how he would reply.

Chris knew a trap when he saw it.

"I wasn't until Hope corrected me on my misconception of backward Cleveland. I have since learned that some of the nation's top chefs have restaurants there. Therefore, I assume that Hope has as sophisticated a palate as do I."

He finished off the last of his undesirable lunch and rose from the table.

"If you ladies will excuse me, I have some work in my office." He swiped his lips and fingertips with his napkin and cleaned his area.

"Chris, do you mind if I stop by your office in a few minutes. I have an issue with a student I'd like to discuss with you." Hope watched the transformation of the man's face. He was delighted she wanted to talk with him. It dawned on her that Chris was really having a hard time assimilating to this town and to the people here. He also probably felt unneeded and underutilized. That made her sad. She would try harder to make him feel a part of things. She would want someone to do that for her.

He left the lounge with a spring in his step, and Hope looked at Pepper, clearing her throat.

"It's not like you to be snippy. I've never heard you say an unkind word. You were kinda harsh with Chris. What gives?"

"He's an arrogant ass."

"Wow, okay so tell me how you really feel." Hope said, laughing despite herself.

"He stopped at Nana's booth and bought an assortment of cookies. He proceeded to sample them there and then talk all about how the best pastries and cookies come from New York bakeries. He went on and on about them in front of my Nana. It was rude."

Pepper's eyes were flashing by the time she was done. Someone slighted her Nana, and Pepper wasn't going to stand for it.

"Okay, I get that. You're right, he was rude, but I think he just doesn't know how to fit in. I think he may have looked at it as a talking point without thinking about how you or your Nana would feel," Hope said helpfully.

"Yeah, but Hope, he's a counselor. He's the last person who should have that problem."

Hope had to agree.

*H*ope knocked on Chris's door. It was cracked open and she could see him at his desk staring at a document on his screen. He turned quickly and clicked off the document bringing up a screen saver of Time's Square.

"Come on in, Hope," he invited, his face lighting up as he looked at her. "What's on your mind?"

She sat in the chair that faced Chris and his desk. In front of her was a small bowl filled with stress balls with a little sign that invited her to feel free to give one a squeeze.

She didn't.

"I think the situation with Rusty has escalated. I can't prove this, but I've received two notes, and I am pretty sure they're from Rusty, especially after what you told me."

"Really? That's troubling," Chris said, his face arranging into a concerned expression.

"Yes. One note was in with my homework papers on Friday. The other was tucked into my screen door on my home."

"That's not good. He is escalating," Chris said, thoughtfully.

Hope thought Chris was a little too calm about it. Having spoken her concerns out loud, she realized just how creepy it sounded. She expected him to react with a little more concern.

"Bridger thinks I should call the police about this. He thinks this sounds like I should be more concerned than I have been."

"Bridger? You discussed this with Bridger? Hope a student's privacy must be protected..."

"Hold on. I didn't share anything about a student. Bridger saw the notes." Hope said, feeling attacked and that her professional judgement had been questioned.

Chris recognized his error and tried to change his tactics

"I'm sorry, Hope. I always try to put the students first, especially those with severe emotional issues. In this case, if the student was aware that others knew of his behavior…well, that would be devastating. I don't know what he would do then."

"You don't think he would harm himself, do you?" Hope asked, immediately concerned for her student, no longer worried about her own safety.

"Now, don't worry. He hasn't given me that kind of indication yet. If he did, I would have pink slipped him, but still. I worry when a student is fragile like he is. You know he looks strong, but that's just a front."

"Okay, so what should we do going forward?" Hope asked, ready to help in any way she could.

"My suggestion is to just continue to act normally. Be his teacher. Be the good teacher that you are. Don't confront him or make him uncomfortable. Report to me any more notes or things that concern you. Together, we will help him be a success. I promise."

"Thanks Chris, I appreciate it." Hope stood up to leave as the bell rang telling her that her lunch was over

"Really Hope," said Chris as he put a comforting hand on her shoulder. "I think it's going to be fine. I'm certain I can help guide him though the things he needs to work out."

She smiled gratefully as he opened his office door to let her out, his comforting hand still on her shoulder.

Two students walked by followed by Pepper. The students started giggling, glancing behind them as they walked down the hall so they wouldn't miss anything.

Pepper raised an eyebrow but didn't stop and wait for Hope. Hope was on her own with this one.

34

*T*hursday, Hope hurried home after school. Chris was going to pick her up at the boat so they could go to the professional development sessions together.

She changed out of her dress finding a more comfortable outfit to wear. She pulled her long hair into a ponytail and scrubbed her face. In her experience, these sessions were attended by tired teachers in blue jeans and sweatshirts. She wasn't willing to dress it down that much, but she was certainly going to push it to that end of the spectrum.

She heard footsteps on the dock approaching her boat.

"Hope?"

Hope slid open the patio door and invited Chris aboard. She didn't miss the look on his face when he appraised her outfit and living conditions. He recovered quickly and settled on a pleasant expression. He was still wearing his light grey dress slacks with pale blue dress shirt and gray tie. Professional all the way.

"Make yourself at home. I'll be ready in just a second." Hope gestured to the bistro table. As she disappeared into the cabin, Chris removed a hanky from his pocket and quickly swiped at the chair before he sat down. He did not look like he belonged on a houseboat on the river.

Hope stepped into the bathroom again and took a look at herself in the mirror. Okay, maybe she pushed it a bit too much. She pulled the band from her hair and let it cascade around her shoulders. She gave her lashes a quick swipe of mascara and glossed her lips. She trotted into her bedroom and grabbed a light sweater and dressy scarf and threw them on. There, instant upgrade.

Lifting the cooler on the way through the kitchen, Hope stepped through the sliding door.

"Okay, I'm ready."

"You look nice," he said, approving of the upgrade. "What's that for?" He gestured to the cooler.

"I just thought we might need something to drink on the drive." She hesitated at the perplexed look on his face. "I don't know. I never go anywhere without a cooler." She suddenly felt a little silly.

"No, it's fine, but it's only a little over an hour."

"Oh, that's right. Hang on." Feeling uncomfortable for a second time that evening, Hope unlocked the door and set the cooler down on the little counter in the galley. "Okay."

"Let's get going so we can avoid traffic." Chris got up and led the way off the boat.

Hope noticed he didn't turn to help her off the boat. She certainly didn't need help, but Bridger always watched to be sure. He started to walk briskly down the dock, then slowed and turned to look at her. He smiled apologetically.

"Sorry, my mind is on the drive and traffic." He looked truly contrite. Hope smiled at him and quickened her pace. She waved as they passed Clarence's boat. Clarence waved at her. Chris nodded at him, then reached back toward Hope to take her hand. He pointed to a loose rope on the dock.

"Careful," he said. "Don't trip."

Bridger heard voices and looked up. He had been sitting at the table on his houseboat having a sandwich and a beer and looking over the finances of the marina. Ever since Jennifer started helping his mom, things were going a lot smoother.

He watched Chris and Hope make their way down the dock toward him. He put a smile on his face even though he felt his gut start to simmer.

Hope saw him and gave him a smile and wave. Chris looked up at the same time.

"Hello, Bridger," he called out making certain Bridger saw him holding Hope's hand.

"Evening Chris, Hope." He casually sipped his beer as Ryker stepped out of the cabin onto the deck.

"Hey, Ryker," Hope called out.

Chris puffed up even more. He grinned at them.

"Hope and I are heading out of town for the evening. Bridger, I hope we don't disturb you when we get back. We'll try to be quiet, but I want to warn you, it'll be late." He put on an air of concern that he might disrupt Bridger's beauty sleep."

Hope looked miserable.

Chris didn't notice.

Bridger did.

"Don't worry, Chris. You won't disturb me at all." He lifted his beer to them and then turned his attention back to the table, dismissing them both.

Chris and Hope stepped off the dock and walked to Chris's waiting car, where he opened the door gallantly for Hope. As she got in, she looked back over her shoulder at Bridger's boat. Bridger caught her eye as Chris turned to walk behind the car. She swore she saw Bridger give her a wink. The tension in her gut loosened. She smiled gratefully at him and turned to smile at Chris as he got in the car. She had figured out that Chris's ego was no match for Bridger, so she didn't want to hurt his feelings, but she was going to have to make certain that he didn't misunderstand her kindness. *Damn,* she thought. *Life was complicated.*

Ryker watched the two of them drive off. He pulled out a chair and sat down across from Bridger twisting off the cap to the beer he had just retrieved from Bridger's fridge.

"You know," he said thoughtfully, "there's something just not quite right about that guy."

"Yeah, but I think he's harmless. He's just in for a rude awakening when he figures out that Hope is a kind, polite person who doesn't want to hurt his feelings." Bridger watched the car disappear down the road.

"I think you'd better rethink that, Bridger. My gut tells me he isn't as harmless as you think." Ryker turned the bottle in his hand, studying the intricate Sperm Whale Ale label. "Just a weird vibe I get."

"I know. I got it, too at first, but Hope thinks it's just the big city boy at odds with small town living. He's pretty uptight for a guidance counselor."

"Maybe," Ryker said, but decided he would make it a priority to watch his friend's back. Something just wasn't right.

35

"*R*eally, Chris, it isn't necessary that you pay for dinner. I've got my own," Hope said as she dug for her wallet in her purse. She had mentioned to the waitress at the beginning of the meal that they would be having separate checks, but the waitress had forgotten or something.

"No, I would like to pay. After all, I did ask you here, suggested this place. The Beef Wellington wasn't completely up to snuff, but it was passable," he said lightly.

Hope thought the meal was exquisite. Not only the beef but the fingerling potatoes and the prosciutto wrapped grilled asparagus was delightful. She could find nothing wrong with the meal, except the cost. It was incredibly expensive, especially on a small-town teacher's salary.

He peeled off several large bills and placed them in the carrier with the dinner check. When the waitress came to pick it up, she hesitated.

"Are we all set?" she asked

"No, I will need change."

"Absolutely," she said, coloring slightly, hurrying off to finish the transaction.

Hope excused herself to visit the powder room. She wasn't interested in knowing what he left for a tip. She was beginning to think it might be an awkward moment.

When she finished, Chris was already standing, ready to leave. She collected her sweater and followed him out of the restaurant. She couldn't help but notice the bills sticking out of the smooth leather folder on the table. She quickened her step. She didn't want to be there when the waitress collected her very inadequate tip. Hope prayed that there were more bills tucked behind the ones that were visible. *That had to be the case,* she consoled herself.

Over dinner, Chris had steered the conversation to Hope, her interests and life in Cleveland. She firmly moved the conversation away from her ex-husband and divorce. She wasn't interested in sharing that. He prodded a little but then stopped, but Hope knew that he would move around to that again. It was obvious he was very curious, so she asked him about New York and the restaurant scene there. She knew that he would expound on that without fail. She wanted to stay away from personal conversation, and she figured that would do it. It worked like a charm.

When they hit the freeway on the way home, Chris tried to gain some intimacy with her, again asking about her past.

"Chris, I'd really rather not talk about it," she finally said, bluntly.

"I understand that it's still raw, but I'm sure that talking it out will help you heal," he said soothingly, in his best counselor voice.

"Truthfully, I'm pretty well healed," she said, realizing that it was true. Her time in Grey's Harbor had already worked its magic.

"Well, you know I am here for you if you ever need to talk." Chris took one hand off the steering wheel and covered her left hand that was resting on her thigh.

The intimacy was more that Hope was interested in. This was going to be a long ride home.

She shifted and then moved her hand, reaching into her purse for a tissue. Wiping her nose delicately, she pocketed the tissue and turned facing him more. The move effectively broke the contact and shifted her further from him.

"Chris, what did Rusty say when you asked him about the notes," she asked. Not only would this move the conversation away from her personal life, but she hadn't had a chance to discuss the situation with him since Monday afternoon when she had mentioned the letters.

"He denied them, of course, but that's what I expected."

"He didn't write them?" Hope's mind started racing trying to think who else may be behind the notes.

"Yes, Hope, he wrote them," said Chris with confidence. "He's just denying it, but his body language said otherwise. His whole demeanor spoke volumes."

"You're sure?" asked Hope, unconvinced. She thought back to Monday when she greeted Rusty. Sure, he was sulky, but he seemed unconcerned, not like a kid who had left those notes for her.

"Yes, Hope, I'd stake my reputation on it."

They pulled into the marina, and Hope reached down to pick up her purse from the floor near her feet. Chris parked the car and got out, walking around to open her door. She was hoping to avoid this, but they were at an inevitable moment.

"Thank you," she said as she stood from the car. He didn't back up from her as she emerged making the distance between them uncomfortably close.

"Hope, I had a very nice evening. I am hoping you did, too. I'm just sorry it was dominated by boring professional development sessions. I am hoping next time, you will allow me to wine you and dine you the way you deserve."

He looked at her earnestly.

Crap.

"Thank you. I actually enjoyed the seminars. I learned some great tips." She stepped back, moving her purse strap to her shoulder. "Now I will have to work on implementing them into my teaching. Thank you for driving, and thank you again for the lovely dinner."

"You are welcome. I'd like to walk you to your door," said Chris, as he moved to walk beside her.

"Oh, that isn't necessary. It's late." She stammered, feeling like an awkward teenager.

"I insist. I don't allow a lady to walk alone to her home." He took her arm and steered her toward the dock. She had no choice but to move with him. She felt like it was easier and more polite to just let him do this.

It was a quiet night. Their footsteps echoed on the water as they made their way down the dock toward her little houseboat.

Hope noticed the lights were out in Bridger's boat, he was probably sound asleep. When they passed Clarence's boat, Hope became aware of just how loud Chris's footsteps were. She was feeling paranoid and obvious. Did he always step so loudly?

Hope stepped onto the deck of her boat and pulled her keys smoothly out of her purse. Chris was right behind her. He took the keys from her hand and unlocked the door for her.

"Good night, and thanks again," Hope said firmly.

"Good night, my dear," said Chris, and he took her in his arms, kissing her firmly on the lips.

His kiss felt like he claimed her.

She didn't like it.

She stepped back quickly.

"Chris…" she started.

"Good night, sleep well," he interrupted, taking charge. He handed her the keys and walked off the boat, leaving her standing there, the rest of her protest unspoken.

Hope stepped quickly inside and closed the door. She didn't like how she felt, out of control, like she had lost at a game of cards. She didn't exactly feel violated. The kiss wasn't overly erotic. It was the kind of thing that happened to every teenage girl, the kiss that they didn't want because they weren't interested in the guy, but as an adult, she should have seen it coming. She should have said something after to end any further advances, but it was awkward. They had to work together.

She washed her face and found herself scrubbing her lips. Then she laughed. If she had any doubt as to her feelings for Chris, she no longer had them.

She slipped into her pajamas and crawled into bed, turning out her light.

ridger watched Chris as he stepped off Hope's boat. He had seen the kiss. He imagined Hope stiffened. If he had to be honest with himself, Hope's boat was too far away to really see her reaction, but he was pretty sure her body language wasn't receptive. Chris's abrupt departure confirmed his suspicions.

He watched Chris slowly, quietly start to walk down the dock then stop. He stood there waiting until Hope's lights went out before he left. Then he walked quietly off the dock.

Bridger remained in his chair in the dark long after Chris had left. *Maybe Ryker was right. There was something odd about that guy.*

36

*H*ope hurried down the dock the next morning, careful not to catch her heel in the cracks. She was running late and in a cranky mood. Her mood continued on the downward trend when she passed Bridger's boats and saw no sign of him. She had grown accustomed to him raising his mug of coffee to her as she passed him in the morning. They always wished each other a good day. She liked that routine, but today it didn't happen.

Bridger's truck was missing, too. For some reason that made her crankier. *Ooof*, she thought. *My poor students today. This is the kind of day teachers show movies to the class*, she teased herself.

As she unlocked her car, she noticed an acrid smell. Normally, she enjoyed the smell of the ocean, the river, and the estuary, but today it bothered her. The smell was different. Not pleasant.

Wow, she thought, *you really are a high maintenance bitch today,* she scolded herself.

Once in her classroom, she tried to work herself out of her mood. She changed the date on her blackboard and wrote out the bell work for each class.

"Here, friend. I saw you come in. I felt your vibes. I bring you coffee," said Pepper, handing over a fresh cup from the cafeteria.

"Thanks. You're a lifesaver. I am in a horrible mood today."

"You and everyone else," said Pepper.

"Really, you, too?"

"Yeah. Wait, you don't know, do you?" Pepper said, realization dawning on her. "You're just in an overall bad mood."

"Know what? What's going on?"

"There was another fire last night. A warehouse down on Briggs street burned. Arson. The volunteers are still down there making sure that the fire is out, and no other buildings are in danger of burning."

"That was the smell I smelled this morning."

"Yeah. We have an offshore wind, so the smoke was blown seaward. If we would've had an onshore wind, this whole place would be covered in smoke and ash."

"Was anyone hurt?" Hope said, thinking of Pappy and Hohner.

"No, not this time. This warehouse was empty, luckily. It has been up for sale for the last six months, so nothing was in it."

"Do they think it's the same guy?"

"Don't know," said Pepper as the bell rang. "See you at lunch."

Pepper walked out as the students filed in. The talk of the hour was the fire. Many of the students' fathers were volunteer firemen, so the kids talked excitedly about what they knew or thought they knew. Hope let them go on for a minute or two, then drew their attention to their bell work and getting them started on their lesson. As she took attendance, she noted that Rusty was missing. That was odd, because he never missed class. He might not like to participate, but he was always there.

Halfway through class, Hope noticed a constant buzzing sound in the room. She had been lecturing about the symbolism of the green dock light in *The Great Gatsby* when she was interrupted. Many of her students were surreptitiously checking their cell phones.

"Manny," Hope asked the boy in the front row who's naturally brown Hispanic face had paled. "What's wrong?"

"The warehouse collapsed," he whispered. "Some of the volunteers were inside." He was trying to be brave, but tears were forming.

"Okay, guys," Hope said, her heart in her throat, her thoughts immediately went to Bridger, Ryker, and Tank. She said a silent prayer as she addressed her class. "Go ahead and check your cell phones. Do what you need to do. If you need help, let me know."

The class waited anxiously as each student checked their phones. The messages were coming in one after the other.

"Dad's fine."

"My brother is good."

"My dad made it out."

"No one can find my dad." Connie's face was pure white, her eyes wide. Hope moved quickly to Connie's desk.

"Okay, honey. Let's hold on to hope that he's okay, just not accounted for yet, okay? Who did you get the text from?"

"My brother," she said.

"Is he there? Is he a volunteer?"

"No. He's younger than me. He heard if from his friend, Bobby. Bobby's dad is a volunteer."

Connie stood up, trembling, looking at her teacher, helpless and miserable. Hope knew she was not supposed to touch her students.

Oh, the hell with it, she thought.

She took Connie in her arms, hugging her close.

"Okay, so far it's just a rumor. You don't have any concrete information." She held on to the trembling girl trying to comfort her. The thought crossed her mind to text Bridger, but she didn't want to bother him in a tense situation, and if something had happened, well, she didn't want to find out here, in front of her students.

A few other students, girls, got up from their desks and wrapped their arms around Hope and Connie, trying to comfort and give strength.

"He's going to be okay, Connie. I just know it," they told her.

A few minutes passed. The room was quiet. Some students' heads were bowed in prayers. Others stared out the windows waiting for news.

A loud buzzing broke the silence.

Connie's phone.

"Mrs. Chandler. I can't," she whispered, holding her phone out to Hope.

Hope took a deep breath and looked at the text on her student's phone.

Thank you, God, she whispered.

"Connie, they found him. He's okay."

Connie burst into tears, clinging to her teacher.

"It's okay. He's going to be okay," Hope said again, knowing that the tears were of happiness, stress, and gratefulness. As she glanced around the classroom, she noticed that almost all the eyes were damp. The ones that weren't were only so because of bitten lips or cheeks. This town was close. The people were family. When one hurt, they all hurt.

They knew Connie's dad was lucky, but there were some that might not be. The day was going to be long.

Before the bell dismissed first period class, Mr. Fender's voice rang out over the PA.

"We are dismissing Grey's Harbor High School today after first period. You are all welcome to return to your homes. If you ride a bus, the busses will be arriving within the next half hour. Those of you who don't want to go home are welcome to stay. We'll have staff and counselors available to you. Please take a minute to pray for our volunteers, that they may all be safe. Again, if you need us, your teachers, counselors, and principal are here for you to talk to or just hang out with. If you need lunch, we will still be providing it to you. Be safe and remember, we will be here for you."

The bell rang to dismiss the school.

37

*H*ope parked her car in the marina parking lot. She breathed a sigh of relief when she saw Bridger's truck. She had gotten word earlier that all the volunteers were accounted for. A couple were admitted to the hospital for minor injuries, but all had escaped life threatening injuries.

She wished he would have texted her, but he didn't owe her that. Yet, he had said he loved her. He hadn't meant to, the time wasn't right, but he had said it. So, in a way, he owed her the news that he was safe.

She got out of her car and headed toward the dock. She was tired, emotionally drained, and she just wanted to get into a pair of pajama pants and a sweatshirt. She wanted to sit on her deck and drink a Hemingway Special or two and just not think.

She walked past Bridger's boats. They seemed empty. Even Clarence was nowhere to be seen. Just as well. She wasn't good company anyway.

She stepped onto her boat and there he was.

Sitting at her table. He was covered in soot and grime. There was a cut over his right eye and his left forearm was wrapped in gauze.

"Hey," said Bridger

"Hey."

She smiled at him, grateful to see he was alive, in one piece.

"I was going to get into my pajamas." Hope said, realizing it sounded childish as it left her mouth.

"Sounds like a good plan. Pizza?" He gestured to a Harbor New York box on the table. She hadn't noticed it because her eyes were all on Bridger.

"Pizza first. What do you want to drink?"

"Water. Just good old plain water. You?"

"I was going to have a Hemingway Special, but water sounds good for now."

She left Bridger sitting there and went into the cabin. She came out with some napkins and two glasses of water. Bridger was waiting patiently for her, but she realized he was famished.

"Oh, for heaven's sake, dig in, Bridger." She flipped open the pizza box and pushed it toward him.

He snagged a piece but handed it to Hope first.

She grinned and took a bite.

He was okay.

After they finished the pizza, Hope turned on her shower for Bridger. He pulled her in with him. They held each other, celebrating that all the firemen were alive.

She washed his back.

That's all there was room for.

Then Bridger lifted her into his arms and carried her to her cabin.

There they celebrated that he was alive.

That night, a summer rental burned to the ground. It was empty and isolated, and well outside of Grey's Harbor.

No one called the fire phone.

*H*ope woke in the morning to an empty bed. Bridger had slipped out during the night. At first, she was hurt, but then she realized that he was probably thinking of her reputation.

She texted him good morning, but there was no answer. She stretched like a lazy cat but forced herself out of bed. She checked the kitchen. *Damn, no hot coffee waiting. He needed some sleepover training.*

She set up the coffee pot and inhaled deeply as it started to drip, filling the cabin with its rich, heady aroma. Then she checked her fridge. Slim pickings. The pantry was low, too. Not even supplies for cinnamon toast. Sighing, she kicked off her slippers and entered her tiny closet of a bathroom.

She took a quick shower and combed her wet hair, leaving it to hang down her back. She slid on a pair of jeans and a flannel shirt, rolling up the sleeves.

Pouring some coffee, she made a shopping list, slipped on her loafers, and grabbed her purse. Bridger would catch up with her later. She felt confident, despite the fact that her text was still unanswered.

Her stomach rumbled as she drove out of the marina, still puzzling over Bridger's absence. She noticed his power boat was gone, too. Again, she felt a little hurt he had gone without her.

He doesn't owe you an explanation as to where he is, she scolded herself. Her stomach complained again as she sipped her thermos of coffee. Instead of heading for the grocery, she turned toward the Cathead Diner. She was going to treat herself to a big country breakfast.

Maeve greeted her warmly taking her to a corner table. As she seated Hope and took her drink order, she casually asked.

"How's Bridger this morning? Is he doing okay?" Maeve looked concerned.

"Yeah, I mean I think so. I haven't seen him this morning. I know he was tired and banged up a bit, but okay," said Hope, touched at Maeve's concern, but then perplexed by the strange look on Maeve's face.

"Right, that fire hurt quite a few men yesterday," she agreed.

"Wait, is there another reason Bridger wouldn't be doing okay?" Hope asked, confused.

"No, no, not at all," Maeve assured her, then switched gears quickly. "Do you know what you're having?"

Hope ordered bacon, eggs over medium and shredded hash browns covered in onions and cheese. Her stomach purred in anticipation.

Within a few minutes, the steaming plate was placed in front of her by a waitress she didn't know, probably Susie, who needed more hours, so Jennifer cut back hers. As Hope dug in Randy stopped by her table.

"Hi, Randy," she greeted him. "I haven't seen that oyster Rockefeller recipe on my desk yet. Your grade is slipping," she teased him.

"I'm sorry. I'll get it for you, I promise. So how is Bridger today? He okay? I know this is always a rough day for him."

"I haven't seen him, Randy, but I don't know any reason he wouldn't be okay, other than being stiff from working the fire yesterday. Is something wrong with Bridger?" she asked, completely confused now.

"No, not at all."

"Then why would today be a rough day?" she quizzed him.

Randy colored then stammered.

"You know, a day after a fire. That's all. It was a rough one yesterday. Well, I'll see you, and I promise I'll drop off that recipe. For sure. Have a good day."

"You, too, Randy."

She put her fork down, her appetite spoiled.

Something was going on, and she was in the dark, and she didn't like it. Not one bit.

38

*H*ope walked up to the bar and waited patiently for Izzy to turn around. Izzy didn't need to. She saw Hope in the mirror. Izzy sighed. She was expecting this.

"Hello, Hope, what can I get you?"

"Do you have unsweetened iced tea?"

Izzy nodded.

"Lemon?"

"Yes, please." Hope waited until Izzy placed the drink in front of her. "Okay, Izzy. What gives?"

"What do you mean," asked Izzy, knowing full well what Hope was getting at.

"Bridger took off in his boat in the wee hours of the morning." She held up her hand. "You don't need to ask how I know. You and I both know how I know." She smiled a wistful smile at Izzy.

Izzy smiled grimly back. She was going to have to handle this carefully. For Bridger's sake, the fool.

"Okay, so he left in his boat. He goes out all the time, sometimes fishing, crabbing, or heading to another marina to do some business." Izzy avoided looking at her.

"Izzy stop bullshitting me. You know something. Everyone knows something except me. Everywhere I go, people are asking me if Bridger is okay. When I tell them sure, why, they get a strange look on their faces, then try to avoid talking to me more. It's like everyone knows this great big secret that I am not privy to, despite the fact that this man proclaims to love me." There she said it. Izzy now knows.

Izzy did not look surprised.

Of course not, because Bridger already talked to her about this. Because Bridger tells Izzy everything.

Hope's eyes narrowed. Her mind spun.

Izzy shook her head.

"Don't go there, Hope. You're not right."

"I think I am. He loves you, doesn't he?" Hope asked, the hurt choking her a little.

"Yes, Hope, he loves me. And I love him. Plain and simple. But that's how it is. Plain and simple. I love him like a brother. He loves me like a...friend." Izzy looked sad for a minute, thinking about her friend.

"Then why doesn't he talk to me? Why you, the great and wonderful Iz." Hope didn't mean to sound bitter. She knew it wasn't fair, but it hurt.

Izzy started to protest but stopped. There was no point. This woman was hurt and rightly so.

A look suddenly dawned on Hope's face.

"He came in late last night, too. He was with you, wasn't he?"

"Yes, he was."

"Why?"

"He needed to talk, Hope. He needed to talk some things out. If it's any consolation, he came home to you. That's a pretty big step up from what he would have done."

"Which is what?" she demanded.

A couple of customers at a table in the corner looked at them curiously then bowed their heads. They knew what was up.

"Which is drinking himself into oblivion, then waking up with a hangover and going out on his boat."

"But why, Izzy? Please tell me. The whole town knows, so why do I have to wait for Bridger to decide to bring me into the biggest secret that everyone knows but me? How often does he do this shit?"

"Once a year," said Izzy, "on the anniversary of his sister's death."

That quieted Hope. Stilled her.

"Okay, you're right. You deserve to know. I have never broken a confidence, but I think it's time you knew."

"I'm sorry, Izzy. Normally, I'd tell you not to, but not this time."

"Come on back to my office. Lonny, you've got the bar."

Hope picked up her tea and followed Izzy. She settled into a soft armchair while Izzy curled up on the couch.

Hope waited for Izzy to begin.

"Bridger had a sister. She was the light of his life. They were good friends, and when they were young, inseparable. The thing is, Bridger was the steady one, the responsible one. His sister had a wild streak. When they got older, they fought a lot. He was worried she would get in trouble."

Izzy took a drink of her ice water. Hope stared at her; the iced tea forgotten.

"She did just that. She got pregnant her sophomore year in high school. I know her girlfriends urged her to give up the baby, but she wouldn't. She and the young man got married. He was an asshole. He hit her. Bridger made him go away."

Hope smiled at that thought, Bridger coming to the rescue. He was made for that.

"It was hard raising a boy alone, but the family helped. You would have thought that getting pregnant that young would have cured her restless spirit, but it didn't. One night, Tammy had been drinking. Bridger was mad at her because she didn't pick up her son when she was supposed to, and Bridger had to leave the marina to get him from day care. Tammy told him she didn't care, and he didn't care about her either. They had a big fight that ended with her taking out a small skiff that Bridger had built.

"Bridger didn't realize she had taken the boat until it was too late. The boat had a problem and needed a repair. He was going to work on the boat that weekend. It didn't matter. Tammy took the boat out to sea and before anyone knew, the accident had happened. They found her drowned. Apparently, she had tried to save herself, because they found a life jacket strapped around her, but it wasn't on right and it didn't keep her head up above the waves."

"And Bridger blames himself," said Hope, her heart tearing to pieces for the man.

"Yes, he does. He went off the deep end. He drank himself stupid and stayed that way for a long time. His friends tried to help them, but he shut them out."

"That's when you rode in?" Hope asked, grateful for Izzy's friendship to the man she was in love with.

"Yeah, I rode in and drug him kicking and screaming to my place. I sobered him up and made sure he stayed that way. Then I told him I would walk the road back with him if he wanted, but he had to decide to do it."

"He still drinks."

"Yes. He's not an alcoholic. He's one of the lucky ones. The day he finally decided to start healing he was able to walk away. Not everyone is that lucky."

"But once a year, he breaks?" Hope asked.

"Not last night." Izzy smiled. "Last night he wasn't drinking. He came to me. Talked more about you than his sister. Then he went home to you."

"I'm grateful, Izzy."

Izzy smiled at her.

"You're welcome. Every year, hung over or not, Bridger takes a boat out to where they found his sister. It's like visiting her grave. Only this time he did it with a clear head and eyes that aren't bloodshot. Hope, you are helping him heal."

Hope let that sink in a little.

"What happened to Bridger's nephew?"

"He's around. His grandmother raised him. He's a quiet boy. Keeps to himself. A good kid, just quiet."

39

*T*hursday morning dawned clear and bright. By afternoon there was a bite to the air, a reminder that winter was on the horizon. That afternoon, armed with a stack of compositions for grading, Hope and her steaming mug of coffee took up residence on her bistro table. She was determined to finish all of her grading and have an open weekend for whatever came up. Bridger had mentioned that he needed to run down the coast to meet with a supplier, hinting that there could be a road trip in her future.

She was game.

The week had been uneventful so far. There were no more fires. Bridger told her that it looked like the work of a single arsonist, but as far as he knew, there were no leads.

"Good afternoon," Bridger called to Clarence as he walked down the dock. Clarence, stopping his calisthenics, greeted Bridger with a cheery smile.

"Good afternoon. I'm happy to see that you have recovered from all of the firefighting you have had to do. You looked like a beaten dog the other night, but I see our Hope has nursed you back to your old self."

Clarence grinned at Hope, waving at her in greeting and flexing his muscles. Hope nearly spit out her coffee with laughter.

"Clarence, if I were older…"

"My dear, age is just a state of mind."

"Back off old man," growled Bridger good-naturedly as he joined Hope on her boat. He kissed her on the lips, and then sat down at the table.

"What are you drinking?" he asked her.

"Why?" she said puzzled as she looked down at her coffee mug.

"Because your coffee breath doesn't smell like coffee breath," he teased.

"Ah, because it is mocha breath," she countered.

"And I used to respect you." He stretched, working out the kinks in his muscles and rubbed his shoulder gingerly.

"Still sore?" she asked, suddenly concerned.

"Just a little stiff, that's all."

"What's wrong with your shoulder, though? You were favoring it the other night, too."

"I got clipped by a beam when the roof collapsed at the warehouse."

"Bridger, you didn't tell me you were in the collapse. I knew you were in the warehouse, but I didn't think you were one of the men that was trapped."

"I wasn't. At least I wasn't trapped. When the roof came down, I got hit by some debris. I was lucky."

I think everyone was lucky," she said shaking her head. "I am so grateful that everyone got out alive. Everyone's going to be okay, right?"

"Yeah. Johnny Ricker's leg is broken, and Sam Husted is going to need elbow surgery, but we are all calling it a miracle."

They sat for a minute in silence thinking of what could have been.

"I see you have a stack of work to do. I can leave you to it," he said as he drained his mug of coffee.

"It can wait until later, if need be."

"I have some work I want to do on one of the boats I'm building. Why don't you come on over after you're done?"

"I'd love to. I just realized I've never seen where you work or the boats you're working on," she said, realizing how little she knew about the man who had swept her off her feet.

"Well, we can remedy that." He pulled her to her feet and held her for a minute, grateful that he was still here to do it. He didn't want to admit to her that his life flashed before his eyes when the roof collapsed. At that minute he knew he didn't want a life without Hope in it.

Two hours later, Hope finished grading the last essay. Her head was swimming. Her students were becoming better writers, but they still had a long way to go. She jotted a few notes about what she needed to concentrate on in her next week's lessons, then she gathered her things and put them away in the cabin.

She slipped on her shoes and walked over to the marina, looking for Bridger and the boat he was working on.

She was familiar with the small white marina building with its laundry facilities and shower house, but she had never been in the big blue metal buildings next to it.

As she approached the first building, she could see that the giant sliding barn doors were cracked open a little. She could hear music playing and the occasional burst of a power tool. She stuck her head in the opening and looked around.

The building was huge with a smooth concrete floor. There were boats of all sizes filling the space. Some were on trailers; some were in wooden cradles. On the far right of the building was what looked like a half finished beautiful wooden hull held up off the floor in a cradle. Bridger's back was to her as he inspected his handiwork. She could see another pair of legs on the other side of the boat. Bridger had a helper.

"That is beautiful," Hope said as she walked up to Bridger. She was in awe of the graceful curves, the grain in the wood as it bent to form the hull. It was exquisite.

"Thank you. I'm pretty happy with her. I just hope the client is pleased."

"Why wouldn't they be thrilled?"

"Hope, the people who can afford a hand built wooden boat are very particular. Everything has to be perfect. I strive to make it that way."

She reached up and ran her hands over the wood. It was smooth as glass. She was astounded.

The pair of legs on the other side of the boat were making their way around the stern, a steady soft scratching sound accompanying the legs. Hope was running her hands along the boat, walking toward the stern, admiring the grain and the curves when the other person stepped around to her side, startling her.

"OH!" she exclaimed, "Sorry...Rusty?"

Rusty glanced up at her, then looked away scowling, grunting a greeting.

"Rusty, say hello to Ms. Chandler," Bridger said, shocked at Rusty's rude demeanor.

"It's okay, Bridger. Rusty, I didn't know you worked here. So, did you help Bridger build this boat?" Hope asked, genuinely interested and proud of her student's handiwork.

"Yeah," Rusty said, turning his back on them and starting to walk away.

"Rusty, what the hell is wrong with you?" Bridger demanded, angry at the way Rusty was treating Hope and confused at the same time as to why Rusty would be like this.

"Nothing," Rusty said, defensively.

"Then why aren't you polite to her? Not only is she a teacher at your school, she's my guest here," Bridger said, his frustration coming to a head.

"Why? Why? Because she doesn't like me. Because she won't leave me alone and keeps hassling me. I do my work. I come to her class, but she just keeps bothering me." Rusty's face had set into an angry teenage scowl.

"Rusty, that's not true. I do like you. I like all of my students. I am trying to get you to engage in my class. That's my job."

"Your job is to give me information. My job is to pass tests and turn in homework. End of story. Your job is not to be involved in my personal life. Your job is not to ask me personal questions like what I did on my summer vacation or any else that juvenile."

"Rusty," Bridger shouted, furious.

"Rusty, if that's the way you feel, then why are you leaving me those notes?" Hope said without thinking, immediately regretting the words as they left her mouth.

The boy was taken off guard. The look on his face was pure confusion. He looked at Bridger and saw the anger boiling to the surface.

"I don't know what the hell you're talking about," the boy yelled and turned on his heels, running out of the building.

"Shit," said Hope. "I shouldn't have said that. I wasn't supposed to confront him about the notes. Damn it."

"You think Rusty sent those notes?" asked Bridger, genuinely taken aback. "There's no way Rusty would do that."

"Bridger, he's a troubled young man. Chris says he is dealing with a lot of issues, mental health issues. I really can't talk about this with you. I think it's awesome that you employ him...he works for you right? I think that is probably a good thing, but I can't share this with you. The fact that I said anything about the notes to him, in front of you...Oh, this is such a mess." Hope said miserably.

"Hope, don't you know who Rusty is?" asked Bridger.

"What do you mean?"

"Rusty's my nephew. He's my sister's child, and he would never write notes like that to you."

"Your nephew? I don't understand. I've called and left messages for his mother to call me back so we could discuss his progress in my class. She never called back." Hope stopped. She remembered her talk with Izzy. Bridger's sister was dead. Rusty's mother was dead. What phone number was in the records? Who was she leaving messages with?

"Hope, my sister died years ago. My mother raised Rusty. Sure, he can be a handful. He's a teenage boy, and he does feel different because he doesn't have a father and his mother is dead, but I can assure you, he doesn't have mental issues, and I can't believe he would leave you those notes."

"Oh, Bridger. I am so sorry." She reached out to touch his arm. She needed contact.

He stood there, stiffly.

He was angry.

He just didn't know who to be angry with.

40

They stared at each other for a minute, each trying to gather their thoughts. Bridger was the one to break the silence.

"Let's go get some dinner." He wiped his hands on the rag in his back pocket and rubbed his hands through his hair dislodging the sawdust that had gathered there. As miserable as she felt, Hope had to fight the urge to smile. She loved the fact that this man worked with his hands, could make something so beautiful and graceful out of pieces of wood, and that he was confident enough to dust himself off and throw on a hat, ready to face the world. She thought about Chris and his careful dressing to success. The image he presented to the world was orchestrated. Bridger's image was Bridger.

Bridger reached down and took Hope's small soft hand in his calloused one and started walking her toward the open barn doors. She felt safe. She knew he was angry and confused, but that small gesture meant he was still connected to her.

"Don't worry," he said softly, "we'll figure this out together."

"Okay, I believe you, but I am worried about Rusty. Bridger, he's so upset."

"Rusty is a man. Sometimes a man needs to be alone to figure things out. Leave him be. He will look at who he is, how he is acting, and I know he will make it right. Trust me, Hope."

Bridger stopped and took her by the shoulders.

"Please, always trust me." He looked steadily into her eyes.

She trusted him with all her heart.

"*H*op in the truck," Bridger told her. "I'll be right back."

She jumped in and watched him as he jogged to his houseboat. He came out a minute later, his phone to his ear.

He opened the door and got in the truck still talking on the phone.

"Did you get any messages from any of Rusty's teachers?" Bridger asked, the frustration only just showing in his voice. He glanced over at Hope. "No, I believe you, Mom. I just thought I would check. Don't worry. I'll take care of it tomorrow. Are you okay? Do you need anything today? Okay, I love you, too."

He put his cellphone on the tray in the console next to him.

"What's wrong?" Hope asked him, worry creasing her forehead.

"I wanted to check with Mom to see if she got any of your messages. She says she didn't, but you never know. She is getting so forgetful. Rusty has been checking the messages for me, but under the circumstances..." Bridger let the sentence trail off and grinned at Hope.

"Yeah, I might not mention to my parent that the teacher called either," said Hope, grinning back at him.

"I wouldn't put it past Rusty. He's a great kid, but he's no saint. Still, Hope, I really can't believe he would send those."

Both of them sat there for a minute thinking the same thing. It would be easy for Rusty to leave the note on Hope's boat. He had easy access. Neither Hope or Bridger decided to voice those thoughts.

*B*ridger swung the truck into the Mizzen Mast parking lot. "Is this okay?" he asked, throwing the truck into park.

"Sure, this is fine," she said, flashing back to the last time she was here and her talk with Izzy.

They avoided the bar and found a table in the corner. The evening was getting chilly, and the patio was only for the brave.

Izzy came over and greeted the two of them warmly.

"Hey guys, drinking on a school night?" Izzy teased.

"I know I am," said Hope laughing. A beer with Bridger sounded like a good idea.

"We have a new handle from Naked Beach Brewery."

"Oh no, what's the name of this one?" Hope groaned with a smile.

"Scurvy Seahorse Stout," Izzy said, wrinkling her nose. "I think they could have thought that one out a bit more, but from what I understand, if you like stout, it's pretty good."

"What the hell," said Hope. "Why not. Bridger are you game?"

"I'm not fond of stout, but I'll give it a go, and Izzy, can we have a basket of fried clams to start?"

"Sure thing." Izzy left the table to get their beer and put the order in the kitchen. Bridger stretched back in the booth pressing his body against the vinyl. He looked tired and stress lines showed on his face.

"You're worried," Hope said, reaching across the table to take his hand. She didn't care if anyone saw.

"I'm just trying to get a handle on everything, that's all. Trying to figure out what to do and where to go from here."

Izzy came back with the beer and sat the stout glasses in front of each of them. She sat down on Hope's side, scooting her butt into Hope and nudging her over with a smile. She gestured with her head at Bridger, grinning as she did it.

Bridger stared at the glass.

Hope laughed at him.

"What the hell? You expect me to drink out of this thing?" he asked.

"I do. It's a proper stout glass. Your guidance counselor friend regaled me for an hour or so on the proper glassware to serve the appropriate beverage in."

"I know it's a damn stout glass, but it's hard to be manly holding a beer in this damn thing."

Both Izzy and Hope laughed at him. Hope took a tentative drink.

"Actually, that's pretty darn good, despite the glass."

"According to Chris, it's the glass that has helped make this beer palatable." Izzy rolled her eyes.

Bridger took a drink of his beer and grunted.

"So, what gives, you guys? You two are wound up tight."

Hope gave Bridger a warning glance. He nodded at her.

Izzy didn't miss a thing.

"Just some trouble with Rusty. He's been surly and rude lately," Bridger answered her.

"You have to expect that this time of year," Izzy said softly, glancing at Hope. "He's a good kid, Bridger. He'll come around."

She slid out of the booth and took the clam basket from the waitress who approached the table.

"Here you go. Let me know when you're ready for something more substantial."

"Wait, Izzy. Before you go, how's Hohner doing?"

"He's making a decision. I'm leaving him to it. I'm hoping he makes the right one, I'm growing fond of him." Izzy smiled a sad smile before she turned from the table and moved on to her other customers.

"Hope, I owe you an explanation," Bridger started as he picked up a clam strip and contemplated it.

"Bridger, you don't have to tell me anything you don't want to," Hope said kindly.

"But I do. Hope, I care for you, and it isn't fair that I've kept you in the dark. It's not fair to you and it's not fair to us."

Hope popped a clam strip into her mouth, taking time to savor it while she let Bridger get ready to speak.

"Hope, my sister was my best friend. She was funny and bright, and a little wild. She really didn't make very good decisions, but she was a really good person at heart. She cared about people and tried to do the right things by them."

He paused, eating a clam strip, choosing his words carefully.

"She fell in love with a kid. They were both just kids. Well, he was a little on the rough side, not necessarily the brightest crayon in the box, and she wasn't careful. They got pregnant. He turned into a jerk, but he married her. They were so damn young."

"I'm so sorry, Bridger." It hurt Hope to see the pain in his face as he talked about his sister.

"They were too young to be married. He dropped out and got a job, my dad hired him at the marina, but the stress of having a job, trying to make ends meet and raising a baby were just too much for him. He started hitting my sister. I didn't find out about it until he had done a pretty good job on her."

His jaw clenched at the memory. Hope's heart broke for him, and she knew there was more misery to come.

"I made it clear to him that he was no longer welcome. He and his family packed up and left town. My sister was now alone in an apartment trying to raise her son. She resented that I, um, encouraged her husband to leave. She was tired and young, and wanted her life back.

"One day, she didn't take care of Rusty the way she should have, and I had to step in. She and I had a fight, and she went off and got drunk. Later that night, she took one of my boats out. One of my boats that was tagged for repair. She either ignored the tag or was too drunk to care. She drowned, because of my boat."

He stared over Hope's head, not trusting to look her in the eyes.

Izzy watched from the bar. Her heart broke for Bridger, but she was proud of him for taking the final step toward healing. He was sharing his pain with the woman he loved. She smiled to herself. Bridger was finally going to be okay.

Hope waited, knowing that Bridger was struggling.

"I went off the deep end, Hope. I gave up on everything. I hurt Pepper, ignoring her, putting our relationship aside. I stayed drunk and didn't work and didn't care for the people I love."

"You were hurting, Bridger," Hope offered.

"Izzy saved me." He glanced over at the bar and saw Izzy watching him. He nodded to her miserably. She smiled at him, giving him strength.

"If it wasn't for Izzy, I don't know where I would be."

"I know," Hope said. "I know what she means to you. It's okay. Izzy is good people."

"I didn't take care of the people I loved," he said again. "Izzy finally decided to step in and kick my ass. She sobered me up. She helped me through the dark times and made me face life again."

He took another sip of his beer.

Hope waited patiently.

"I couldn't salvage what I had with Pepper. God bless that woman; she didn't hold it against me. I came back to work and stepped in to be there for my nephew. I tried to be like a dad to him. I did the best I could. For so long he was angry, hurt that he had been abandoned by his father, my fault, and orphaned by his mom, my fault again."

"Bridger," Hope started.

"No, I know that none of it was really my fault, but I was an instrument in it, and in a boy's eyes, I could be the person he blamed. It took a long time, but eventually Rusty came around. We learned to respect each other. Now, I don't know what to do. I just can't believe."

"Then maybe you don't have to," Hope said suddenly.

"What do you mean," Bridger asked, looking at her steadily.

"What if Chris is wrong? What if Rusty didn't write those notes. Honestly, Bridger, he was surly when he saw me there, but he looked absolutely shocked when I accused him of the notes. He looked bewildered, not like someone who was busted."

Hope ran her finger around her empty glass, thinking.

"Did Chris have any proof?" Bridger asked, his mind starting to work.

"Not that I know of. He said he had been counseling him, that he was angry and had mental issues. Wait," Hope said suddenly, "who is listed as his guardian?"

"Technically my mom, but I am also listed as a contact from the school."

"Bridger, I would have noticed that in his records when I looked up his contact information. That's really weird."

"Hope, these clam strips weren't enough. Now that I've talked that through, I need a burger. You?"

"I thought you would never ask," Hope laughed, happy that the tensions were gone.

Bridger waved Izzy over.

"You two decide you were ready for something else?" Izzy asked, noticing that they were smiling and a lot more relaxed. Score one for the good guys, she thought.

"A couple of cheeseburgers, Izzy, please. Is that okay, Hope?"

"Perfect, and I feel the need for onion rings."

"Make that two, Iz. Thanks." Bridger smiled at her. "Thanks for everything," he said meaningfully.

"What was that all about?" Hope teased as Izzy left the table.

"She suggested, quite strongly I might add, that I talk to you. I should have listened and not waited so long. I should have trusted you, Hope. I'm sorry."

"You trust me now, and that's all that matters."

41

The next morning, Hope got up extra early. She wanted to get to school to have a chance to talk to Chris before she had to get ready for her students. She just hoped he would be there for her to talk to.

As she turned down the hall, she saw that the door to his office was open. She popped her head in to ask if she could have a minute with him.

The office was empty. She walked to his desk and pulled a page off the sticky notepad and picked up a pen. Jotting a quick note that she needed to speak with him a soon as possible, she returned the pen and looked for a good place to stick the note.

She figured his computer screen was as good a place as any. As she pressed it front and center, she happened to notice a note on his desk. It was like all the others Hope had received full of veiled threats and declarations of affection.

What the hell, she thought to herself.

She heard a noise behind her.

"Just exactly what are you doing in here?"

She turned. Chris was standing in the doorway, and he looked very angry.

"Good morning, Chris. I needed to talk with you this morning. I saw that your door was open, and I popped in to see you, but discovered you weren't here. I wrote a note and left it on your computer screen."

She gestured weakly to the screen. She was shocked at the growing anger that was written on his face, the fury in his eyes.

"I'm sorry if you feel like I've invaded your privacy, but I have to ask you. Where did this letter come from?"

She gestured to the letter on his desk.

He crossed the room in two steps. Hope shrunk back, suddenly frightened.

Chris recognized her fear and adjusted his demeanor.

"I'm sorry," he said contritely. "I didn't mean to frighten you. I just need to protect my student's privacy. You understand," he said as he picked up the letter and placed a hand on Hope's arm to put her at ease.

"Oh, yes, this is another one of Rusty's letters," he informed her.

"I don't know, Chris. I'm beginning to think maybe Rusty isn't responsible for the notes."

"What would make you say that? I told you Rusty penned these. What, did Bridger come to the young man's defense?" Chris's words were biting, accusatory.

Hope moved further into the room, moving away from the desk and closer to the door. Chris calmed down and tried for a soothing voice.

"Hope, we found this letter this morning during a locker check. I was concerned about what we might find there, so I ordered a check, looking for anything; notes, drugs, weapons."

"Weapons? Seriously?"

"I told you, Hope, he is a seriously disturbed young man."

Something didn't feel right to Hope, but she couldn't put her finger on in. She didn't like the wary look in Chris's eyes, the mistrust that he had. On the other hand, she shouldn't have come into his office when he wasn't there. It wasn't professional. And she shouldn't second guess him. He was, after all, an expert. He had all the degrees on his wall that affirmed he was highly qualified at what he did. Maybe she was not being professional. Maybe her personal relationship was clouding her judgement. After all, they found another letter this morning in the kid's locker.

"You're right, Chris. I'm sorry I doubted you. It's just, this is starting to wear on me."

Immediately he was at her side, consoling her.

"Hope, I can't imagine how you feel, to be the target of a disturbed student's ire. I am here for you whenever you need to talk," he said soothingly. "Look, I even have chamomile tea if you want some to de-stress." He gestured to his shelf where several beautiful tins of herbal tea shared a prominent spot.

He really was ready to help.

She felt like such a bitch.

The bell rang. *Damn*, she wasn't ready for her students.

"I feel like such a witch. Again, I apologize, and I might take you up on a cup of tea at lunch, but right now, I really need to get to class."

"No need to apologize, my dear. Stress does strange things to a person. I'll bring a tea bag with me to lunch. Do you need a mug, too?"

"No, I at least can contribute that. Thanks," she said gratefully as she left his office and hurried down the hall to her room.

The students filed into her room, and Hope was at the door as usual, greeting them as they entered.

"Connie, how's your dad?" Hope asked.

"He's good, just sore. Thanks for asking." The girl smiled gratefully at her teacher for caring. Hope couldn't imagine what it would have been like if the news they had gotten wasn't good.

"Good morning, Rusty," she said as she was getting ready to close the door on the last stragglers into the room.

"Whatever," he said, not looking at her.

"Wait a minute," she said, her voice cutting.

Rusty, startled, stopped and looked at her. She usually didn't speak crossly.

"Class, please get started on your bell work. I need to take care of an issue, and then I will be with you."

She turned her attention on Rusty, ushering him back out the door into the hall. She closed the door all but a crack, so she could still hear what was going on in the classroom.

"I didn't realize your uncle was Bridger," she started.

"So, now you know, so what."

"So, nothing. It was just a conversation starter. Rusty, seriously, we need to get past this. I know you said you don't think I like you. I do like you. I think you're a smart young man. I've seen that in the extended responses you've written on your tests and homework. But I also know that you're angry and confused. Bridger told me about your mom."

"He had no right. It's none of your business," he hissed.

"He did it because he cares. Just like I care, but I care about you as a student."

"What the hell are you talking about? You talk in riddles and don't make sense," Rusty said, backing away from her, stepping out into the hall more.

"Rusty I know they found one of the letters like I've been getting in your locker this morning. I know you've denied it, and at first, I believed you, but now there's evidence. I don't think you're a bad person. I know that you're hurt because your mom is gone, and maybe you're looking for a substitute for her, but I can't be that."

"Look. I don't know what you're getting at, but I didn't write any notes. I am sick of this shit, and I am sick of you. You could have just left me alone, and I would have done my work. You're a pretty decent teacher, but you always look at me like I'm going to steal your stuff. I don't need this, and I don't need you, and I don't need Bridger, either. I don't need anybody."

With that Rusty turned on his heels and walked down the hall, passing the guidance counselor and out of the building.

Chris walked up to Hope.

"What just happened?" he asked.

"He was angry coming in this morning. I tried to talk to him, but he just got angrier and said he didn't need anybody. I need to let the office know we have a student who has gone AWOL," Hope said grimly.

"Don't worry. Teach your class and I'll take care of that. He probably needs some time to cool off. I'll talk to him later, maybe make a home visit."

Hope looked at Chris startled.

"Yes," he said. "Sometimes we still do that." He gestured toward her door, and she opened it and moved to step in. "and Hope, I shouldn't need to caution you on this, but you can't discuss a student with a non-guardian. You could lose your teaching license. Please don't forget that." He noticed the shock on her face. "Hope, I'm just trying to protect you. I know you care and want to help, but don't jeopardize your career needlessly. Please let me handle this."

She nodded miserably. "Please let me know when he's found and that he's okay. Please?"

"I promise," Chris said, crossing his heart with his index finger.

The day crawled. Chris brought the promised chamomile tea for lunch, but it didn't do anything to steady her nerves. Pepper tried to cheer her up, by now knowing that Hope had a run in with a student. After all, it was all over the building. She didn't know all the details, but she didn't pry either.

When the final bell rang, Hope was grateful. She didn't know why, but she just had the feeling of impending doom all day. She didn't like it and didn't know what to do with it

On the way home, she stopped for some groceries that she sorely needed, then changed her mind about going on home and headed for the beach. The groceries would be okay in the car for the little time it would take to walk on the beach and clear her head.

She slipped off her shoes and started across the sand to the water's edge. The waves were good size, crashing onto the beach, the foam running out in front of them. Seagulls and sandpipers ran along the receding waves, snatching up the small crustaceans tumbling in the foam. She walked and walked, letting her thoughts go, thinking about the last couple of months, her interactions with students and her interactions with adults.

The ocean was healing. Her mind was clearing. She knew what she had to do. The first thing was to talk with Bridger. She turned and started back toward her car. She was surprised how far she had come.

She was alone on the beach except for a lone figure in the distance, back where she had parked the car. It was so far away that she couldn't make out who it was. No doubt it was another soul who needed healing from the sea. As she walked closer the figure turned and disappeared over the dunes. She understood the desire for privacy. This quiet walk alone had worked its magic.

42

*H*ope sautéed the diced pancetta and onions until the meat was crispy and the onions soft. She removed them from the skillet and added sliced baby portabella mushrooms and a splash of olive oil. While they were cooking, she put a pot of salted water on to boil. As the mushrooms cooked, she added a handful of fresh thyme. The cabin was filled with the savory aroma of her cooking.

It was calming, just like the ocean. She had left a text message for Bridger to join her for dinner if he had the time. He hadn't responded but she figured he was busy, and he would either show up or not. It wasn't a big deal.

When the water came to a boil, she added a pound of orecchiette, little ears pasta, and stirred it to make sure the little disks of pasta wouldn't stick together.

When there was a minute left to go on the pasta, Hope added the pancetta and onions back into the skillet and added a cup of the pasta water to make a light sauce.

As she drained the pasta, her heard footsteps on the dock.

"Come on board, Bridger," she called as she returned the pan to the stove and lifted the strainer, shaking the excess water off the pasta.

Bridger knocked on the screen door and Hope gestured for him to come on in as she tipped the pasta into the skillet, tossing it with two wooden spoons to coat it well.

"Wow, that smells amazing," Bridger said. He had come to tell her that he really didn't have time for dinner, but the smell had side-tracked him. He watched as she tipped the contents of the skillet into a colorful, hand painted pasta dish then garnished it with fresh thyme and shaved parmesan cheese.

"Hungry?" she asked as she set the dish on the galley counter where two colorful place mats set with plates and silverware were ready for them.

"Yes, I guess I can take a few minutes to eat. I'm going to wash up first."

Bridger walked down the hall and washed up in the bathroom while Hope added two salads to the counter bar.

"What would you like to drink?"

"Just water," Bridger said as he eyed the wine bottle on the counter.

"Coming up," she said, getting two glasses out and filling them with ice and water.

She gestured for him to sit and she joined him. She dished up a plate of pasta for him first then herself. He waited until she had hers, and then he dug in.

"This is incredible, Hope."

"Thanks. It was my grandmother's recipe. I make it when I need comfort food."

"You need comfort food?" he asked looking at her sideways, his mouthful.

"Yeah, I do. It was a rough day. Did the school call you?"

"About Rusty? They called Mom. Said he'd left school. I called the school back and told them to leave him be, that I would talk to him. What happened?" Bridger asked as he finished his plate of pasta, eyeing the bowl that was still half full.

Hope started filling his plate without missing a beat,

"Thanks," he said.

"I went to talk with Chris this morning," she said.

She filled him in on the conversation in the office, leaving out the silly fact that she felt intimidated for a minute. It was obviously her overreaction to the situation.

"Then I spoke with Rusty. I didn't intend to, but he lashed out at me again this morning. I wanted to let him know that I wasn't angry with him, but he didn't want to hear it. I mentioned the new letter that was found in his locker. That made him really angry and he left. I'm sorry, Bridger. I obviously didn't handle it well."

Bridger's phone rang and he pulled it out of his pocket to see who was calling. It was his mom.

Her voice was panicked

Rusty was gone.

His things were gone.

He'd left a note.

He'd run away.

Bridger tried to soothe his mother, convince her that Rusty just needed some time to himself, but his mother wasn't having any of it.

"Bridger?" Hope said as he hung up the phone.

"It looks like you did it this time," he said, frustration getting the better of him.

"I did what? What's wrong with your mom, and what do I have to do with it?"

"Apparently, your conversation with Rusty and your buddy, the counselor's intervention was enough to drive him away. He's packed his things and run away."

"Oh no, Bridger. What can I do?" Hope asked, wringing her hands, frightened at the cold tone in Bridger's voice.

"You've done enough, Hope. I told you he couldn't have been involved. I told you to leave him be, but you couldn't. You didn't. And now he's gone. I need to go find him. Thank you for dinner," he said stiffly, and he pushed back his stool and stalked out of the cabin.

Hope stood there, her arms wrapped around her, tears streaming down her cheeks. *How had this happened?* She was just trying to do what was right.

Restlessly, she cleaned up the kitchen, washing the dishes, and wiping up the crumbs on the counter. All of the earlier calm the sea had provided had vanished, replaced by a gnawing guilt in her gut. She had come to the conclusion while walking the beach that something didn't add up, she just wasn't sure what it was. She didn't like the way Chris's demeanor had changed so rapidly in his office, and she didn't like the anger she had seen behind his eyes, but because she was kind and polite, she always gave the benefit of the doubt to others.

The walk on the beach had made it clear that things may not be what they seem, and something just didn't mesh. She had planned to talk it over with Bridger after dinner, but she didn't have a chance, and now everything had blown up in her face.

When she was done cleaning, she found herself pacing. She was at a loss, wanting to help Bridger, but knowing he didn't want her. Her heart was breaking, and she didn't know how to fix it.

It crossed her mind to go to see Izzy, but she didn't want to go running to Bridger's best friend. She thought about Maeve or Jennifer, but she didn't want to air their dirty laundry. In the end, she just paced.

Finally, she couldn't take it anymore. She put on a fleece jacket, the night was chilling down considerably, and she slipped off her boat onto the dock. Night had fallen. Usually the lights on the dock cheered her, but tonight nothing could bring up her mood. Nothing but finding Rusty safe and having Bridger forgive her.

She called out to Bridger at his houseboat, but there wasn't any answer, the same with his sailboat. She should have known that he wouldn't be there. He'd be out looking for Rusty. She stood in the gravel parking lot, turning around, looking around her, for what, she didn't know. She had never felt so helpless in her life.

She walked a path by the river toward the estuary until the path narrowed, then plunged into tall grasses and marsh. Hope could go no further, and she was chilled to the bone. Realizing it was hopeless, there was nothing she could do to help, she turned and walked back to her boat.

All of the sudden, she felt incredibly alone, but at the same time, she felt like she was being watched. It was like when she was a little kid walking from the bathroom in the middle of the night back to her bed. The closer she got to her bed, the faster she walked, feeling like a hand was reaching out to grab her. She always ended up running the last few feet certain something bad was going to get her before she reached the safety of her bed and blankets.

Stop it, she scolded herself. *There is nothing out here that is going to hurt me.* She forced herself to slow her steps, to calm down. She was just feeling jittery and letting her imagination get to her.

She emerged from the tall grasses that fringed the estuary and continued toward the marina on the wide path along the river. The moon was rising, lighting up the world around her. She thought it would make her feel better, but it cast more shadows, alerting her imagination to more made up dangers.

Her feet crunched on the gravel as she reached the parking lot. She had no idea how long she had been gone. How far she had walked. Usually walking would clear her mind, but not this time.

She stepped up on the dock, not even glancing at Bridger's boats. She was defeated and destroyed. He didn't believe in her or trust her. He blamed her for Rusty deciding to run away. He was done with her and she knew it.

Despite the cold, when Hope got back to her boat, she left the sliding door open, just shutting the screen. She wanted to hear if there was any activity on the dock, if there was any indication that Bridger had found Rusty. She didn't know what she would be listening for, maybe Bridger bringing Rusty back to his boat to talk to him or something. She just wanted to stay connected.

She slipped off her shoes, but her feet were cold, so she padded to her bedroom and pulled a thick pair of woolen winter socks out of her dresser. They felt cozy on her feet. She pulled the comforter off of her bed and carried it with her into the tiny living room. She wrapped herself up like a cocoon on the couch and waited, hoping to hear something that would let her know that Rusty was safe and Bridger was back.

She sat that way for hours, her mind slowly turning, hashing over the things she thought about on the beach. Something just kept nagging her. Eventually, she fell asleep, sitting up, wrapped in her comforter.

*S*tealthy footsteps fell on the dock. They stopped at Hope's boat. In her sleep, she stirred. A warning flashed in her brain. Everything was quiet again. She snuggled deeper into the warmth of the comforter.

The quiet footsteps moved again, stepping over the side of the boat and onto the deck. Cautiously they approached the patio screen door.

He could see her lying there, wrapped up in a blanket, a sock clad foot hanging off the couch.

Hope was dreaming. Rusty was coming for her. She didn't know what to do. He was just a kid. A smart kid who was lost, but he was coming to get her, to hurt her.

She struggled to see where he was, but it was dark. She knew he was there, but where?

Suddenly, she felt his presence near her. Rusty was there, close to her, but it wasn't Rusty. It was Chris. It was Chris who was there, who wanted to hurt her.

Hope's eyes flew open.

A man was standing over her.

What the hell? She shook her head, trying to clear the fog. She must still be dreaming.

No, there was a man standing above her.

She tried to stand, but she was wrapped, trapped in her comforter. It didn't matter, because two strong arms grabbed her and pinned her down.

"You couldn't let it go, could you?"

The face was close to her, within inches. She could smell the alcohol, strong and stale on his breath.

"Why are you here?" she asked, turning her head to increase the distance between them.

"You could have just minded your own business, but you wouldn't. You just kept sticking your nose in, talking to people."

"I didn't mean to upset you," she said, realizing she had to try to talk rationally to him. To remind him of their relationship.

"But you did. And then you had to bring Bridger into it. That was a huge mistake on your part."

"I'm sorry," she whispered. She looked into his eyes and saw pure soulless hate. She suddenly understood that she was in terrible danger.

"Now, I can't let you continue to run your mouth. I can't let you destroy what I have been trying to build, and you will destroy it. So, it's quite simple."

He reached into his pocket and pulled out a glass jar.

"I'm sorry, Hope. I'm afraid this is not going to go well for you."

Before she had the chance to react, he struck her hard in the head. She felt the impact and her head snap sideways, then darkness. Sweet, oblivious darkness.

He unscrewed the lid to the jar and splashed the contents around the cabin.

Then he leaned over and kissed Hope on the lips. It's too bad, he thought to himself. We would have made a cute couple.

He slipped out the screen door as he lit a box of wooden matches, sliding them across the floor to rest against the throw rug and soft chair, both of which had been doused with light kerosene.

The rug quickly caught fire, the flames running up the side of the chair, igniting the curtains within seconds.

Chris stepped off the boat and onto the dock, slipping into the shadow of Clarence's boat. He knew he needed to leave quickly, but the fire was mesmerizing. He wasn't worried about the old pervert seeing him. He knew that the man was in town at the Mizzen Mast trying to woo some new ladies, and Bridger was out looking for his precious nephew.

"Hope!"

He heard shouting.

Bridger.

Chris slipped off the edge of the dock and into the water. He ducked under the floating dock as three men ran past him. They never saw him hoist himself back up on the dock and move quickly away into the night. Their attention was on the burning houseboat and saving the woman inside.

Bridger jumped onto the boat, Ryker behind him, Tank bringing up the rear. As Bridger crashed through the screen door, flames were licking the walls and running along the ceiling. Tank yanked the spigot handle up on the dock hose and Ryker uncoiled it, wetting down Bridger as he followed him into the cabin.

Black smoke filled the small room, but Bridger saw the comforter on the couch. Ryker turned the hose on the blanket, soaking it as Bridger gathered the still form in his arms. They backed out of the cabin and onto the deck.

Hope moaned and began flailing her arms, trying to fight the blanket and the person who was holding her. The world was burning. Her world was burning, and she had to stop it.

"Put me down," she croaked, still fighting against the comforter. Bridger set her on her feet, freeing her from the fabric. He circled his arms around her, but she would have none of it. She was wild with fear, striking out at him as she saw the little boat in flames. He dropped his arms, giving her some space.

Suddenly, before Bridger could react Hope ran back to the boat and into the cabin.

"Damn it," Bridger yelled. "Hope!"

He followed her, Ryker behind him. He spotted her ducking beneath falling, burning debris, reaching for something. The photo of her parents. He grabbed her arm and yanked her toward him, spinning as he did so she would end up near the door.

Ryker reached for her and hauled her out. The last thing she saw was Bridger engulfed in flames.

"Bridger," she screamed and passed out in Ryker's arms.

Tank was there. He pulled the hose from Ryker and doused Bridger as he crashed back out of the cabin, Hope's school tote and computer bag in his right hand.

"You're an idiot," Ryker yelled at his friend.

Tank grinned at the two of them.

"I think our friend is in love."

43

*S*irens screaming, an ambulance arrived followed by a fire truck and a slew of other men. Two paramedics took the unconscious Hope from Bridger's arms and quickly loaded her into the ambulance while a volunteer tended to Bridger, who kept waving him off.

"I need to get to Hope," he protested.

"She's already on her way to the hospital." He pointed to the ambulance leaving the parking lot.

"Damn it. I wanted to go with her. She needs me with her."

"You need some attention to those burns, Bridger."

"I'm heading to the hospital in a minute, but I'm going to see if I can save my boat."

Bridger pulled away from the man and ran back down the dock. The men were already putting out the last of the flames.

"You've got your work cut out for you, buddy," Tank said as he wrapped an arm around his friend's shoulder, "but I think we were able to save it. Your joints are so tight in that woodwork that the wood didn't catch fire. Not enough oxygen seeping through. The soft stuff, well, that's toast."

Bridger looked into the cabin. The furniture was burned, and what wasn't burned was water damaged. Soot marked the walls, and he knew from experience that all of Hope's things would need professional fire cleaning to rid it of the acrid smell. Still, there was hope for the little boat. He smiled at the thought. Hope for the boat. His Hope, his boat. They were perfect together.

"I've got to get to the hospital," Bridger said, turning and patting his pockets for his truck keys.

"I'll drive you," Ryker said. "You're in no condition. You need to get checked out, too."

"No, I don't want to be without my truck. I'll drive."

"Damn it, you stubborn ass. First you run back into a fire for some homework and a damn laptop, and now you want to go gallivanting off in your truck. Tank will drive you in your truck and I'll follow. If, and that's only if, you check out okay, I'll give you your keys back, and Tank can give me a lift home."

The three of them walked down the dock, leaving the rest of the men to finish the job. Bridger handed his keys to Tank and they left for the hospital.

When they pulled in, Bridger didn't wait for the truck to stop before he jumped out. He ran to the emergency room doors impatient with the line ahead of him.

A nurse came out to see him.

"Bridger, you look like your seen better days. Are you okay? There was an accident on the freeway. The ER is filled."

She was doing triage as she talked to him, noting the wild look in his eyes.

"Patty, I'm fine. It's Hope I'm looking for. Is she okay?"

"He's not fine, Patty. He has third degree burns on his arms," said Ryker as he came up behind them.

Patty glanced down at Bridger's arms, the charred sweatshirt revealing blistered flesh.

"Well, that's not good, but you're not going to die from it, so you're going to have to wait," she said good-naturedly.

"Patty, what about Hope?"

She looked at him with pity. His heart clenched.

"Bridger, you aren't related. I can't give you any information."

Bridger roared in frustration.

The ER got quiet.

Patty turned stern, reducing Tank and Ryker to high school boys with their heads hanging.

Not Bridger.

He stared her down.

"Bridger, I know you're concerned and frustrated, but the law is the law, and my job is my job." She softened as she looked at the anguish in his face.

"I will say that I have some critical cases with the traffic accident. Nothing else has come in tonight that is as urgent as those." She winked and patted his shoulder, careful not to touch any burns.

Tank handed Bridger a cup of coffee and led him to a quiet corner of the waiting room where Ryker had already retreated.

They settled down to wait.

Bridger's pocket vibrated.

He pulled his phone out and glanced at it.

Rusty.

"This had better be good," he answered.

"It was Mr. Komat," the voice sputtered.

"What?"

"It was Mr. Komat who started the fire. I saw him. After you, Ryker, and Tank ran for Ms. Chandler's boat, I was going to follow, but I saw someone climb up on the dock behind you and walk away.

"I was going to help you, but I figured I should follow whoever that was. He walked a long way to his car. It was parked alongside the road, kinda hidden in the bushes. I wasn't sure who it was until he opened the door and the dome light lit his face."

"Okay, slow down. Where are you now and are you okay?"

"I followed him."

"I know, you said that."

"No, I mean I followed him to his house. I ran back and took grandma's car, sorry about that Bridger, but then I was able to catch up with him."

"I'm guessing you didn't follow any traffic rules," Bridger said wryly. By now he was pacing, Tank and Ryker trying to make sense of the conversation.

"Bridger, here's the thing. I think he is going to try to leave town. He is packing a bunch of stuff, and Bridger, Ms. Chandler's pictures are all over the walls in this guy's bedroom. It's creepy as hell."

"Are you still at his house? What the hell are you doing?" Bridger asked, on the move now.

"I'm looking in his windows. Don't worry, he can't see me. I'm wearing camouflage."

Despite his worry, that brought a smile to Bridger's face. He guessed his nephew had been hiding from him in plain sight. Brilliant kid.

"Okay, stay out of sight, I'm on my way."

Rusty gave Bridger the address and Bridger walked out of the hospital despite Patty's protests that he needed treatment.

*B*ridger drove this time. Ryker and Tank knew better than to argue. Tank called the police dispatch as Bridger sped toward the apartment. They parked down the street and walked in the shadows toward the address.

"Psst."

The sound came from the bushes on the side of the cottage.

Ryker and Tank ducked into the shadows while Bridger stood on the sidewalk deliberating his move.

He didn't have to make a decision.

The front door opened, and Chris stepped out carrying a briefcase and a large duffel bag. He was sorting through his keyring to find his car keys, so he never saw what hit him.

Bridger took him to the sidewalk,

Rusty landed the first punch.

Tank and Ryker stood back watching as Bridger and Rusty took their turns making sure that Chris couldn't go anywhere.

As the police cars rounded the corner and headed toward them, lights flashing and sirens blaring, Tank and Ryker looked at each other.

"Guess it's time to stop the fun," Tank said as he hauled Bridger off the bleeding man.

Ryker lifted Rusty to his feet and held him at arm's length. Rusty apparently wasn't done, because his arms were still flailing.

"Settle down, boy," he told him. "You've done your job."

"This asshole set me up," the teen swore. "And he tried to hurt my uncle's girlfriend, and he burned the boat. I think he probably killed Pappy, too." With that he renewed his effort to get back to the job he had started.

Tank was having some trouble with Bridger, too.

Bridger was seeing red and had no intention of stopping. He fully intended to kill the man. Tank couldn't let that happen.

The police cars came to a stop and officers piled out of the cars.

Chris sputtered from the sidewalk.

"These men attacked me! Arrest them!"

"Shut up, counselor," a young patrolman spoke, then proceeded to read the man his Miranda rights.

"You okay Bridger, Rusty?" an older officer asked. "That man didn't hurt your fists any did he? We can add to the charges if that's the case."

"How did you know to arrest him?" Rusty asked.

"Well, Tank here called in what you told him, but we also got a statement from Ms. Chandler. She said he had struck her over the head with a jar full of fluid. She said she was certain he started the fire."

"Hope's awake? Is she okay?"

"I think she'll be fine, Bridger."

"Sir, that asshole, sorry, I mean Mr. Komat has all kinds of pictures of Ms. Chandler hung up in his bedroom. It's really creepy."

The officers entered the house. Bridger, Tank, Ryker and Rusty followed.

"You stay here," the older officer ordered Rusty.

He didn't listen and trailed after them anyway. The officer pretended not to notice.

The house was fastidiously clean and very upscale. Everything was in its place with stunning artwork on the walls, but his bedroom was the den of a demented man. Large glossy pictures of Hope covered the walls. Pictures of her at school, working with students. Pictures of her at the beach, walking by herself, bending over picking up a shell. There were pictures of her with Bridger, too. Or at least it looked like Bridger, but it was hard to tell with his face hacked by razor blade slices.

Then Bridger saw a picture that made his blood boil. It looked like it was the night of the warehouse fire. It was the two of them, embracing on her boat. The focus was on her face, which was sliced several times by a blade. The edges of the photo had been burned.

44

*B*ridger drove to the hospital with Rusty by his side. Tank took Ryker home. On the way, Bridger and Rusty had a heart to heart. Rusty felt terrible for the way he treated Hope. At first, he didn't see it, his surly disposition towards her. He just felt like she was an outsider, and he would have to explain his personal life to her. Everyone else knew and let him be. He felt like she was prying. He also mentioned that Mr. Komat had told him that she didn't understand him, and he was going to have to just put up with the fact that she had zeroed in on him to make an example of. He realized now that he was being set up and so was Hope. He also realized that Hope really just cared about him as a student and wanted him to be successful.

He felt miserable.

"Bridger, she's going to be okay, isn't she?"

"She's awake and talking, so I'm sure she's going to be fine."

"What about you?"

"What about me?" Bridger said, looking at his nephew.

"Bridger, your arms are badly burned. I wish I would have seen him sooner. I wish I could have stopped him," said Rusty.

"Rusty, are you kidding? You did stop him. He's in custody and can't do this to anyone else. Where were you, by the way?"

Rusty grinned at him.

"Holed up in Mr. Anzlovar's boat. I knew he was going to be out of town for a couple of weeks because he called and wanted me to check to make sure the bilge pump was working okay. I checked. It's fine." He grinned at Bridger.

"And you were there the whole time we were all looking for you. I should knock your block off."

"Nah, I was tortured enough."

"How," asked Bridger, confused, knowing just how elegant Mr. Anzlovar's boat was appointed.

"I could smell that dinner Ms. Chandler cooked for you. My stomach was growling. The only thing on that fancy boat were some damn peanut butter crackers and a bunch of fancy schmancy wine."

Bridger laughed a hearty laugh and grinned at Rusty.

"That dinner Hope made was damned good. It's too bad you didn't get any."

As they pulled into the hospital Bridger got a text. It was from Hope. Bridger's eyes got moist as he read it.

Bridger,

I'm sorry about your boat. I know it meant the world to you. It was your connection with your dad, and now I am sure it's destroyed. They told me you were okay but suffered some burns. I am sorry for that. It's my fault. I should never have done anything to risk your health. I understand if you don't want to speak with me again. I didn't trust you about Rusty, but I know now he didn't have anything to do with it. It was all Chris. Chris clouded my judgement, and I didn't trust myself. I don't know if I can ever trust my professional judgement again. I know Rusty will never forgive me. What I did to him is reprehensible. Let me know what I owe you for the boat. If there's anything left, I will clear it out as soon as I can. I will be in touch with a rental agent tomorrow to find a new place to live. Thank

*you for all you've done. You've been an amazing friend. I'm so sorry
I've let you down.*

~ Hope

"Bridger, what's wrong?" Rusty asked, alarmed.

Bridger handed the phone to Rusty and let him read the text.

"That's bullshit," he exploded. "She's a great teacher. She even made the stupid *Scarlet Letter* interesting. Who does that?"

Bridger grinned despite himself.

"How about we tell her. Maybe we can get arrested forcing ourselves into her room. What do you say?"

They stalked into the hospital, a formidable force to be reckoned with. One man covered with soot, his arms blistered raw, another covered in mud and sweat, dressed in camouflage. Both ready for a fight.

Patty walked up to them, cool and efficient.

"Patty, I don't mean to be disrespectful, but I'm going to see Hope, even if it means opening every damn door in this hospital looking for her. You aren't going to stop me, and neither is anyone else."

"And that goes for me, too," said Rusty, mustering up the deepest voice he could.

Patty suppressed a smile.

"Room 236," she said.

"Patty, I mean it," said Bridger. "Stand aside."

"Bridger, she just gave you her room number," Rusty said, plucking at his uncle's sleeve.

"What?"

Patty just smiled and shook her head.

"Pain getting the best of you Bridger?" she asked looking pointedly at his arm.

"No, I'm fine," said Bridger as he started walking.

"Bridger, um, this way," said Rusty following the direction Patty was pointing and outright laughing now.

Bridger hesitated at the closed door, afraid of what he was going to see. He braced himself then knocked.

"Come in." Hope's voice was hoarse, and he detected pain behind her words. It broke his heart.

He opened the door and poked his head in.

"Can I come in please? Can I come in and apologize and ask your forgiveness?" he said, frightened at how small she looked in the sheets, a gauze pad over her forehead.

"Bridger," she said, smiling a tired smile. "Hey."

"Hey. I'm sorry, honey, so very sorry." He moved quickly to her side and took her hand gently. "I wasn't there for you. I let this happen to you."

"Bridger, there was nothing you could have done. Chris is crazy. He set this all up." Tears formed in her eyes.

"I know, honey. I know." He smoothed her hair, careful to avoid the swelling on her head.

"Hey, Mrs. Chandler." Rusty hung by the door, unsure what to do.

"Rusty. Thank God you're safe. I'm so sorry I doubted you. Can you ever forgive me for it?"

"It's cool. We're cool," Rusty said awkwardly, suddenly very uncomfortable.

Hope, her years of experience kicking in, smiled at the young man.

"Okay, as long as we are cool and you're safe, don't forget you have to have a project idea ready for me on Monday." They grinned at each other, bridges mended.

"I'm going to get a soda. Do you guys need anything?" he asked as he edged back toward the door.

"No, thanks for asking," Hope said warmly.

"No, thanks. You need money?" Bridger asked, knowing his nephew was just looking to escape.

"Nah, I got it."

Rusty left closing the door behind him.

"It looks like I can save the boat," Bridger told her, stroking her hair, convincing himself that she was going to be okay.

"Thank goodness. It broke my heart seeing it burning," she said. Then her eyes went wide, memories flooding back.

"Bridger, I just remembered, I saw you burning!" She sat up

quickly trying to check him, making sure he was safe, but she became immediately dizzy. Bridger saw it and eased her back on her pillow.

"Easy tiger, I'm fine," he assured her.

Her eyes spotted his arms.

"Oh no, Bridger."

Tears sprung, running down her cheeks, and she grabbed her call button, hitting it repeatedly.

Patty came through the door with an intern on her heels.

"Bridger, he's hurt badly," Hope cried, pointing at his arms.

"We know. We were on our way even before you summoned us. You're still okay, right?" Patty asked as she gave Hope a quick glance.

"I'm fine, but Bridger is burned."

The intern looked at Bridger's burns.

"Okay, you have a bunch of second degree burns and these third degree. The third degree are small. I think we can avoid skin grafts if you heal quickly, but you have to follow my orders. Do I need to admit you, or will you behave?" the intern asked, earnestly.

"Oh, he'll behave," Hope promised. "Or he'll have to answer to me."

Bridger started to protest then realized it was futile. He followed Patty and the intern out so they could clean up his wounds. He knew it wasn't going to be pretty, and he didn't want Hope to be any more distressed than she was.

An hour later, he joined her. He had given the keys to Rusty so he could go on home, then he settled himself in a reclining chair next to her bed. Her doctor wanted to keep her overnight for observation, and he had no plans on leaving her side. Not now, not ever.

When Hope woke in the morning, she found Bridger next to her, his hand resting on hers. She smiled to herself. She had her Bridger back, and she was never going to let him go again.

"What are you smiling about?" he asked, sitting up stiffly. His arms hurt like a son of a bitch, but he wasn't going to let her know that.

"I'm smiling that you're here. I'm here, and Rusty's safe."

"Those are good things to celebrate."

Patty opened the door and stepped into the room.

"Ready to go home, Hope?" she asked, nodding a good morning to Bridger at the same time.

"I am," she said, but then hesitated. Her home was gone. "But, I—"

"She's ready to go home, and I am ready to take her there," said Bridger, forgetting he didn't have his truck with him.

"As soon as she signs these papers, we'll process her discharge. It should only take about half an hour."

Patty gathered the needed signatures and left, Rusty walking in as Patty walked out.

"Here're your keys, Bridger." He tossed them to Bridger who caught them, wincing. He was going to have to remember to take it easy for a while. Skin grafts were not high on his to do list.

"Hang on, I'll take you home when we leave," Bridger told him.

"No need, Connie will take me. She followed me here," said Rusty shyly.

Connie poked her head in and waved.

"I hope you get better soon, Ms. Chandler," she smiled at her favorite teacher. "Just so you know, Rusty and I are going to start working on our projects this weekend. We have a really cool idea." Typical Connie was bubbly and full of positive energy. Hope knew she would be a good influence on Rusty. Things were looking up.

"Well, Ms. Chandler, are you ready to go?"

"I'm not sure where I'm going," she said. "I didn't have a chance to call the rental agent." Her face was serious, not a hint of a smile.

"I thought we were past that," Bridger scolded. "You're coming back to the marina. You can stay in the houseboat, and I'll stay in the sailboat. There won't be a hint of impropriety to jeopardize your standing in the community or your reputation as a teacher. These will be the arrangements until you take my name and become Mrs. Cadigan."

He looked at her earnestly.

There were no sounds.

He waited, watching her considering what he said.

"What do you say, Hope? I love you. I have since the day you stepped on my boat. Please, Hope. Will you marry me?"

She smiled, and the world lit up.

"Only if we can get married on a boat," she said teasing.

"Oh, I can make that happen," he promised. "That will not be a problem."

"Then yes, Bridger Cadigan. I will happily marry you!"

Turn the page for a sneak peek of Harbor Tides- A Grey's Harbor Story

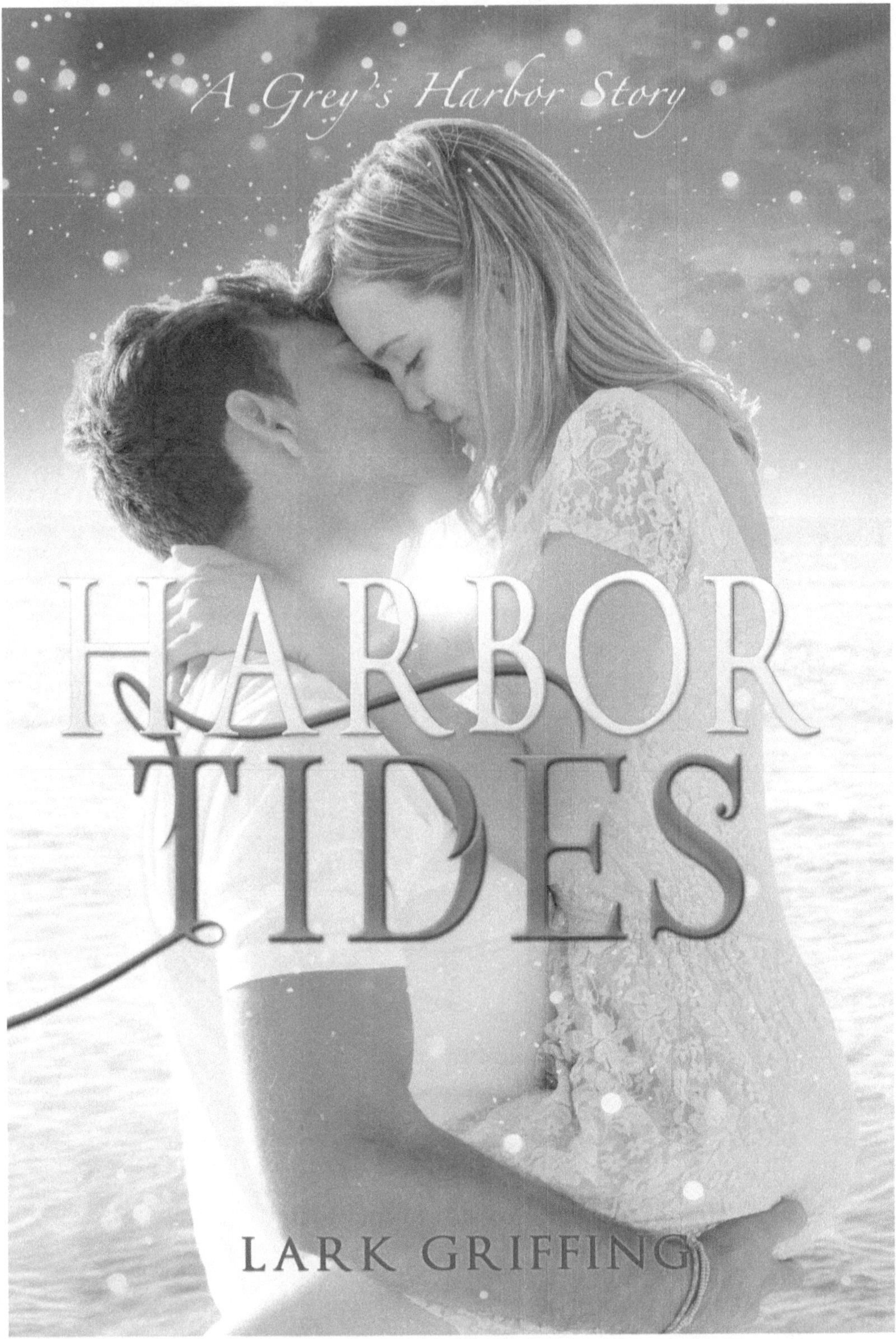
A Grey's Harbor Story
HARBOR
TIDES
LARK GRIFFING

CHAPTER ONE

"Maeve, I'm sorry, but I'm just not ready." Tank moved to draw Maeve into his muscle-bound arms, but she stiffened and took a step back. Seagulls wheeled above them, and the wind whistled past the old lighthouse sounding like a ghost woman crying in grief.

"I don't think you'll ever be ready, Tank. I'm sorry. I love you with all my heart, but I can't keep waiting, hoping that you'll someday decide we belong together forever." She turned her face away, not wanting him to see the tears glistening in her eyes.

"It's because you want a family, right?" He reached for her again, lifting her chin with his finger so she would look him in the eyes.

"No, well, yes. Damn it, Tank. I'm not that young anymore, and I guess my clock is ticking, but that's not the reason I want us to make this relationship permanent..." She stepped away again and kicked a piece of driftwood, frustrated with having to explain. "I want commitment. I want security. Is that really too much to ask? And if you won't or can't give it, then I understand. It's just not who you are, but Tank, this is not who I am. I can't keep going on like this. I'm sorry, but I have to end it. For me." She looked at him, the misery she was feeling written all over her. Her blonde hair covered her face, partially because the wind blew it there, partially because she wanted to screen herself from him. Protect herself from the man she loved.

"Maeve, I love you," Tank groaned, angry at himself, angry at Maeve, angry with the world.

"I love you, too, Tank, but I'm not going to waste my life waiting for a man who won't commit to loving me forever." With tears streaming down her face, she stretched onto her tiptoes and kissed the man. She loved him, but it would be the last time, she told herself. She was done.

Tank stood stock still. Shocked as he watched the beautiful lady walk away. She bent over, sliding her sandals off her tanned feet and walked toward the surf. The tide was coming in and the waves beat a steady rhythm against the shore. Maeve moved into the water, holding her sandals in her hand, letting the waves rock her body as they hit her calves.

She walked. Away from Tank.

And he let her.

"Hey, sis." Ryker walked across the diner and wrapped his sister in his arms, giving her a bear hug. Her blonde head disappeared in his arms as he pulled her against his chest. "Rough couple of days, huh?" he asked, whispering against her hair so the diners couldn't overhear.

It was a silly attempt at privacy. Everyone in Grey's Harbor knew that Maeve Wynn and Tank Harmond had broken up. Maeve looked up into the deep green eyes that matched her own and smiled.

"I'm hanging in there. Thanks for checking on me, or did you just stop in because you know it's meatloaf night and you adore my meatloaf?"

"I could never lie to you, sis. It's the meatloaf that brought me here."

Maeve swatted her brother and led him to a booth.

"You have lied to me plenty of times and don't forget it, but I forgive you the sins of your youth. Meatloaf, mashed potatoes and gravy? Salad or broccoli?"

"Seriously, Maeve. You know damn well I don't want broccoli. Oh, and extra ranch with that, please."

"Of course. Malt?"

"Not tonight. I would feel guilty having a malt without Jenny."

"Where is she tonight?" Maeve asked, not used to seeing her brother without Jennifer Creely by his side.

"She's over at Cadigan's Marina. There are some more problems with the books. She's with Bridger trying to figure out what's what."

"I thought she took over the accounting for the marina. What happened?"

"She did, but Bridger's mom decided to help out again. No one realized she 'helped', and now there's a mess to clean up." Ryker shook his head sadly.

"Poor Emmeline. She was such an efficient person. Dementia sucks."

"Yes, it does. Bridger needs to make some decisions, but he keeps putting it off. I don't blame him. It has to be hard."

Maeve put a hand on her brother's shoulder. She knew he was hurting for his best friend. She went into the kitchen and came back out with a large salad and two ranch containers. She delivered them to her brother and went back into the kitchen. A few minutes later, she placed the early evening special, her bacon-wrapped grilled meatloaf slices and creamy mashed potatoes, in front of him. She'd been careful to make a deep well in them and poured on the brown gravy, just like her brother liked.

"Thanks. Maeve, if you need to talk. I'm here for you. Hell, I'm here for both of you. Tank is sulking around work, pissed off, and no fun to be around. For the tough guy he is, he sure is a baby." He was hoping he would get a smile from his sister. It didn't work.

"Is he okay?" she asked softly, her eyes misting.

"No, he's not, and neither are you. Can't you guys work it out?"

"I don't think so, Ryker. It's over. I need to move on."

"But you two are meant for each other."

"Ryker, if we were meant for each other, he would've put a ring on my finger. You've said it a million times. You told him to make an honest woman of your sister. The writing's on the wall. Now eat that before it gets cold and let me get back to work. I'm getting ready to close."

She bent down and planted a kiss on her brother's forehead, then hurried away so he wouldn't see her cry.

CHAPTER TWO

*M*aeve locked the front door to the diner. She was tired. She was used to long hours on her feet, and she loved running the diner. That's not what made her tired. She was just weary from sadness. She didn't remember a time when she had ever felt so alone. She moved down the sidewalk oblivious to the silky summer air that touched her skin, the ocean salt leaving its mark. Normally she would savor a night like this, but not tonight. Tonight, she was pulled inward, her thoughts on Tank and the wounded look in his eyes when she had convinced him it was over.

"Head's up."

Two hands reached out and caught Maeve just before she plowed into the man who had stepped up onto the sidewalk.

"Oh, I'm so sorry," Maeve stammered, still not looking at the man's face but checking her feet which had tangled up on themselves. Those hands were stopping her from hitting the dirt.

"No problem, Maeve. Preoccupied tonight?"

"A little. Oh, Jeff, hi. Thanks. I'm sorry."

He tilted his head and looked the leggy blonde over. She looked good, as always, but her normally easy going face was lined with something...worry, regret?

"No reason to apologize. Forgive me for saying this, but you look like you could use a friend, Maeve." He smiled at her and his eyes crinkled at the corners.

"Ha, it shows, huh?" Maeve looked up at Jeff and decided that he was being sincere. She didn't know him well. He had moved to town a couple of years ago when Jones and Johnson Architects had lost an associate. He filled the bill and seemed to assimilate into Grey's Harbor fairly well. He had been to the diner on many occasions and had made a nice donation to the Oyster Festival fund each year. He seemed like an easy going kind of guy, but he moved in a different crowd and they didn't cross paths often.

"I was going to have some dinner, but I didn't realize it was so late. The diner is closed, I see." Jeff mused as he reassessed his plans.

"I'm sorry. We closed an hour ago. I decided a long time ago that I wasn't interested in the late evening crowd. Early morning breakfast and early dinner and I'm done," she said with an apologetic smile.

"Does this mean that you've already eaten your early dinner?" Jeff asked, his eyebrow cocked, his deep brown eyes searching her face.

"No, I didn't manage to do that tonight," Maeve admitted. Much to her embarrassment, her stomach announced its hunger pangs. Jeff laughed, and after an embarrassed second, Maeve joined him.

"How about you join me at the Mizzen Mast for a bite to eat? Bar food wasn't what I had in mind, but Izzy does make a good burger. What do you say?" He stepped back a little and waited for her response. He didn't want to make her feel at all pressured. He wasn't that kind of guy. From what he remembered, Maeve dated a very muscular, testosterone filled kind of man, and he didn't want to step on anyone's toes.

"You know what?" she said, a slight smile forming on her lips, "I think I'd like that."

"Do you feel like walking there?"

"Sure, it's a nice night. I'm fine with that." She smiled at him making sure he knew that hoofing it wasn't a problem for her. They turned and fell into step together heading down the sidewalk to the Mizzen Mast.

"Hey, Maeve," Izzy called over her shoulder as Maeve stepped into the bar. Izzy nodded at Jeff as he walked in behind her. "Hi, Jeff."

"Hi, Maeve," Jeff said, "Does it matter where we sit?"

"Nope, just find a place, and I'll be with you two in a minute. Ryker, Tank, and Bridger are out on the deck," Izzy said with a meaningful look at Maeve.

"Deck or inside, Maeve?" Jeff asked, oblivious to Izzy's meaning.

"Inside would be nice, if that's okay with you." She wasn't in the mood to chit chat or have to deal with Tank once he saw her with Jeff.

Jeff led her to a table at the back wall where the windows looked out onto the river as it flowed lazily by on its way to the ocean. He pulled out her chair for her, seating her, then sat himself and picked up a menu.

Maeve knew Izzy's menu by heart, so she watched Jeff as he looked through the selections. His soft brown hair was cut neat and short, typical of the business set. Overall, he was a good looking guy. He filled out his white business shirt well, but not like Tank who had trouble getting shirts to fit his extremely muscular build. Her heart squeezed at the thought of Tank and those strong arms that used to hold her. It was her own fault that she was sitting here instead of by his side on the deck with their friends.

"Hey, what's wrong?" Jeff was looking over his menu, studying Maeve's face. Her green eyes were filled with pain.

"Nothing," she said lightly. "Just trying to decide if I should go for broke and get a big greasy bar burger or suffer with a salad."

"Bar burger," they both said together, then laughed.

"You have a great laugh, Maeve," Jeff said as he looked back down at his menu. It was an offhand comment, not sounding like a sleazy pick-up line. With that, Maeve decided to relax and just enjoy the evening with an acquaintance she thought she should get to know better.

An hour later, Maeve wiped her fingers on her napkin for the umpteenth time. True to the genre, Izzy's bar burgers were juicy and delicious. She enjoyed her time with Jeff. He was easygoing and interesting. He could hold a conversation and asked questions of her and shared about himself but didn't dominate the conversation like so many of the transplanted young businessmen who had come to this sleepy seaside village.

"You never told my why you came to Grey's Harbor," Maeve said, suddenly realizing she knew about his beer brewing hobby and his love of kayaking but didn't know what had brought him here.

"I had an internship my last year of college in a large architectural firm who had offices in Baltimore. I discovered I loved the ocean but wasn't fond of that big of a city. So, when I graduated from college, I started looking for a firm somewhere on the East Coast who did large projects but was headquartered in a small town. Not an easy find." He picked up his beer and drained the last of it. "The rest is history."

"Is living in a small quiet town like Grey's Harbor everything you hoped it would be?"

"It is. I grew up in a smallish town. I thought I wanted to live in a bigger city, enjoy the amenities that city living offered. Honestly, it grew old. I decided living within driving distance of a big city was good enough for me."

"Hi, Maeve." Tank's mellow voice still could make her stomach flip, but this time it hurt her heart, too.

"Hi, Tank." She smiled up at him, her eyes glistening slightly.

Jeff didn't miss the chemistry between them, but before it turned awkward, he stood and offered his hand to Tank.

"Hi. I'm Jeff Mitchell."

"Tank Harmond."

They shook hands sizing each other up. Jeff was no dummy. This was the guy Maeve dated, and by all indications, it was past tense.

"You're the architect who worked on the new health clinic out by the mall, aren't you?" Tank asked, surprising Jeff.

"Yeah, I'm lead on that project. Are you involved with it?" Jeff asked, gesturing for Tank to have a seat. Tank shook his head and declined.

"I work for Ryker Wynn. We're doing the interior finishes on that. I like what you did. You met all the requirements for a health facility but made it feel inviting and warm. So many of those places are cold."

"Thank you. That was my absolute intention." Jeff smiled at him. Tank's appearance was misleading. Obviously, this was a man who was intelligent and paid attention to details.

"Well, have good night," Tank said to Jeff, "Maeve…" his voice just dropped off as he made his way toward the men's room.

Izzy watch the exchange from the bar. What could have been an extremely awkward, volatile encounter had gone very well. She didn't like drama in her bar. She didn't expect it from her friends, but you never knew. She snagged the bill from the waitress and delivered it herself to Maeve's table.

"Can I get you anything else?" Izzy asked pleasantly, her eyes on Maeve. The girl was hurting, and the man sitting across the table from her wasn't oblivious to that fact.

"No, thank you, Izzy." As he handed her several bills Maeve protested.

"I've got my share," she said, reaching into her pocket.

"Not tonight," Jeff said firmly. "It's my treat. Tell you what, you can get the next one. Keep the change, Izzy." He was trying to put Maeve at ease and stop her from feeling awkward. Izzy was a pro at handling these situations.

"Thanks, Jeff." She patted Maeve on the shoulder. "It looks like it was good karma that you ran into a friend tonight. Everyone needs a friend now and then. Now I'm going to go chat Tank up. You have a good evening." She gave Maeve a quick hug and headed toward the bar. "Hey, Tank. You promised to move that big barrel for me out back. You slackin' on me?" She hooked her arm through his and led him back out to the deck chewing him out for breaking a promise.

PURCHASE HARBOR TIDES

From Amazon

or

Click the linked cover below

SIGN UP FOR LARK'S NEWSLETTER

Would you like to know when Lark releases her next book? Do you want a sneak peek at sample chapters? If so, sign up for Lark Griffing's newsletter.

Subscribe now

Or use this URL to subscribe

http://eepurl.com/dH1mzz

ACKNOWLEDGMENTS

So many people touch my life and contribute to a book without even knowing it. Sometimes it's a look or a kindness that sparks my creativity. To all those souls, thank you for the inspiration.

To my editor, J.C. Wing of Wing Family Editing, thank you for always listening, for stopping what you are doing and reading a passage I want to share, too excited to wait until an edit comes back. Lady, you are patient and kind.

And thank you to my family, especially my husband who has taught me the coast can hold your heart and soul the same way the mountains can. Thanks, Joe for those many hours on the sand, and in the water, both above it and below it.

ALSO BY LARK GRIFFING

Grey's Harbor Stories

GREY'S LANDING

GREY'S HARBOR with various authors

HOPE ADRIFT

HARBOR TIDES

Gone To the Dogs Camper Romance Series

TEARDROPS AND FLIP FLOPS

TEARDROPS AND REST STOPS

Young adult novels:

THE LAST TIME I CHECKED I WAS STILL HERE

THE STARFISH TALISMAN

Short Story Collections

DOG ON THE DOORSTEP

ABOUT THE AUTHOR

Lark Griffing is all about stories of adventure and romance. Whether writing about a recent Widowed women discovering life in a teardrop trailer or a teenage girl dealing with evil spirits in her aunt's ancient house on the cliffs above the sea, Lark sets the story in motion and the reader is never really sure where or how it's going to end. Often that reader gets a surprise they weren't expecting, and Lark likes that.

Lark Griffing is a dabbler. Her hobbies are many and varied, from SCUBA diving to backpacking, kayaking to knitting. You never know what you're going to get on any given day if you hang with her.

Her husband and boys are used to her running off in all directions, and they humor her because they know that with Lark, an adventure awaits them. The only members of her family who are not up for the fun are her tabby cat, Dickens and her golden doodle, Maggie. The two of them would prefer staying curled up together holding down the fort until Lark comes bursting back through the door.

Keep up with Lark at her website:

www.LarkGriffing.com

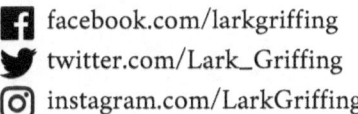

facebook.com/larkgriffing
twitter.com/Lark_Griffing
instagram.com/LarkGriffing

www.ingramcontent.com/pod-product-compliance
Lightning Source LLC
Chambersburg PA
CBHW020413260626
47156CB00007B/2358